avenge

The Spiral Series

lisa silverthorne

REPRISE

Book 3: The Spiral Series

Chaos descends on the Between as demons take control. But Heather Billott has stopped running. After discovering a rebellion brewing among the shadow creatures, Heather tries to unite forces and strengthen her pale army with unexpected allies. But, caught in a whirlwind of emotions, Heather is torn between her love for Ross and her undeniable attraction to Knox.

When trapped souls start to disappear from the soul tree, Zakhart and the pale angels wield a dangerous new weapon of light against the shadowy landscape. With time running out for the missing souls, Heather and her pale army must engage the demons. On Mulciber's treacherous turf.

As Ross struggles against Mulciber's influence and Heather's distance, Knox wages his own war to win her affection while the pale army trains to take the fight to Mulciber. And destroy the Mechanism.

Forcing Heather to choose between Knox and Ross.

Avenge is the *third* book in ***The Spiral***, an epic dark fantasy tale of love, sacrifice, and redemption. Prepare for a tense journey through shadows as the fate of the Between hangs in the balance and the destinies of its inhabitants intertwine in ways they never imagined as they fight to reach the Spiral.

SUICIDE IS PERMANENT

Trigger Warning: **This work of fiction is about suicide and its aftermath. Suicide isn't a solution. It won't fix anything.**

Suicide is ***permanent***. It isn't romantic. It can't be undone. It doesn't resolve your pain. Every person who jumped off the Golden Gate Bridge and lived said that they regretted their decision the moment they stepped off the bridge. But it was too late.

- **TEXT or CALL 988** for help
- **TELL** someone
- **ASK** for help
- **REACH OUT** no matter how much it hurts

There are ways to fix what seems unfixable. ***You are worth fighting for*** no matter how much it hurts or how much you think you don't matter. **You *DO* matter.** Your light is unique. Without it, the world's entire spectrum darkens.

If you feel suicidal: Text or Call 988
***Because* YOU MATTER**

Science Fiction Writing as L.S. Silverthorne

Standalones:

REDISCOVERY

Experiencing True Purple series:

RECOMBINANT, Book 1

HELIX, Book 2

SPLICE, Book 3

one

. . .

THE HORRIBLE MOMENT moved in slow motion, inching forward frame by frame, Heather just out of his reach.

A muffled screech. Rush of air.

Ross' strangled shout tore through the chaos like it had come from someone else. He couldn't move. Couldn't stop it. Couldn't stop that —thing from carrying off Heather.

"Ross!"

Heather's cry ripped through him.

Feathers rustled. Flash of black. Another scream.

"Ross, help me!"

Ross turned.

Demon claws raked across his chest, pulling him to the ground. They swarmed over him, tearing, scratching. He gagged at their stench, slinging vicious grey demons off him as he scrambled to his feet.

Heather!

Step. By. Step. He tried to get to her. But...she was just out of reach.

He stretched his arms as far as he could, his feet pounding the hard ground toward the soulstalker as it stretched its black wings wide and lifted on the air currents.

Heather clutched in its arms. She fought hard, but couldn't break free.

"ROSS!"

Heather's shout was a razor to his chest, the sound frozen and stuck in his head, playing over and over.

"Let her go!"

His body trembled as he ran underneath the soulstalker that still flew low over the tall, swaying grass. He leaped at its legs, clawing the air to catch the edge of its wings.

"Heather!"

His feet were cement blocks slogging through heavy mud.

Every step. One moment. Too late.

Screaming in frustration, he sprinted faster, his legs pumping hard as he fought for every step.

The soulstalker rose through the air currents and he jumped after it, lunging, throwing himself at the dark flying thing.

He grabbed it around its legs, but already, his hands were slipping.

The soulstalker oozed upward, sliding free of his grasp. Greasy black feathers slipped through his fingers, her name on his lips as he demanded, pleaded—begged for that horrid thing to release her.

To take him instead.

"Heather! HEATHER!"

His voice was raw, aching, her name floating on the air as a handful of black feathers swirled in the breeze, eddying in the updrafts and twisting slowly to the ground.

Scattering at his feet.

For several long moments, he could only stare at the sky, watching the love of his life carried away. He'd loved Jessie, but those emotions paled to the white-hot passion that had built like a firestorm between him and Heather.

Despondent, he sank to his knees, unable to look away from the speck on the horizon.

Heather was gone. Torn from his grasp.

Finally, the red haze of rage won out, fueling his attack when two demons wrapped their slimy limbs around his arms, claws tearing into his skin.

"Mulciber isn't done with you yet," one of the demons hissed against his ear.

He swung his arm around, punching the demon in the throat. Knocking it to the ground.

Stumbling backward, he turned. And threw himself at the tangle of grey demons as more surged out of the forest. Followed by several larger demons.

The red ones.

He gritted his teeth, nurturing a special hatred for them. Remembering the endless beatings. Countless hours of digging tunnels. And twisting his thoughts and memories until he wasn't sure of anything. Not his life before the Between. His time in the great tree.

Or his time with Heather.

God, he felt so weary. He sighed, his chest aching. But regardless of everything the demons had warped and tried to change, they couldn't touch what he held deep in his heart. Protected even from Mulciber.

His undying love for Heather Billot.

But he refused to forget the constant pain they'd inflicted on him. The torture. The incessant probing thoughts that had sliced through his consciousness, trying to disguise themselves as his inner voice. Trying to compel him to do their bidding. To make him believe only the worst in himself. And everyone else—even Heather.

It made him sick. Tormented him even now.

He winced at the memory of being herded into a crowded, hot chamber filled with bright lights and a large metal cage in the center where they locked him inside, pitting him against other souls and demons. He shuddered. And hideous creatures he'd never seen before. Forcing him to fight or be tortured.

While the demons bet on him. For their amusement.

Ross pivoted right, ducking under the claws of a red demon, and turned, delivering a roundhouse kick that staggered it. Rolling out of the confused creature's reach, he turned, and pounded it with a right cross and an uppercut to the chest that dropped the hulking thing at his feet.

He'd become their unwilling Champion, forced to defeat a long line of other souls and demons, something that filled him with despair and guilt even now. But somehow, he'd survived. He was grateful that he hadn't known any of those souls. That would have been too much. Now, shaken, angry, and wounded, he was never quite sure if his thoughts were his own.

Long ago, Thraecius had hinted about some of these horrors in a quiet moment by the great tree's hearth, when it had been just Ross and the Roman gladiator. At the time, Ross saw how those moments had haunted Thraecius, but he had little understanding of what Thraecius had endured. And he never dreamed that he'd follow Thraecius into that hell. Alone.

The former gladiator had even confessed to him that it was the reason he'd remained behind in the caves. Thraecius couldn't face his parents again after that, knowing what he'd become. He spat when he said he'd become Mulciber's Champion. The last thing Thraecius said was that afterward, the strain turned him into a volatile mess. When Mulciber realized that the gladiator had become unpredictable in the cages, he gave up on his plans to take Thraecius deeper into their SoulSport.

Ross understood what those plans had been now. Mulciber had planned to take Ross into the depths of a realm the demons called NetherReach, forcing him to battle in this shadow world's darkest depths. In its darkest pleasure. SoulSport. A guaranteed one-way trip to oblivion in Ross' eyes. When he'd refused, Mulciber chained him to the wall and left him there to either fade from existence or fight for him in NetherReach. Thankfully, Heather, Zakhart, and Knox rescued him. Saving him from a slow fade of his life force from existence.

Or a short trip to oblivion in NetherReach.

From the demons' broken conversations, Ross had figured out that this SoulSport was anything but a sport. It was some sort of gathering where demons chose their leaders and gained power through combat —now that Hell no longer had a king. The lesser demons used lost souls as currency and lesser demons to fuel and populate their twisted campaigns. He sighed. And competitions.

Zakhart and the others had no idea what hell these creatures had put the lost souls in the Between through. The coalfields and the Mechanism were just the surface of their depravity. And he was grateful that he'd only seen a minor part of it.

Ross glanced over at Zakhart who battled two demons to his left. The pale angel looked rattled, his gaze not leaving the sky as he flung a bolt of lightning at the demons, disintegrating them into piles of ash.

The air stank of sulfur, burnt hair, and scorched demon flesh.

Ross covered his nose, gagging.

The sight—and smell—of demons made him ill even now. He hated the stench of them, the squishy smacking sound of their sticky skin as they brushed against him, like slimy meat left too long in a refrigerator. He hated their oozing movements and the scritching of their shriveled feet shuffling across the dirt. Like rats running through the sewers.

Most of all, he hated the empty, hungry expression in their eyes. And their leering smiles. Lesser demons weren't smart enough to recognize that their hair was on fire, much less understand this SoulSport beyond kill or be killed. They seemed to function on impulses, leaping at a bite of meat dangled in front of them or cowering at the sound of their master's voice.

Mulciber. He gritted his teeth. That monster.

Disgusted, Ross beat down every demon that attacked him. He felt only fury and despair right now, his chest a raw ache, the panic rising as he tried to think. Tried to plan. To find Heather and bring her back to him.

Where had that thing taken her? Oh God, would she become like Jessie?

Had that bastard taken her to the poppy fields? Was she already a posed figure lying frozen in one of those poppy graveyards, her soul left to crumble into dust as pollen drifted like fog around her?

He couldn't even count all the poppy fields now, there were so many. So many horrible things had happened since they'd carried him below.

Before he and Heather found the Spiral, there had been some semblance of order in the Between. He sighed. Some inborn instincts that had governed the Between creatures' behavior. Now, it was chaos. Creatures once forbidden to attack human souls had gone crazy, attacking anything—everything—on sight. Flocks of soulstalkers crowded the dusky skies, clutches of demons gathering in caves and outcroppings, and even prides of wild sand runners prowled the grasslands.

Human souls were the prey—even for Death herself—with very few safe havens to avoid these creatures.

Shouts and thumping footsteps beat the ground behind him. He turned, looking back at the soul tree.

Dozens of souls and pale angels rushed out of the glowing ring of trees, throwing themselves into the fight.

He smiled. Two or three at a time, they attacked the flurry of demons as more left the tree to join the fight. Almost a decent force of lost souls to battle these shadow creatures. Maybe it wasn't completely hopeless to fight back? To go out there and bring Heather back.

He didn't care. He was going out there and find her. No matter what happened to him.

Ross wondered if any souls remained at the great tree. The tree that had been here from the beginning. When Ester and Matthew first came to the Between. And Thraecius. If enough souls had survived the demons' assault on the great tree, maybe they'd come here—to this new place. Maybe between those two groups, they'd have enough souls to create a solid defense?

He grimaced. Or an assault.

How had they created this new soul tree so quickly? Had it grown out of the dark or had the pale angels created it?

He had so many questions and only fleeting memories of Heather mentioning the great tree and this new one last night. He winced.

When she'd still been safe in his arms.

Cora and Javier fought their way through the massive force of demons to him. Barb shoved ahead through the thick swarm of demons, her five-ten frame towering over them as she picked them up and threw them out of her way.

He recognized many of the human souls fighting beside him, still struggling against their inner demons (like him). And so many others that he didn't recognize.

When had the other souls ever banded together to fight the creatures in the Between?

Then he remembered, a smile softening his snarl. Heather had come back. Doing what she did best—uniting people. Bringing out the best in them.

Like she had in him.

Two more demons leaped at him, knocking him to the ground. Ruining the moment.

He got to his feet, side-stepping two more, and stumbled into a third demon.

It sank its talons into his thigh, the others ripping fistfuls of claws across his chest.

Shouting, he picked up the writhing, little monster with its claws stuck in his thigh, ripped the claws free, and heaved it into the trees.

Another one rushed at him, but Lamarr Dunkirk was at his elbow now, grinning as he kicked it away like a soccer ball.

"Going 'for the goal," Lamarr muttered with a chuckle and

punted two more demons away from Ross. He slapped Ross on the back. "Good to have you back again, man. Missed you."

Ross patted Lamarr's shoulder. "Can't tell you how glad I am to see you, too, Lamarr."

With a nod, Lamarr moved toward Barb to clean up another surge of grey demons. The smarter red demons were falling back now.

Ross watched the souls working together, fighting side-by-side, and aggressively attacking the demons.

He couldn't remember a time when all of the souls had banded together into a single force like this. He'd tried since the day he arrived in the Between to spur them to action, but no matter what he did, they just cowered and hid in the great tree. Leaving him to go slowly crazy as the years passed. Every day, he became more and more like them, going through the motions of a life he'd voluntarily extinguished.

Avana had been right about him. He'd given up, too.

Until Heather Billot showed up one night in the Between and took his breath away. So beautiful with her burgundy-streaked hair and those black Converses, crouching in the tall grasses, a determined gleam in her haunting big green eyes.

She'd enchanted him with her patient but fiery spirit. And always made even the most mundane things exciting. Meaningful. He couldn't even count how many times her stubborn persistence had gotten him to act. Yet, no matter how bad things got, she never stopped believing in him. Loving him.

It stunned him silent just thinking about how she'd given up her new life to come back to this—this wasteland. Giving up everything on a slim chance to rescue him.

He vowed to do the same.

Ross grabbed a demon by the shoulder, spinning it around, and wrapped his arm around its neck. With a grunt, he flung it into three other demons running toward him.

The little grey demon spun like a top, slamming into the others, scattering them like bowling pins across the grass.

By that time, a flood of lost souls had joined him in the fight. To even the odds a bit.

He and Zakhart were no longer outnumbered.

No, Heather's compassion was endless and sometimes, Ross forgot that she'd ended her life like the rest of them. It hurt him deeply to think about her in a moment of quiet despondence so deep that she had killed herself.

Three demons tackled him, holding his face against the cold ground.

Anger burned deep as he kicked a nearby demon's legs, tripping it. He struggled until he'd worked his arms free and knocked one demon off him. He slammed the third one against the ground, pounding it until it stopped moving.

His hands were sticky and slick with inky, black demon essence, his face and clothes spattered.

With a feral scream, he scrambled to his feet. Propelled himself into the next wave of grey demons shuffling out of the forest.

He beat another demon into the ground, straddling it, and pounding it with both fists.

"I'll destroy you! Every last one of you until I find her! You hear me, you slimy bastards! I'll destroy you!"

Black sludge splattered his face, flecking his cheeks and chest as the horrid thing beneath him shuddered and heaved a final breath.

But she was still gone and he was still blind with rage.

"Every last one of you! You hear me? You're all dead!"

The memory of her frightened green eyes, so large and luminous, burned through him as that thing carried her off. Like a pike through his chest. Eyes that had cried over him, smiled at him—flirted with him—loved him like no one had ever loved him. He winced, still hearing the screech of that soulstalker in his ears, tearing at his soul.

"I'll find her!" he shouted, pounding the lump of cold demon flesh. "If I have to go through every single demon to locate her, I will!"

A hand squeezed his shoulder and he jolted, body turning, fist cocked, and ready to launch, but another hand slowly wrapped around his fist with a gentle squeeze.

Zakhart.

"Ross," he said in a soft, concerned voice. "It's dead. It's over."

Ross froze, staring into Zakhart's intense pumpkin-orange eyes, at last, aware of the silence and the retreating demons.

He glanced past Zakhart's shoulder, the pale angel's robes mottled with black, inky demon blood.

The demons *were* retreating.

The pale angel reached out and slowly slid his arm around Ross' shoulders, pulling him to his feet. Away from the dead demon.

"Where's Heather?" Ross asked, his voice so small and frail that he wasn't sure he'd even spoken out loud, but the watery expression on the pale angel's face told him he had. "Zakhart, tell me. You must sense her somewhere in the Between. Can't you?"

Zakhart shook his head.

Ross pulled away, rubbing his hand over his face, eyes smashed closed. His cheeks were sticky with black sludge and he swiped at them with his sleeve.

"We don't even know if the soulstalker that took her was one of Mulciber's." Ross sucked in a breath. "Or Death's. And there are thousands of poppy fields now. Thousands!"

The pale angel scanned the horizon as Razasha and Lairz burned away the remaining demon carcasses.

"Then I know you understand that it would be impossible to search for her among the poppies, Ross."

Zakhart took him by the shoulders again and this time, Ross let him. He was too heartsick and distracted to think straight right now. He felt Zakhart's angel light engulf him, burning away the demon blood.

"We need to take a step back and figure out our next move, Ross. Plan our actions instead of rushing headlong into a trap."

Ross nodded. "You're right," he said, winded. "Let's take a moment. To organize some search parties. Plan out a route through the warrens. Maybe if we divide up into groups—"

"That's suicide," Knox snapped, stepping toward them.

Ross bristled at the tall, curly-haired soldier. How did Knox fit into things? He had to be fairly new to the Between. Nevertheless, he'd been awfully close to Heather in the caves. Had there been something between them?

A cold chill shot through his chest. Had Heather fallen for this tall, dark soldier?

Ross sighed. He'd already lost his heart to Heather. She meant more to him than his own life. Little more than an empty promise here, but he would give up this shadow existence to save her.

Maybe she preferred Knox after she saw what he'd become in the Demon Veils? Had he already lost her to Knox?

Ross was six-foot-one, but he looked short—pale and weak—standing beside Knox who had to be at least six-foot-four. This soldier was tanned, broad-shouldered, and muscular with pale blue eyes that made him look like a movie star—like a curly-haired Paul Newman. Ross frowned. Unlike Knox, he was devastatingly average. How could Heather pass that up for average?

But dammit, he'd fought for her!

He'd given up everything to get Heather through that Spiral, away from Death, putting himself in Death's wake. He'd barely escaped her deadly embrace when the demons grabbed him first. And he went through hell because of it, too. He wouldn't give Heather up that easily.

Not to Knox. Not to anyone.

She had been leaving the Between with him. Not Knox—him. And he would keep fighting for her.

"You got a better idea?" Ross demanded with a snarl, his tone sharper than he'd intended.

He squared off, hands on his hips as he glared at Knox. He wasn't intimidated and the last thing he wanted was another competition. Especially another fight to the death.

With another soul.

"Ross," said Zakhart, stepping between them.

The pale angel reached out and laid his hand on each of their shoulders, drawing both of them onto more neutral ground.

"I don't think the two of you have formerly met. Ross, this is Knox. He's a recent arrival to the Between."

Knox studied Ross a moment, looking him over carefully. Trying to intimidate him.

Ross tried to look behind the man's game face, but that mask was on tight.

"Former Sergeant Knox Travers, United States Marines, but it's just Knox here." He extended his hand.

Ross gave him a sharp nod. "Ross Shepherd," he said and shook Knox's hand.

Knox's upper lip curled into a scowl and he pointed toward the sky, in the direction that soulstalker had carried off Heather.

"Don't know how long you been out of commission, Ross, but this place isn't the same as it was before you were captured. It's a hot zone now, insurgents everywhere. We're gonna need to recon the field for intel, redefine the perimeter and safe zones, and locate egresses so we have an exit strategy before ever sending out a patrol."

"Last I checked, I wasn't drafted," Ross snapped, glaring now. "So I'm not under your command."

Knox snorted. "Drafted? Damn, dude—how old are you?"

"I came here in 1961," Ross replied. "When I was twenty-two."

"Sounds to me like you don't know shit about S&R either," Knox said, pressing past Zakhart, getting in Ross' face. "So why don't you leave this to the experts?"

"You? Someone who's barely seen what's out there?" Ross shoved him backward. "Don't think so. Besides, this isn't a pissing contest! Our goal is to rescue Heather, got it?"

"I should have left your ass locked up in that demon hole!" Knox shouted. "Think you can just walk in here and take charge?"

"Enough!" Zakhart shouted, his voice deep and rumbling with thunder, silencing them both. "Bickering like this isn't productive. Now, the two of you better find a way to work together right now or I'm going to get mean."

Grudgingly, Ross held up his hands.

"Okay, okay—truce. I've seen you mean, Zakhart. I don't want to go there." He extended his hand to Knox again. "Truce?" he repeated.

Knox's expression was dark and he looked like he was sulking, but finally, Ross shook the curly-haired soldier's hand.

"All right," Knox said with a sigh. "Truce. For Heather, we'll work together."

Every time that guy said her name, Ross felt a chill brush down his spine. What had happened between the two of them? Did he kiss her? Tell her that he loved her?

Ross looked at Zakhart again. And nodded.

"All right, boss," Ross replied, folding his arms against his chest. "What happens now?"

Zakhart watched the two of them in silent concentration for several moments.

"Ross, you have more knowledge of this terrain than any of us. And Knox, you have a lot of combat experience. I want to combine the two. Working together, I want you to draw up a map of possible locations where that soulstalker might have taken Heather. Then we'll form small groups and go out to search for her according to likely hot spots."

Ross scanned the horizon. It was as good a plan as any and as long as they were doing something to find her, he was in.

"I'm on it," said Ross finally.

Zakhart turned to Knox.

"And Knox, I want you to step up training these souls. You're the best person we have for the job. Because we need to build an army. Quickly."

"Army?" Knox and Ross said in unison.

"Why?" Knox asked. "We already rescued Ross."

The pale angel didn't turn around, his gaze still on the horizon.

"That wave of demons was just child's play," Zakhart said, his tone grave. "You both know that if Mulciber was serious, he'd have sent an overpowering force against us. I want to know why he didn't."

"Maybe this skirmish was a cover-up?" Knox asked, beginning to pace in front of Zakhart.

The pale angel nodded.

"Possibly. I feel like he's trying to distract us from something, but what? I think he has another target in mind, but until we know if that soulstalker was Mulciber's or Death's, we have to assume that Mulciber has captured Heather."

"You're right, Zakhart," said Ross, watching the horizon. "Mulciber's after something else here. The shifts for digging tunnels beneath the Mechanism were increased tenfold. And the coalfields are now bringing in three times the amount of rock." He ran his fingers through his sandy blond hair. "And Mulciber was absolutely obsessed with his work with those shiny, carved rocks. I could only hear what he was doing out there. Didn't see it."

"We need to figure out what he was researching, Ross," said Zakhart. "And the purpose of this Mechanism that he's fueling with souls. It's critical to understanding what his goal is in the Between."

The pale angel walked behind Knox, laying a hand on his back.

"In the absence of knowing Mulciber's plan, we have to assume that he's going to harm us. Like he destroyed the great tree."

Ross' eyes widened, his stomach dropping.

"Destroyed the great tree?"

Zakhart nodded, his eyes sad. He motioned toward the south.

"Yes, Ross. The demons destroyed the great tree. They dug tunnels beneath it until it collapsed. The demons poured inside it and captured many of the souls, carting them off to the caves. We managed to rescue some of the souls who escaped into the forest, but a lot of the souls were taken to the caves."

Sickened, Ross bowed his head.

"Most of them were probably enslaved to the Mechanism or forced to dig more tunnels. Or wagered into the SoulSport. The ones they can't control end up in the coalfields. But usually, the end result is annihilation."

Zakhart fell silent. He turned away, his gaze connecting with a few of the other pale angels near him. He toned some somber tenor notes that played like a requiem, three other angels joining him in the conversation. Their harmonies were melancholy, the notes aching in the quiet, carried away on the wind. Ross had never heard them sing notes so dark before.

Finally, the pale angel turned around to face them again.

"The best thing we can do right now is prepare. Learn to work as one unit—souls and angels. Because the demons have chosen to break the Golden Edict. That means they will do anything and everything to achieve their goal—like harm souls and physical humans. So, we have to stop them. Using whatever tools we have at our disposal."

Knox shook his head. "Too bad we're fresh out of tools."

A curious smile brightened Zakhart's face.

"Not exactly. In certain circumstances, Archangel Uriel has allowed certain individuals to channel the Maker's Light."

Ross stepped toward Zakhart.

"Individuals? You mean angels?"

The pale angel shook his head.

"Souls. We have a few possible candidates. If they can control it, we'll train them to channel the light like we do."

"Does that include the wings?" Ross asked with a smirk.

To his surprise, the pale angel didn't crack a smile. His face was shadowed with an intensity that Ross hadn't seen before.

"We'll have to see how this progresses," Zakhart replied. "If we have one or two channelers, then maybe we can become a serious opposing force against these demons. Stop them before they complete this Mechanism. And find Heather. Heather is the glue that holds all of us together."

Ross watched Zakhart pace through the ashes of demon carcasses. The pale angel looked rattled. Concerned. Pensive. He remembered when Zakhart had always brought optimism and hope to the great tree, but now, the angel seemed almost jaded. Like Ross. And militant.

"I don't understand what the poppy petals accomplished and I've never seen that strange grey pearl that Mulciber took from Heather," Zakhart declared, hands on his hips as he turned back to Ross. "Mulciber wanted her for something and honestly, he seemed surprised when the soulstalker took her."

"Do you think that soulstalker belonged to Death?" Ross asked, fear washing cold against his chest.

"I don't know," said Zakhart in a quiet voice. "But I'm certain that soulstalker didn't serve Mulciber. So, we need to get to Heather before that demon."

Dozens of thoughts spun through Ross' head like fan blades as he chewed on Zakhart's observation. The pale angel was right. Mulciber had been as surprised as Zakhart when the soulstalker carried off Heather. But Zakhart didn't seem convinced it was one of Death's creatures. If it wasn't demonic or part of Death's domain, then who controlled it? Who was it stealing souls for? And why?

Regardless, they had to find Heather fast.

Before anything else in the Between found her. Like Death.

"Zakhart," Ross asked, turning toward the pale angel. "What if that soulstalker didn't belong to Death or Mulciber? Who else could control them? Someone in the Red City?"

The pale angel opened his mouth to speak, but stopped, staring at Ross as his gaze tracked toward the horizon.

"Is that even possible?" Zakhart asked finally. "That something else we don't know about could be controlling soulstalkers?"

"I've seen a lot of strange things here—including within the Red City," said Ross, turning to scan the forest surrounding them.

"Anything's possible. Especially now that the demons have declared war on the human souls here."

The Between was a huge place and he'd only seen a fraction of it. Zakhart and the others had only seen small swatches. But Ross had only spent a short time inside the Red City—long enough to search for Jessie. He'd go back there again if it meant finding Heather. There was no telling what else prowled past the sea of grasses and poppy fields. But drastic changes had happened to the Between since he'd been trapped in the Demon Veils. They needed to delve deeper. Find out if new enemies lurked out there. Something else they hadn't even considered yet.

Something else that could destroy them.

two

. . .

DANGLING HIGH ABOVE THE BETWEEN, clutched in the arms of a hideous soulstalker, Heather stopped struggling. The distance to the ground terrified her even though she was already dead. What would happen if she hit the ground? Would it shatter her soul into a million pieces or would she bounce off like nothing happened?

Regardless, her fear of heights had taken hold.

This was the first time she'd ever seen the Between's entire expanse laid out before her. The Between's persistent greyness held even from this height. The forest seemed concentrated in the Between's center, the swamplands (and caves) separating the forest from the mountainous area to the north (what felt like north, at any rate). Where the Spiral gleamed, even though she couldn't see its brilliance through the pervasive grey mist that hung like clouds of pollution across the terrain. To the west and south, a sea of silvery green grass stretched far into the distance, poppy fields dotting the landscape as small, ashen grey squares. To the east, the forest thickened, darkened—appearing misty, tree trunks obscured. But, as the edge of the grasslands, something deep and metallic blue-grey loomed, covering a huge area.

The soulstalker flapped its great black wings in a steady, staccato rhythm that thrummed above the swift air currents until the creature caught an updraft and soared higher, wings spread wide.

At this height, the air felt cold, pressing against Heather's face. She shivered, chills dancing across her skin. The air tasted sweet against her dry lips, the smell of dirty rain dissipating.

The shadow creature squawked a bright soprano note that lingered on the wind like an eagle's call, its steely black gaze focused ahead on something in the distance. Its face was long, human-like features angular, its skin smooth and putty-colored. It had large, round dark eyes, widely spaced, a beak-like human nose, and pointy teeth resting against thin lips. Its thick, black hair was shaggy, wavy, and wild against a long, slender neck as the flowing locks trailed like a banner in the wind, brushing across rounded shoulders.

Dark, shimmery fabric draped its chest, crisscrossing across small breasts that revealed a shapely waist and torso. More fabric crisscrossed its hips and pelvis and wrapped in loose folds around its legs to the knees. At last, Heather realized that this creature was female.

Where was it taking her? The poppy fields? Death's hovel?

They'd already passed over several poppy fields until the landscape became an unbroken sea of silvery green grasslands. Pristine, not a single foot trail winding through them. Not a single poppy poked its heavy grey petals through the undulating meadows of grasslands. If this creature belonged to Mulciber, then it should have been headed far to the northeast, toward the demon caves. Maybe it was carrying her to Death's doorstep? Heather had no idea where Death resided in the Between. She'd only traveled through the center of the Between, never to its edges—not even when she'd entered the Spiral which lay at the edge of the northern mountain range.

Then she saw the heavy black fog that curved like a snake

through the forest, obscuring a crystal-clear stream where the heartlilies grew in a blushing glow of orange in the dark. Just north of where Zakhart and Razasha had built the new soul tree. The soulstalker was flying directly south from the soul tree. If she could get to the ground without shattering everything, she'd head north toward the mountains. Get back to the new soul tree.

As the soulstalker soared farther west, a large, flat area took shape. It was gunmetal blue, its surface almost mirror-like, covering a great distance as it stretched far to the west.

A body of water?

The whole landscape changed as they got nearer to the water. A lake? Maybe an ocean?

Abruptly, the grasslands shifted into taller, thicker blades that were golden almost like wheat or straw.

The wind picked up, carrying a dry, musty scent.

The creature caught another updraft and sailed on the currents, the feathers of her great black wings fluttering in the cool winds. She drifted a long time, gliding on the updrafts until Heather saw trees below. They weren't like the spindly, bone-white tree trunks that filled the central forests. Those trees had always reminded Heather of river birch or aspens. The trees ahead reminded her more of the old-growth trees that had become soul trees. Huge, thick, dark trunks, but the bark was patterned like herringbone.

With a soft trill, the winged creature banked right and made a graceful turn, heading toward the water.

Her wings beat the air with steady thumps. They were descending.

The staccato rhythm quickened until Heather felt an upsurge of wind that seemed to take hold of them and lift them higher in the sky. Heather's feet dangled, touching clouds that hung in the sky as the soulstalker accelerated. They passed through the low-hanging clouds, edging closer to the ground.

The occasional thump of wings echoed in the silence as the soulstalker corrected course.

The water was so close now. Heather saw it lapping at the Between's grassy edges, a gentle tide nuzzling sandy banks.

The soulstalker passed through the fog banks that collected at the edge of the water, sinking softly toward land. All along the shoreline, Heather saw massive, egg-shaped spheres, woven from the golden-brown strands of dried grass that hung from the massive trees growing along the water's edge. The trees reminded Heather of Redwoods or the Live Oaks that grew in Georgia with tufts of something that resembled Spanish moss clinging to the branches. A cottony soft blue that trailed in long, delicate strands from the massive trees' bare limbs. Like wisteria. Everything in the Between was perpetually autumn, so the pale blue stuck out.

As the soulstalker soared nearer to the ground, Heather heard the din of noise below. Like a colony of seagulls. Her fingers turned cold, her stomach falling into her feet. Worse than that.

A colony of soulstalkers.

Would this creature toss her out to them? As their evening meal?

Screeches and shrieks chattered around her, making her skin crawl. Flashes of black wings passed in front of her, above her—below her—as three of the creatures took flight, sailing past. Heather began to shake. Their faces were fierce, eyes wild, expressions angry as they soared in packs across the lake.

As the soulstalker got close to the colony, Heather realized that the fog banks she'd seen were steam clouds rolling off the lake. From geysers spouting water high into the air. As they passed over the water toward a jutting finger of land on the edge of the colony, hot steam roiled over her. The water bubbled and hissed with vapor as the soulstalker landed beside an isolated tree.

She stood Heather on her feet, but her taloned claws were still wrapped around Heather's arms. Heather felt their sharp points pressing into her flesh, but not puncturing it. As the soulstalker stood up straight, wings folding against her back, Heather realized how tall she was. The creature towered over her, well over six feet tall. Taller than Knox.

The heat from the nearby sea almost knocked her down. It boiled like a pan of gravy, thick, gloopy bubbles churning across the surface, steam rising.

The soulstalker let out a soft, scratchy call as she pulled Heather alongside her, toward a huge, woven structure that hung about twelve feet off the ground. It resembled the soulstalker warrens she'd seen in the grasses near the forest, but these looked different somehow. These hanging nests looked larger, wider.

Shadows flashed across her from all sides, so many soulstalkers that she lost count. Their wings looked fuller than the soulstalkers she'd encountered. They were shiny and the fabrics they wore seemed different somehow. Shimmery, not smoky like the grasslands soulstalkers. Their skin was a soft putty color, not fleshy and pink like the almost human skin of the other soulstalkers. The grasslands soulstalkers looked spongy, their faces bloated and shadowed.

The faces of these soulstalkers seemed a little different, more refined, and natural with their hawk-like noses and softer cheekbones. At first glance, their eyes looked black and empty, but looking closer, she found their eyes intense, animated with large, owl-like pupils and irises flecked gold and brown like illuminated tortoiseshell. They didn't have the wild-eyed, hungry gaze of the other soulstalkers she'd seen.

No, these water soulstalkers were different.

"What do you want with me?" Heather demanded as the soulstalker dragged her toward the looming tree with its hanging nest.

The soulstalker cocked her head, staring at Heather with a confused stare. She let out a tiny chirp and then pushed Heather forward, prodding her toward the tree.

"Why did you kidnap me?" Heather shouted, unable to dig her heels into the soft, sandy ground. "Take me back. Now!"

Finally, Heather's foot hit a root and she dug her toe underneath it, pulling back from the shadow creature when she finally got some leverage. The stumble broke the soulstalker's grip.

Heather bolted left, zigzagging across the ground, trying to dodge the soulstalker's talons.

She bolted right, turned left again, running toward the nearest tree, but the shadow of wings fell over her.

That's when her feet left the ground.

Heather kicked and screamed as the soulstalker lifted her off the ground, floating high in the air. She kept screaming and fighting until the soulstalker smashed her hand over Heather's mouth, carrying her up toward the nest.

"No!" Heather shouted against the creature's hand, her voice muffled. "Let me go!"

The soulstalker threw her into the dark structure and slipped inside behind her in the darkness. She pulled a woven grass mat over the opening and tied it into place as Heather struggled to sit up in a dry pile of grass. It had a crisp, pungent scent like freshly mown grass or cilantro, but the dried grass was surprisingly soft, not prickly or scratchy. It also held in the heat.

Her eyes began to adjust to the darkness as she watched the soulstalker spread parts of the weave apart with long, taloned fingers. Letting in the light, Heather realized. She looked around the small structure that was larger inside than she'd expected. Maybe about eight feet across. There were three piles of grass against the nest walls and what looked like four wooden crates arranged in a circle in the center of the nest. Three tin cans sat on top of one of the crates. From the ceiling hung several cloth sacks and what looked like three hammocks.

The soulstalker moved toward her and she scrambled backward, huddling against the nest wall.

What did it want with her? Was she a prize? A meal? What exactly did these creatures eat? Lost souls?

The soulstalker folded her wings tightly against her back and knelt on the ground about three feet in front of Heather. Staring. With those intense, luminous tortoiseshell eyes.

Studying her, Heather wondered, keeping as still as possible. Or getting ready to eat her?

three

...

THE LAST THING Ross wanted to do was fight. Or train to fight. He'd seen enough violence to last a lifetime in the Between. That was before the demon uprising.

And his capture.

Ultimately, he felt responsible. He'd initiated it. He'd started the violence by killing himself. They all had, but for Heather, he'd embrace all of it again to find her, to save her from going through the horrors that he'd experienced at Mulciber's hands.

He paced the ring of trees, watching the others train from a distance. Knox swaggered through the grounds like a tyrant, watching the small groups of souls and angels training. Practicing hand-to-hand combat.

Man, this guy got under his skin! Sure, he'd helped save Ross from the demons, but only done it to please Heather. And every time the curly-haired soldier looked at Heather, he wanted to explode.

Turning away, he focused on Lamarr and Razasha who were teaching others some acrobatics. Flips, somersaults, and rolls. Lamarr seemed to have springs on his feet, his body lithe and fluid as he bounced through the air. Razasha seemed fascinated by his movements and did her best to imitate them. She caught on quickly which delighted Lamarr.

"Join us, Ross!" Lamarr shouted, motioning him over.

His South African accent was gentle and appealing. He was well-educated and soft-spoken, a perpetual smile on his ebony face. Ross admired his positive outlook and wondered what dark moment had befallen him, made him give up on everything and end his life, but they'd never discussed it. He'd mentioned something about Apartheid, but Ross died decades before Lamarr and had never heard the word before.

He had never asked questions because Lamarr didn't like to talk about it, saying only that the violence had been horrific. It was hard to think about how the world went on without them, making the same horrible mistakes every decade. And Ross couldn't help but wonder about the events that had happened in the world since he'd left it.

How different had his world been from Lamarr's? And Heather's?

Ross shook his head, shoving his hands in his pockets, his thoughts spinning with worry.

"Come on, Ross," said the tall South African, his black hair sculpted close to his scalp, smile bright against his dark skin. "It'll take your mind off everything."

"Maybe later," he said, offering Lamarr a warm smile.

Razasha gave him a sympathetic look and returned her attention to the other souls learning to tumble.

Lamarr trotted over to him, a hand on his arm.

"Hey, bru—don't you worry, we'll get her back. If you need someone to watch your back out there, you know I will."

Ross gripped his forearm a moment. "Thanks, Lamarr. That means a lot to me."

The taller man patted him on the shoulder and hurried back to Razasha and the others. He launched into a chain of flips, his body appearing weightless as he landed on both feet in front of Razasha who clapped wildly.

"That's amazing, Lamarr!" she cried, delight in her eyes.

Lamarr grinned and bowed.

"Will you teach me that?" she asked.

"Of course," said Lamarr.

Ross turned away, continuing across the courtyard where Javier and Barb trained a bunch of souls and a couple of pale angels how to use a staff that they'd fashioned from a tree limb. Their grunts and shouts filled the courtyard, crack of wood against wood like thunderclaps, competing with the noise emanating from Knox's loud hand-to-hand groups. The clash of wood and thump of footsteps echoed in the silent forest, overshadowed by Knox's booming voice shouting out orders.

Some gangly, black-haired kid scurried after the tall soldier, following every step, mimicking every movement. She looked about fourteen and had stars in those large, doll-like hazel eyes. In a few years, this kid would have grown out of her awkwardness. But maybe she was older than she looked. Still, it made his chest ache to see such a young teen here in the Between.

What made someone so young quit right at the beginning of her life like that?

Knox seemed calm and patient with the kid who was like a puppy following him around. If it weren't for Heather, he might have been friends with Knox, but the stakes were too high. The thought of losing her to this man made his insides twist into knots.

Heather meant everything to him. He couldn't lose her to the soulstalkers. He winced. Or Knox.

Ross glanced up at the bare tree limbs clacking in the wind, missing the soothing rustle of leaves, and the chittering of birds perching on branches in the treetops. He missed their calming song on the wind and the flash of green leaves. He missed watching squirrels skitter up and down the trunks, bushy tails twitching as they chased each other from tree to tree. He missed so many things he'd taken for granted.

At the edge of the courtyard, Cora sat in the grass, watching the others train. She huddled into a tan shawl wrapped around her shoulders, dark blue eyes stormy, fearful. He walked over, startling her.

"Ross!" she said with a gasp, her hand against her chest, eyes wide.

"Sorry for scaring you, Cora," he said. "Mind if I sit?"

"No, of course not," she said, a smile curving across her pale face.

She'd gone through hell in her short life, the horrors of the Civil War nearly destroying her soul. He remembered how terrified she'd always seemed, huddled in the great tree like a statue. She'd been one of the many fixtures in the great tree (like Ester and Matthew) when he'd first arrived.

Avana had pointed out a bunch of hopeless souls to him that day, telling him to forget about them, not to bother. Like Ester and Matthew. And Cora. She'd been beyond hope, Avana had said, that she'd been there a long, long time and couldn't escape her tortured thoughts. So Ross made it his mission to get her to open up to him. He nearly quit several times, until one night, he asked her name as he'd asked her a million times. Finally, she whispered it to him like it had been the location of pirate treasure.

Every day, he spoke to her, tried to engage her in conversation, offering her comforting words and all the patience he could muster. At first, it was just the one whisper, her name, so he'd sat with her and carried on an awkward monologue about his life, telling her whatever stories came to mind. After a while, it felt more like he was just talking to himself, Cora whispering here and there, occasionally uttering a word or two. But one night, as Ross struggled through a story about his grandparents, Cora's whole awful story poured out.

She told him about the soldier that had raped her, the ones that had also killed her Ma. Once she got through that first, horrible story, she began to blossom. He'd never forget the moment he first saw her smiling on the staircase, a thick tan shawl bunched around her shoulders. It was the first time she'd come downstairs since she'd arrived in the Between. As horrific as those events had been, they hadn't scarred her delicate features or marred her fine porcelain skin.

"I was just daydreaming," she said, a slight pout to her mouth, fine hair reminding him of corn silk from his detasseling days in the Indiana cornfields.

She had a small pert nose and a tiny mole above her upper lip that she covered with her fingers when she talked. A sprinkling of freckles dusted her cheeks and the bridge of her nose.

He smiled. Jessie had freckles. She always got so mad when he counted them before kissing her. Or whenever he touched the small, raised mole on her right cheek. Jessie hated that mole, always trying to hide it with that horrible pancake makeup that smelled like paint primer. She'd always complained about her heart-shaped face— something that Ross never quite understood. The shape of her face had been as beautiful as her heart, but she could never see that. No matter how many times he told her.

Cora reminded him so much of Jessie, sweet and insecure. Sincere, kind, and concerned.

Ross dropped down beside Cora, folding his legs underneath him.

"How are you holding up?" Cora asked, a finger against her mouth. She reached out and rubbed his shoulder.

"I'm not," he said with a sigh, brushing his sandy hair out of his eyes. "Going out of my mind, to be honest."

"I'm sorry about Heather, but don't give up, okay? We'll find her."

Cora reminded him so much of Jessie, reassuring but self-conscious, always hiding her body underneath that thick, bulky shawl that she never took off. Her body was thin and trim, yet she hid it.

"She didn't give up on me," he said, smiling. "So I won't give up on her."

Heather was straightforward and tomboyish (the word in his time period) with her lithe gymnast's body, slim hips, and slender legs, oval face smooth and clear with that adorable, upturned nose, and the clearest green eyes he'd ever seen. He loved how her nose crinkled when she laughed.

Every time Jessie saw a woman with an oval face, she pointed it out, telling him how much she wished her face had that shape. She would have found Heather beautiful and she would have stressed about how perfect Heather's hair and face were. And hurting over how she looked nothing like that.

He sighed. Jessie never understood how beautiful she was and how much he'd loved her for that heart-shaped face, those freckles—and the mole on her cheek. Things that made her look unique to him. She could never accept that he'd fallen in love with her differences. The cute freckles, the hip-hugging black skirts, the long ponytail at her shoulders.

Looking back, he realized that those little insecurities had been her first steps toward taking her own life, even before she got sick. He was relieved that those things didn't seem to matter to Heather. She seemed comfortable with her body and her looks, but not the feelings she tried to hide from others. Like she felt broken on the inside, missing pieces of her life, and felt ashamed to show her emotions.

And he'd done everything in his power to find her after he survived the first suicide attempt, succeeding on his second. But a year in his time had passed. That had been a lifetime in the Between and he'd had no idea that it was already too late to save her when he got here.

"You've got that right," said Cora. "Heather never gave up, Ross. Zakhart said that she'd even carried her loss into the new life he'd given her. Even though she couldn't remember you."

He frowned. "What do you mean?"

"Zakhart had two possibilities for her when she entered the Spiral. He said she chose the young woman with a defective heart because she knew hers couldn't be whole without you."

Cora's words sliced through him and he winced like she'd struck him in the face.

"A defective heart? What do you mean?"

"Apparently, Zakhart had a corresponding life picked out for you, too. You were to meet Heather at fourteen and live out a short life with each other. Dying together. But your soul wasn't there to enter that new life. So she continued living the young girl's life who had a bad heart."

He was stunned, staring at Cora in disbelief.

"Is that the truth?" he asked, a lump in his throat.

Cora nodded. "I wouldn't make that up, Ross," she said in a soft voice. "Heather told me and Zakhart confirmed it."

He turned away, overcome with emotion, his arms folded against his chest. Pulling in breath after breath to control the stinging in his eyes. And moisture welling there.

Cora slid closer, putting her arms around him. He felt her shawl against his cheek. She'd always been kind to him, but he'd felt the hint of an attraction between them. A tiny spark, like the scritch of a match just under the surface. But it had never caught fire in him—not like his love for Heather. Cora had never flirted with him, never acted on it, and she had never pushed herself on him like he'd seen other souls do.

Over the years here, he'd watched other souls wrapped in each other's arms, seen them kiss and grope each other, even wander off together. Had they been able to have sex? He'd always wondered. If he and Heather had stayed any longer in her bed upstairs, he'd have probably found out.

"I'm sorry," she whispered against his ear, her voice soothing. "Maybe I shouldn't have told you that, but I just wanted you to know how much she cares about you. Heather and I used to talk a lot in the great tree. I always told her how much I admired her, how she threw herself into the action. Or made her own. She'd just laugh and tell me that she admired my restraint."

He turned out of her embrace, studying her dark blue eyes, like sapphires. Not a hint of malice or jealousy.

"Women are weird," he said with a chuckle. "You each want what the other one's got. Looks, clothes—possessions."

Men. He kept that thought to himself though.

He'd loved Jessie, but she had a knack for falling for other girl's boyfriends in high school. She'd chased after him his entire sophomore year when he'd been dating Wendy Brenner. One afternoon, Jessie cornered him in the malt shop, *Don't Be Cruel* thundering from the jukebox. He'd just broken up with Wendy after he found her kissing Ben Healy behind the bleachers. Football practice had gotten over early that day. Wendy hadn't expected him for another thirty minutes.

"That's not true," Cora said with a laugh. "Most of the time anyway. Okay, some of the time."

He'd gone to drown his sorrows in a chocolate malt and listen to the devil's music that Momma wouldn't let him play at home. He'd just put a nickel in the jukebox, Elvis' velvety voice getting everyone up dancing when Jessie made a play for him. But this time, he didn't tell her that he and Wendy had broken up. Sometimes he wondered if Jessie would have made a play for him if she'd known he was already available.

Cora let him go, adjusting the folds of her shawl around her shoulders.

"But you and I both know that men are shallow," she replied, sounding a little distant now.

"Visual," he countered. "We're very visual. And pretty straightforward actually."

Cora smiled, shaking her head as she wrapped her arms around her knees and leaned back against a tree trunk.

"We were taught from an early age that beauty and manners were the only things that mattered, Ross. The prettiest women marry the rich and powerful. Their fathers use them as bargaining power. And heaven help women who are plain or homely—unless they're sit-in' on a fortune. Or women that didn't know how to conduct themselves at galas and socials."

In Cora's time, that was probably true.

"Did that happen to you?" Ross asked. "Promised to some old rich guy?"

She shrugged. "Long before the war, Daddy inherited Bougainvillea, one of the largest cotton plantations in Georgia. I grew up part of Atlanta's gentile society, manners and piano classes, etiquette—all of it preparing me to marry General Stallons' oldest son. Harvey. But all of it was just cotton candy, just spun sugar hiding bitter truths about our lives. The violence and slavery. Something I learned here—in the Between."

She shuddered, a haunting look in her eyes as her memories took her far away for a moment.

Ross swiveled around, watching her eyes now. He understood about the spun sugar and how everyone in his time had made segregation look happy and acceptable. But it wasn't. It was arrogant and wrong, something he'd felt as a child, but was promptly silenced when he asked why his friend had to use a different water fountain or couldn't sit with him at the lunch counter.

"I take it you weren't very fond of General Stallons' oldest son?" Ross replied.

"I despised him," said Cora, almost spitting, her eyes narrowing. "He was dirty and conniving. His Daddy paid good money to keep several young debutantes quiet after he'd assaulted them." She folded her hands into her lap, her eyes lightening. "I remember my sixteenth birthday. It was the grandest ball of the summer! Daddy and Momma bought me the most beautiful dress. It was silvery pink and sparkled like star shine. I'll never forget walking down that sweeping walnut staircase that night at Bougainvillea while a quartet played Beautiful Dreamer. Such a shame that Mr. Foster passed on shortly after writing this beautiful song." Her voice grew wistful, her eyes turning misty. "That's when I saw Billy Baxter standing at the bottom of the stairs in his pressed black suit."

Abruptly, Ross saw the pain creep into her face, her voice tight now.

"But Daddy didn't like Billy's parents. Their farm wasn't big enough. They weren't true Southerners, being only two generations in Georgia. Daddy had his heart set on Harvey Stallons. He was a nasty man who parroted his Daddy's opinions as his own. Billy spoke his mind. About the economy. About politics. About slavery. And they hated him for it."

Ross laid his hand against her forearm. "You loved him, didn't you?"

Cora looked up at him, nodding, eyes wet with tears.

"With every bit of my soul, Ross. He was beautiful and passionate. Such a good man who loved people and hated war. He went north to fight for the Union because he despised slavery. I tried to follow him, but Daddy locked me in my room."

She got to her feet, pacing the courtyard. Ross walked alongside her.

"Did you ever see him again?"

She shrugged, fine blond hair curling around her face.

"As the war raged on, the plantation fell into ruin. Cotton rotted on the vines, what little remained after the Yanks burned the fields. By the time the Union army reached Atlanta in 1864, Daddy had fallen in the battle at Petersburg. Momma and I sold what we could and were forced to live in a small sharecropper cabin on the property, fearing for our lives after raiders gutted Bougainvillea. Then my little brother fell at Jonesborough and the next night, Atlanta burned, Bougainvillea with it. I'd have traded my station and my looks for an ounce of courage, a dram of skill."

Ross took her hands in his, caressing her fingers.

"You had great courage that night, Cora. The way you fought off those soldiers, stood up to protect your family. You did your best. You were brave and you fought for your family when it mattered."

Cora looked away, her gaze falling on Knox. Her hands trembled as she adjusted the taut braid that hung down her back (like Jessie who always wore a ponytail).

Such a contrast to Heather's wild, honey-warm brown hair, so loose and flowing around her shoulders. He closed his eyes, remembering her cool, clean scent that reminded him of an Indiana spring rain. He could almost feel her buttery soft skin like pure silk against his fingertips which made his chest ache. Cora seemed reserved and calm—like his Jessie—content to wait until the right thing happened.

Heather was more intense and passionate, determined to make the right thing happen. It was that stubborn, raw fire that made him ache for her, long for her when she wasn't there. She was the most genuine person he'd ever met and she brought out the best in him. Just thinking about what might be happening to her right now was driving him crazy.

"But I lost everything," Cora said with a hiss. "After I'd struck one of the Yanks in the head, I rolled him away from her." Her breath caught, her voice turning into a guttural squeak. "The one who raped and killed my momma."

Tears slid down her face now and Ross held her hands tighter.

"It was Billy, Ross."

She sank into the grass and Ross dropped down with her.

"All our pride and grand ideals—on both sides. Reduced to rabid animals snarling hate to our dying breaths. Union, Confed—just animals in different fur coats who'd rather kill each other than say we were wrong. Who'd rather burn everything to the ground than say we're sorry."

She leaned into him, pressing her face against his chest, and Ross held her.

"That was a barbaric time, Cora," he said in a quiet voice. "But sadly, we never seem to learn from those dark times. Every generation seems to repeat them."

"Were there other wars?" Cora asked.

"Two World Wars," he said. "And others. I left the world in 1961, almost a hundred years after you did. I'm guessing there were more."

"And now this," said Cora. "A war against demons. I'm not sure I have the strength to face this. To watch everyone turn into animals again."

Ross felt her trembling, her gaze settling on Knox.

"Like that one," she said, a growl in her voice. "Frankly, he terrifies me, Ross. When I look at him, I see Billy in his eyes. I see that night outside Atlanta all over again. The city and Bougainvillea burning. Momma's screams. The Yanks' laughter rising above the flames—just makes me sick."

She pressed her hands to her ears, eyes smashed closed.

"I can still hear them asking Momma where her pretty daughter was."

She couldn't hold back a sob and the sound hurt his chest, her gaze needle-sharp as she stared at him now.

"Here we are, Ross, taking up arms to rescue a beautiful woman and Knox will harm anyone and everyone to get to her. Beauty causes nothing but pain and misery." Cora sighed. "He's in love with her, you know."

Ross winced, his stomach twisting into knots. It was obvious to him that Knox had feelings for Heather, but what he needed to know was whether Heather had feelings for Knox. It was a terrifying question he'd been too afraid to ask.

"Is that what you think this is about, Cora? Just Knox and me fighting over who gets to rescue Heather?"

Cora shrugged.

He took her by the shoulders, forcing her to look at him.

"Cora, look at me," he demanded, his voice sharpening. "Do you actually think that the only reason any of us are taking up arms is a schoolboy fight over Heather? And only because she's—beautiful?"

She wouldn't look at him now, but the shallowness of her accusation burned in his gullet.

"So, if Heather had one eye in the middle of her forehead, a unibrow, and size fifty hips, you don't think I would bother saving her? Because I'm so shallow that I only think beautiful people are worth saving? Is that what you're saying?"

Anger churned in Cora's dark blue eyes, her gaze snapping toward him.

"And are you telling me that if she'd been fat and homely, you'd still be motivated to save her?"

Cora's words made him pause. Was she projecting her prejudice on him? Yes, Heather was beautiful, but that wasn't what made her worthy of rescue. He and Heather had entered the demon caves to save other souls, not to judge their worthiness of rescue based on their looks or their intelligence. They were worthy of rescue because they were human souls. Because it was the right thing to do. And he'd leave the judging to horse shows and Heaven.

"I'm motivated to save her because I love her, Cora."

He couldn't quite hold all the annoyance out of his voice. And he resented her accusation.

"I went into the demon caves to rescue other souls and I never once based the decision to rescue them on how they looked."

Cora stared at him now, pain in her expression.

"Momma and I muddied our faces and dirtied our clothes, even cutting our hair. So the soldiers wouldn't..." She was trembling, teeth chattering now. "Wouldn't notice us. Wouldn't...see our beauty. Wouldn't—hurt us." She could barely choke out the words. "Or rape us."

He understood now. It wasn't jealousy. Cora had gone through hell that night and because of it, she couldn't separate beauty from worthiness—or violence. To her, beauty was the cause of it all.

He held her tighter.

"I'm so sorry that you went through that, Cora. Those attacks weren't your fault for being beautiful—no more than those soldiers attacking someone they saw as ugly. The assaults weren't about you. They were about rage and power and sickness. About force and control. It wasn't your fault."

She cried in his arms. Probably for the first time since she'd killed herself.

When her sobs quieted, she slipped out of his arms, wiping her eyes with her shawl. She was shaking.

"I can't tell you how glad I am to have you back, Ross. I never told you this, but you were always my rock here."

He smiled. "And you were always a friend I could count on, Cora."

Cora turned toward him, her eyes watery.

"I mean that, Ross," she said, her voice intense again. "Things were so different when you disappeared. Everything just fell apart after that. The great tree was destroyed and we were all running from demons and soulstalkers. Lamarr and I hid for days at a time in the forests, dodging soulstalkers and sand runners, not knowing what to do or where to go. I kept hoping you were all right. But I was so scared."

"That was a horrible time," he said in a distant voice.

She nodded. "You'd always been there for us, guiding everyone. Even when we didn't want to listen. But when the great tree fell, there was no one around to help. And so many souls were taken away by the demons. It was terrifying."

She motioned toward Knox.

"Then he arrived."

"Knox?"

Cora pointed toward the small groups practicing hand-to-hand combat. Where Knox paced back and forth, shouting directions and shuffling around, correcting postures, and adjusting stances.

"The soldier," she almost spat, her gaze unblinking as she glared at him.

Had something happened between the two of them? Had they argued or was it something else? Had Knox made inappropriate moves on her?

"Did something happen between the two of you?" Ross asked.

She shook her head, staring at Knox with a wary expression. She pulled her shawl tighter around her shoulders, rocking now.

"He's a soldier," she whispered, anger in her voice. "That's more than enough to hate him."

Ross shrugged. "Like a lot of soldiers who've passed through here, I'm sure. Hate and rage take so much energy to maintain. Especially when Knox hasn't done anything to deserve that—as much as I hate admitting it. Use that energy for something better, Cora."

She ignored his comment and kept glancing toward Knox.

"He's new. He's been ordering everyone around, too." She fixed Ross with her gaze. "And he's gotten really close to Heather. He better not have touched her either."

That statement made Ross shudder. That was the one other unanswered question between him and Heather.

"Cora, what do you mean?" he asked, the first flicker of anger welling inside him. "Did he do something to Heather? Hurt her in some way?"

"All I know is that she tried to avoid him and he liked to get her alone."

If that guy had hurt her in any way at all, he'd damage him.

He watched as Halea shuffled across the courtyard to stand beside Knox, watching him in silent fascination as the curly-haired soldier sparred with Javier, hand-to-staff.

"That pale angel is never far away from him either," Cora said, her tone dark as she crossed her arms. "I'm going inside. Watching these preparations makes me ill."

"Cora, wait!" he called as she shoved past him, gripping the shawl around her shoulders, and running toward the soul tree.

She paused at the doorway, casting a long look around the courtyard between the ring of trees, and disappeared into the soul tree.

Ross stood at the edge of the trees, glaring at Knox. He didn't like this cocky punk who thought he was the best at everything. Had Heather fallen for his bad-boy charm? Why did women fall for bad boys? They always fell for them and then later, they complained about the very things they'd found so appealing. Boy, did women confuse him.

But as much as he wanted to hate Knox, he couldn't. The guy had helped free him from demons. And Knox hadn't done anything to earn his—or Cora's—hatred.

The rustle of wings made him look up. Zakhart. Descending from the sky. He landed beside Ross and put an arm around his shoulder.

"Ross," he said in a quiet voice, a smile on his face. "Walk with me."

Nodding, Ross followed Zakhart toward a small footpath that led out of the courtyard, following the crystal-clear stream toward the familiar clearing ahead. He knew that clearing and the trails around here like the back of his hand. The air was gritty, smelling like rain when it came through a dusty screen. The forest felt cool, the wind slicing through the trees.

"What's up, Zakhart?" he asked.

"Heather," he said in a dark tone.

Ross sighed. "You have any ideas yet? Any leads?"

"I took a flight around the Between, observing the demons and the poppy fields. I studied the soulstalkers that flew in and out of the caves. They were smaller and dumber than the soulstalkers living in the grasslands."

"And?" Ross snapped.

"And I've seen enough soulstalkers to last me an eternity. The soulstalkers of the grasslands are ferocious and quick. They look bony, their skin almost shadowy. With fierce faces. Their movements are lightning fast."

Ross shrugged. "Okay, but what does that mean?"

"It means," said Zakhart, his voice hushed, "that the soulstalker that took off with Heather didn't match either of those descriptions." He held up his index finger. "And...it flew toward the south. Not north like the demons' creations. I watched their movements. They flew the same route every time. They were also slow and a bit sluggish. But this one didn't fly into the grasslands like Death's shadow creatures. This one flew south, past the grasslands, and kept going."

Ross pointed toward the south. "Is there something beyond the grasslands?"

"The Lake of Despair."

Ross frowned. "A lake?"

Zakhart let go of him, his hands behind his back as he paced ahead a step or two.

"I had to go into the Archive blueprints to identify it. There is so much about the Between that I don't understand yet. So many structures and places. This task has been a difficult one."

"What task?" Ross asked.

He shoved his hands into his pockets, kicking a stick off the dirt path.

"Securing the Between," he replied.

He paced in a small circle now, treading on the stream's bank and then turning back toward the dirt path again.

"After you and Heather entered the Spiral, Archangel Raduriel took great interest in this realm. Of course, it helped when I told him that demons had infiltrated this supposedly neutral ground. That's when he placed a whole phalanx of pale angels at my command." He looked at Ross sheepishly, shrugging. "Well, sort of. Actually, I asked for more angels and he granted my request."

"That's all that matters, Zakhart," he said, smiling at the disheveled pale angel, his white hair ruffled, robes askew.

Ross studied Zakhart a moment, the wind rising. Tree branches clattered, mixing with the stream's steady trickle. He was anxious about something, but eager to share it.

"What does it have to do with this Lake of Despair?" Ross asked.

"This one is a forgotten relic of the Dusk Wars," said Zakhart. "The last battle was fought here to the south. In the grasslands. Every creature of the light faced every creature of dusk. The light prevailed, casting the darkest creatures out of the skies, and into the lowest reaches of the realm. The NetherReach. The boiling lake of salty tears is all that remains of that battle. All the tears shed by angels of light and angels of darkness, suspended in the Maker's rage at the betrayal. Another betrayal. It was used to grant wings to pale angels and souls that had been elevated in times of need."

"Cool story, Zakhart," said Ross, pausing by the stream.

Ross trailed his fingers through the cool water. The burble of the water was soothing.

"But why should we care about a lake with a good folktale tied to it?"

Zakhart frowned, closing one eye. "Folktale?"

"Folktale," Ross repeated as he leaned against a spindly, bone-white tree trunk, arms crossed. "A tall tale. A creative story attached to a mundane object to make it sound more interesting."

"A fib?" Zakhart snapped, his whole face scrunching into a mix of annoyance and confusion as he stopped pacing. "You think I'm lying to you, Ross?"

A hurt expression burned in the pale angel's pumpkin-orange eyes. Ross felt guilty now. He hadn't meant to make Zakhart feel badly. Zakhart didn't always understand human sarcasm or other facets of humor. He hadn't meant to insult him or question his honesty.

"No, Zakhart, not a lie," Ross replied with a shrug and held out his hands. "Humans love a good story, so sometimes, we attach little embellishments to make things more exciting. To be more entertaining." He gestured toward the flowing stream beside them. "You know, like saying this stream—or a small lake—is full of angel tears." He chuckled. "Because it's not really angel tears...it's just water. Right?"

Zakhart's mouth twisted into a grimace as he crossed his arms. A deep furrow shadowed his brow.

"Ross, you don't know much about angels, do you?"

Ross shook his head. "Only what I've observed and what you've told me."

The pale angel's pacing began again, slower this time.

"You see, angels—even pale ones—are compelled by our natures to tell the truth. But because I am half human, I tell you the truth not because I have to, but because I choose to."

"You're serious about this lake," Ross replied.

Zakhart nodded, pausing again in his pacing.

"Yes, Ross. The lake is made from angels' tears. And the reason that's important is because there is great power in those tears. Power that can be transferred to others."

The word surged over him. Power. Was it something they could leverage against the demons? Something that might give them an edge over the growing numbers of those demons spilling out of the caves?

"What sort of power?" he asked in a quiet voice, stepping closer to the pale angel.

Zakhart slid his arm around Ross' shoulder as he unfurled both wings. The wings sprang forward, the sound like a sail catching the wind, and stretched into two beautiful curves of cream-colored wings that framed his body. He bent toward Ross' ear and whispered.

"Flight," he said. "And wielding light."

"How?" Ross gasped.

Was that even possible? Would it level the playing field? And save Heather?

Zakhart let him go now, pacing with renewed vitality, his footsteps already deepening the grassy footpath.

"Within the lake's depths lie all the powers stripped from the rebelling angels. Powers that Archangel Raduriel, Archangel Afeziel, and Archangel Mikhail removed in the Dusk Wars rebellion. As the Maker's General, Archangel Mikhail struck the rebelling angels down like the Maker did in the first Rebellion."

"How?" Ross asked.

Zakhart's voice was intense, deeper than usual.

"Mikhail rained down pure white fire on them, burning away their wings. Then Raduriel summoned massive bursts of thunder that knocked the rebels from the highest plane in the realm. They fell a great distance, finally landing in the Between—an event unforeseen by the general. Where Raduriel and Saraqael pursued them. Raduriel summoned hundreds of angels to defend the realm and the fiercest battle I've ever seen raged. As fierce as when Lucifer was thrown from the Heavens in the first Rebellion. And the night of the Enochian Apocalypse that raged above the Earth."

"Sounds brutal," said Ross, glancing at Zakhart. "But weren't the fallen angels powerless without their wings?"

Zakhart shook his head.

"In the Dusk Wars, they no longer had their wings, losing them in the Enochian Apocalypse. But they were still angels. They still had all their abilities, which made the battle seem endless, both sides equally matched. Only the Lightbringer and the archangels of death had the power to kill an angel by then. Azrael, Sidriel, and Turiel. And the Maker, of course. But then Dariel joined the rebellion."

Ross saw the pain sharp in Zakhart's eyes as the pale angel stared at the ground. He could almost see a string of terrible memories flash past in Zakhart's eyes that had turned dull copper, a grey cast flushing his face and skin.

"Where's the Maker now?" Was that another term for God? He'd never heard that term before.

"The Maker of all things. Crafter of knowledge and all the Realms. Maker of humans and angels. A being of many names."

"God?" Ross asked.

He felt dense now. He should have known that already.

Zakhart shrugged.

"You know, like from the Bible?"

"I don't read the works of humans much." His voice fell to a whisper. "Too much fiction."

"Those sound like ugly battles," said Ross in a quiet voice. "Could the dead angels be raised?"

"Only the Lightbringer and two angels of death have the ability to resurrect an angel. And peripherally, Archangel Eosphoro, my—"

Zakhart stopped abruptly, eyes wide as he stared at Ross,

indecision on his face. He inhaled sharply, brushing his ivory hair off his forehead.

"My—mentor. Only those two angels and the Lightbringer have the power of resurrect. Later on, Archangel Eosphoro was granted the power of decision. He decided which angels were allowed to be brought back. After the return of the Lightbringer." Zakhart's voice took on an edge, bitterness dripping from every word now. "Archangel Eosphoro. Bringer of Dusk and Dawn. Beginnings and Endings. And the second rebellion."

"So, an archangel started another rebellion?" Ross didn't know why, but it surprised him.

Guess even angels got tempted and did terrible things, too.

Zakhart nodded. "So many angels fell in the Dusk War. Creating the pool of tears to the south. The Lake of Despair. The war continues, but that lake is one of the last remnants of the battles in the Between." At last, the hint of a smile touched Zakhart's face. "And it just might help us fight the demons here."

"How can we extract power from a dormant lake?" Ross asked.

"Leave that to me," said the pale angel, gazing deep into Ross' eyes, looking into the depths of his soul. "But I have a difficult request to make of you."

Ross tensed, his muscles corded, his stomach twisting into a knot.

"Go on," he said.

Zakhart's grip tightened on his arm and Ross swallowed a nervous breath.

"Besides Heather, you are the only soul among us who has felt the light's pure white fire in the Spiral and the Dusk's deepest shadow. You, two are the only souls here that I can infuse with the Lake's power, but I can't do so without your consent."

Ross stared at him, a chill trembling through his stomach as he studied Zakhart's expression, but the pale angel had his game face on, revealing no emotion.

"If I accept this—this power, what will happen to Heather? And me?" Ross asked.

"You'll be able to summon the light's pure white fire," Zakhart explained as he summoned a ball of white light in his right hand. "Deadly to shadow creatures, but life-giving to creatures of the light."

Sounded powerful. And too good to be true—even from a half-human, half-angel. And what was the cost of having that power? He needed to talk to Heather. No, first, he needed to rescue her.

"I'll have to uh—think about that, Zakhart. Can you give me a little time?"

"Of course," said Zakhart. "But don't take too long. We don't have a lot of it to spare."

Zakhart tossed the ball of white light to Ross and Ross caught it. A sense of warm peace fell over him, the light washing over him in healing waves.

"I could do that?" Ross asked, pointing at Zakhart's hand. "What you just did?"

Zakhart nodded. "Yes, and there's something else."

"What?" Ross asked, frowning.

The pale angel bowed his head, taking in a deep breath.

"You would eventually grow temporary wings."

Ross couldn't speak for a moment. He stared at the pale angel's magnificent span of powerful ivory and sparrow-grey wings, a million thoughts tumbling through his brain.

Holy shit! Wings?

four

. . .

THE DARK NEST smelled musty and pungent with dried grass, only pinpoints of light trickling into the huge hanging nest. Outside, feathers rustled, sharp trills and chirrs echoing on the wind.

Heather rubbed her eyes, trying to adjust to the lack of light and strange smells. The female soulstalker crouched about four feet from her, a soft warble occasionally filling the silence as she watched Heather, unblinking.

Her warm tortoiseshell eyes were intense, her gaze darting toward any sound or the slightest movement. A stretch of Heather's foot, a twitch of her elbow. Even a sigh.

Was she waiting for Heather to try and escape so she could tear her apart? Shred her soul with those sharp, shadow talons? Did soulstalkers play with their food like cats? Like orcas tossing salmon back and forth in the Puget Sound?

Outside, the wind had picked up, the nest creaking and swaying, stirring up that musty smell of decaying leaves.

Heather grabbed hold of the nest walls to keep from pitching forward, right into the soulstalker. The muffled sounds of creatures scrabbling across branches and squawking outside the nest unnerved her. An occasional, sharp screech punctured the calm, startling her. And the calls reminded her of the laughing seagulls along the piers that ran along Alaskan Way and Seattle's Elliott Bay.

Every time she moved, the soulstalker shifted forward, its unblinking eyes never straying from her face.

"Look," said Heather, holding up her hand in a calming gesture. "I don't know why you brought me here, but if you're going to eat me, I wish you'd get it over with."

The soulstalker tilted her head like a dog that had heard a strange noise, pupils in her owl-like eyes widening. She chirped a quick note, her head tilting left then right.

"This place is way too creepy for my taste," said Heather, shifting her legs, the dry grass rasping against her jeans. "Do you even understand me?"

The soulstalker trilled a series of high-pitched notes, head tilting from side to side again, but it kept its position in front of Heather. Blocking the only exit out of this swaying nest.

"Do you understand?" Heather repeated.

The soulstalker's expression didn't change.

How could they understand each other when they couldn't speak the other's language? But she'd heard soulstalkers speak before. Was it just mimicry—like a Mynah bird? Or something more?

A huge gust of wind struck the nest, banging it against the tree.

Heather fell onto her side, getting a face full of grass. She spit out a twig and sat up.

The soulstalker was no more than a foot from her face.

Startled, Heather scrambled backward, pressing her back against the nest wall.

The nest shifted again.

Heather grabbed hold of the rough sides to stay upright, but this close to the soulstalker, it didn't seem quite as scary.

Heather studied her features for a long time, the downward curve of her mouth, sharp jut of her chin. A line of black dots ran the length of the soulstalker's jawline, trailing across her chin. Underneath her intense eyes, little black dots ran in a half-moon around the outer corners of her eyes. A column of black dots ran down from the soulstalker's forehead to the tip of her beak-like nose.

Decoration? She smiled. No, makeup.

Glancing around the nest, Heather touched a patch of dirt on the floor of the nest. Licking her fingers, she dipped them in the dirt, and pressed dots from her forehead down her nose. She pressed her fingers into the dirt again and pressed a dot under each eye. And turned her face toward the soulstalker.

The soulstalker trilled an excited string of notes, like a piccolo playing sharp tones, her wings twitching as she stared at Heather. Heather laid her hand against her chest.

"Heather. Heh-thur," she repeated phonetically.

And waited, watching the soulstalker.

Heather couldn't tell if she was angry or intrigued as her wings fluttered, feathers shifting dry grass across the nest floor.

"Heh-thur," Heather said again, saying it slowly as she laid her hand against her chest one more time.

The creature squawked, making some sort of scratchy sound. She paused, cheeping out another note or two. The sounds were almost melodic, reminding Heather a little of how the pale angels intoned to each other.

A third time, Heather said her name, slowly enunciating each syllable.

The soulstalker shifted back and forth, wings fluttering again as she crouched in front of Heather. The creature closed her eyes, her entire body trembling as she struggled. One shrill note. Then two. But to Heather, they were just sounds.

Agitated now, the shadow creature threw itself against the wall of the nest, warbling the same notes over and over as she beat her fists against the nest's woven walls.

Heather rolled into a ball and covered her head as the creature screamed and threw handfuls of grass through the space. Her taloned feet stomped against the spongy floor, punctuated by an almost throaty growl. Rusty notes and syllables rasped together, sounding more like nonsense to Heather.

Okay, that hadn't gone well.

After throwing herself at the walls of the nest a few more times, the soulstalker slipped between the folds of the door and the nest wall, leaving Heather alone in the darkness.

She let out the breath she'd been holding and leaned her head against the nest wall.

Did these creatures share a language? Were they even intelligent enough to communicate? The soulstalkers she'd seen carrying off souls seemed like dumb animals, almost blindly obeying commands. But they still spoke. Taunting her with their words, calling out to her from the skies to try and terrify her into running.

She crawled toward the opening and forced her head between the thick, woven mat covering it and the nest wall.

Flocks of soulstalkers darted across the boiling lake and flew north. They were an inky black smear on the horizon, blotting out the thin traces of light that cut through the steamy mist clinging to the ground and settling in the treetops. Their chattering became a sharp roar drowning out the rush of wind and the ebb of water against the sandy banks. The air smelled humid and dusty like dryer lint. It left some sort of residue behind that coated her lips and tasted almost metallic with a touch of sulfur. It clung to her skin, making her feel grimy.

Below, in the shadows, a small group of soulstalkers—four or five—clustered together, wings extended, dragging the ground as excited chitters hung in the air. They reminded her of a bunch of ravens fighting over the season's last apples.

Were they no more than animals? If so, then why hadn't they carried her off to the demon caves? Or given her over to the sand runners in the poppy fields like Death had commanded them to do? That was their job, right? Their function? Capture souls and put them to sleep among the poppies.

Not once had Death shown even a glint of her deadly scythe

since Heather had come back to the Between. According to Zakhart, she'd been furious at losing Heather to the Spiral. And Ross to the demons. Wouldn't she sense Heather's presence again? And pursue her relentlessly like she had before?

What had changed?

The soulstalkers below flitted into the air, rolling into somersaults and barrel rolls, their chatter filling the silence. They hit the ground and rolled across it, wings and legs tangling.

Were they fighting or playing? She didn't care as long as they were preoccupied. And left her alone.

The shadow creatures continued their display as Heather squeezed outside between the mat and the nest wall, sliding through the opening. She tucked her fingers into the strands of woven grass and climbed across the nest. The material was rough, cutting into her hands, and chafing her arms as she shimmied up the nest, one hand over the next until she was on top.

The nest swayed in the wind, dangling high above the ground. At least three stories up, she realized, her stomach sinking into her feet.

Even though she couldn't see them, the soulstalkers' shrill calls and trills echoed below. She hoped they didn't see her as she grabbed hold of the thick coil of grass rope that connected the nest to the massive tree. Trails of sky-blue moss hung from the bare limbs, floating weightless when the breeze caught them.

With a grunt, Heather hooked her foot into the thick twist of grass and pulled herself up toward the tree branch.

She forced her foot into a small notch in the rope and hefted herself up, stretching her hand as far as she could, but she couldn't reach the branch. Struggling, she poked and dug her left foot into the rope, trying to find a toehold to pull herself up.

The rope bit into her hands, tearing. She did her best to ignore it, concentrating on the next place to wedge her foot. This time, her fingertips brushed against the tree branch.

She was so close!

Grabbing the rope in both hands, she pulled her body up the rope and dug her feet into the braided strands of grass again.

She tested her weight and the rope held.

Reaching up, she grabbed the tree branch with both hands and struggled to pull her body up. Finally, she slid her torso onto the wide limb, gripping the tree with both hands until her body was flush against the branch. Only when she had her balance did she pull her legs up onto the large tree limb and lay against it on her stomach as it swayed in the strong winds.

She crawled on her belly across the limb until she reached the junction point with the tree's thick trunk. In the crook of the limbs, she folded herself into the small space, turning her body around.

Another wind buffeted the tree, bending the branches against the force, and carrying a pungent whiff of the fetid, salty lake below.

Heather hugged her body against the trunk, closing her eyes against the grit as she waited out the gust.

But the throaty growl forced her eyes open.

Intense tortoiseshell eyes glared back at her, a trickle of quiet but forceful noises above the hiss of the wind.

Heather vaulted to a lower limb, her fingers clamped to the rough wood, but the soulstalker ripped her off the branch, twisting into a quick climb toward the nest. She shoved Heather between the mat and the opening as she chirped out a frenzy of sounds.

Tumbling into the tangle of dry grass, Heather scuffed against the coarse weave, her cheek and shoulder burning from the contact.

With wings stretched wide, the soulstalker surged toward her. She pressed her face an inch from Heather's, an urgent but menacing cry escaping through gritted teeth.

Heather froze, holding her breath as she stared back at the creature.

The soulstalker worked her mouth, thin lips struggling into unfamiliar shapes as she stuttered sounds at Heather, those owl eyes piercing, daring her to move.

Wind rattled the nest, the thin light beginning to fade as Heather faced off with the soulstalker.

"What do you want from me?" Heather said in a steady voice, not breaking her stare down with this strange creature. "If you're going to eat me, do it already!"

She bared her teeth, glaring as she leaned forward, tired of this game.

"Do it!"

Tilting her head from side to side and finally in a half circle, the soulstalker matched her stance, eyes unblinking. She had the look of a golden eagle, a simple, majestic beauty like those huge birds except that her colors were charcoal, black, and watery greys. She looked nothing like the leering, pointy-toothed monsters that Heather had battled in the grasslands. The bony, wraith-like creatures that had wanted to devour her and the other souls when they'd attacked the soul tree.

"Doo. Eet." The soulstalker's raspy alto voice forced out the two guttural notes and cocked her head.

She'd repeated Heather's words!

Heather pressed her hand to her chest. "Heh thur," she said in slow, clear syllables and patted her chest.

"Het. Tur."

Was she trying to communicate or just parroting back the words?

Moving her hand slowly, Heather reached out and very gently laid her hand against the fabric crisscrossing the soulstalker's chest. She gave the fabric a deliberate pat and locked her gaze with the creature's intense eyes. Waiting for the soulstalker to respond with her own name.

The soulstalker stared, unblinking as she cocked her head slightly to the left.

Once more, Heather laid her hand against her own chest.

"Heather," she said with a gentle tap. "Heh thur," she said, saying her name slowly and clearly. "Heather," she said again, pressing her hand against her chest one more time.

Again, she tapped the soulstalker's chest and waited for a response. But none came.

Sighing, Heather sank back against the nest wall. It was no use. The female soulstalker didn't understand. She was just repeating everything mindlessly. It wasn't the creature's fault. She was only doing what she had been created to do. Heather would have to wait for another opportunity to escape—or make one on her own.

Why couldn't she have had more time with Ross? She struck the nest wall with her fist. Why!

They'd been apart for so long and she'd only spent a few hours at his side while he slept in her bed. But those moments in his arms had soothed that aching need to be with him.

She propped her elbows on her knees, resting her face in her hands. Poor Ross was probably going crazy right now, Zakhart struggling to keep him from doing something reckless. And she hadn't had a chance to even thank Knox.

How did he feel now that Ross was back? How did Ross feel about Knox?

She felt so conflicted now. Guilty. Confused.

She couldn't deny that she'd been attracted to Knox. He'd been there for her through much of her pain, watching her back, teaching her to fight. He'd fought for her, helped her rescue Ross, knowing what that meant for his chances with her. Now what?

Everything was all jumbled up and confused now.

If she and Ross had gotten through the Spiral like they were supposed to, she'd have never met Knox. And if she'd refused to return to the Between, she would have lost Ross forever. Even after returning to the Between, there'd only been a slim hope of success. Everyone—even Zakhart—had insisted that even together, they might never save Ross.

Why'd she have to meet that tall, gorgeous soldier? And why had Ross been so hot and so wonderful? Becoming so much a part of her world that she'd have chosen eternal sleep over a future without him.

She winced at that awkward moment when she'd finally stood

between both men, feeling so conflicted (and horrible for feeling that way). Seeing the pain on Knox's face when she'd held Ross' hand in the soul tree. He looked so dejected.

The last thing she'd expected was to have feelings for Knox Travers.

How had that happened? Did he feel used now? Like she'd just led him on so he'd help her rescue Ross?

It wasn't fair. Not to Ross, not to Knox, and especially not to her. She'd wanted to talk to Zakhart about what she was feeling, hoping for guidance. Now, she was trapped in this soulstalker warren on the edge of the Between. While Ross and Knox were together. Would Knox hurt Ross? Would they fight with each other?

She kicked the wall of the nest.

"Dammit! This is all just a big mess and I can't even be there to straighten it out."

Would Ross and Knox get along? Would they work together with Zakhart or would they be at each other's throats right now? Either way, she hoped Zakhart could handle it. Heather sighed, glancing at the soulstalker crouched in front of her.

Until she could escape from this damned nest!

Something grabbed her sleeve, tugging.

Heather's gaze snapped up, staring into the soulstalker's brightly flecked tortoiseshell eyes. The soulstalker thumped her fingers against Heather's shoulder.

"Heh'tur," she said, her alto voice throaty, the timbre of her voice rusty like an old crank struggling to turn again.

Great, she'd created a mynah bird that would now drive her crazy by endlessly repeating her name in the soulstalker's broken voice.

Heather groaned, rubbing her face, and wishing she'd kept quiet now.

Inhaling sharply, the soulstalker laid her hand against her chest.

"San-dri-ana."

The syllables rasped against the soft hush of wind rustling past the nest.

For a moment, Heather could only stare, stunned by the soulstalker's throaty response. She squinted at the creature.

"Heather," she said, pointing at herself.

She paused a moment, her gaze concentrating on the creature's intense expression. Her brow was pressed into a series of hard lines above her owl-like eyes that were flecked with fire, watching Heather intently.

With two fingers, she nudged the soulstalker's shoulder.

"Sandriana?" Heather asked, flowing all the syllables together.

Delight gleamed in the creature's eyes. She bounced up and down on her haunches, the corners of her thin lips rolling upward. A smile?

"San-dri-ana," she repeated and touched her chest.

The soulstalker tilted her head right then left, pointy teeth showing now.

Was she grinning?

The creature poked Heather's shoulder, the talon sharp against her skin, but the soulstalker didn't put any extra pressure against it.

"Heh'tur."

Heather grinned. Had she just communicated with a soulstalker? Maybe now she could find out if this creature intended to eat her or drop her into a field of poppies.

Or...maybe something else entirely.

Things were looking up. Well, sort of.

five

. . .

THE PUNCH TO ROSS' face staggered him.

He shook it off and lunged at Knox, but the soldier side-stepped him, slamming a blow into Ross' back.

An uppercut hammered his left kidney.

"That's pathetic, Shepherd! That all you got?"

Dozens of souls and pale angels had gathered in a loose circle around them, shouting and egging them on. Cora stood at the edge of the group, looking distraught, hands clutching her shawl tight around her shoulders, eyes sharp with fear.

Knox circled him, grinning as he motioned Ross up from the ground with both hands.

Slowly, Ross fumbled up from the hard ground on one knee as he searched for his opponent's weaknesses. Knox was nearly six-foot-five and had at least thirty pounds on him.

He couldn't outgun him, so he had to out-maneuver him.

Struggling to his feet, Ross dug his heels into the dirt and waited for the right moment to launch a well-timed blow. He focused on Knox's movements, tracking every twitch, every step.

Ross had taken three or four punches already and each time,

Knox had feigned left with his left foot, throwing all his weight behind a right-handed punch.

"What's the matter, Shepherd? Scared?" Knox taunted.

Knox's right hand twitched, left foot shuffling forward, left knee bent, feigning a move left.

"Of you?" He smiled. "Never."

Wiping his mouth with the back of his hand, Ross shifted forward, balancing his weight as he moved with Knox, matching his movements, not letting the guy come at him from the right.

Knox danced around him, ducking, and pivoting right then left with light-footed bounces.

Ross countered, bobbing and weaving, fists up to block a miscalculated blow.

They shifted back and forth until Knox's whole body leaned left. He taunted Ross, holding out his left arm, right fist dropping low at his hip.

Keeping his center of balance low, Ross leaned left and then dodged right, maintaining an agile defensive stance as he matched steps with Knox. He pasted on his game face, not letting emotions cloud his expression, and signal his next move.

Outwitting this bigger, tougher soldier was Ross' only way to defeat him.

Knox closed the distance between them, a fierce expression on his face.

"What are you waiting for?" Knox shouted, fists pounding his chest, his shoulder muscles taut and corded as he raised his fists. "Come at me, bro!"

Ross kept quiet, knowing his silence was pissing off Knox. He enjoyed putting him a small step off balance as he watched for the right moment.

Only when Knox's head tracked slightly right, foot sliding left did Ross launch a punch at the guy's smug face, just moments before the soldier's right fist sliced up from his hip toward Ross' gut.

The punch hit Knox low in the ribs.

Knox gasped, the air exploding from his chest.

He stumbled, falling to his knees, eyes wide, mouth bobbing for air. Knox hadn't expected that punch.

Ross pivoted right, landing a left to Knox's gut then a right kidney shot that wilted the taller man.

Knox groaned as he hit the ground.

Backing away, Ross gave the soldier room to recover.

"Damn, Shepherd," he coughed. "Where'd that come from? That was some nice work."

"Thanks," Ross replied and extended his hand to Knox, helping the taller man to his feet.

Knox bent forward, leaning his arms on his legs as his chest heaved. He struggled for a few more moments before finally straightening up and facing the now-silent crowd of souls and pale angels.

Now, Knox scowled at Ross, mouth twisting into a frown.

"Thought you were a noob, Shepherd. Where'd you learn that move?"

Laughing, Ross patted Knox on the back.

"I didn't," he replied. "It just took a few punches to learn how you fought. You tilt your head right then lean left before you throw that right uppercut. So, I just waited for the tilt and lean."

Studying him for a moment or two, Knox's surprised expression shifted into a look of respect. Before this hand-to-hand exercise, Knox had lumped him in with everyone else who wasn't used to fighting, but Ross knew he wouldn't make that mistake twice.

Knox had no idea about the forced training Ross had endured at the demons' hands. No boot camp training or combat experience could have been worse. There were so many times when he'd spent days and days (whatever a day felt like here) locked in a metal cage, fighting for his life. His soul. To amuse demons.

There'd only been one rule: survive.

"Now can we go out and search for Heather?" Ross demanded, his gaze falling onto Zakhart who looked away.

In the demon caves, Ross had learned to be fast on his feet, to take a punch, and to sum up his opponents quickly. Instincts he never thought he'd cultivate, but they were a part of his soul now. At times, he'd felt like a rabid animal in that cage and he wondered if letting him out of it had been wise.

Maybe they shouldn't have rescued him? Maybe Heather should have left him to splatter his soul across the NetherReach and finally put an end to the terrible memories and experiences that haunted him now. Like poor Thraecius.

Knox held out his hand and Ross shook it. Even as they called a truce, Ross felt a future challenge in that shake, saw it shining at the dark edges of the guy's blue eyes.

And it wasn't about combat either. He stiffened. It was about Heather.

Poor Heather. His chest ached at the thought of her caught in that soulstalker's arms. He winced. What were they doing to her? Feeding on her? Laying her beneath the poppies. In one of the thousands of poppy fields where he'd never find her again?

He knew more than he'd ever wanted to know about this place. Nevertheless, Heather had no idea what she was facing at their hands.

And she had no idea what he'd become.

An animal. A thrall to demons. He bowed his head. It clung to him like a second skin, wove itself deep into his soul in ways he couldn't have ever imagined. Could he ever shed that skin and go back to the man he'd been before the demons caged him? A man that had given up, but someone that still prized his humanity. But he'd had the heart of a demon beating in his chest. And it had changed him.

Could he ever change back again?

Zakhart and Razasha had extracted that demon heart from his soul, but sometimes, when he closed his eyes, he could feel the memory of it in his chest, hear its faint thumping reverberate through his body. And he felt its violent tremors shudder through him as the demon heart pumped that black sludge deeper into his soul. Along with hate and malice. A heart that whispered his name at the blackest moments of the night.

Taunted him, summoning him to that shadowy cage for one more taste of combat. One more kill.

Every night since his escape, that ravenous appetite had hollowed his belly, made him hunger to rend another soul apart, and absorb its essence.

Was it even possible to have removed all of that? Would it forever taint him?

He was afraid to tell Zakhart or Razasha about it, fearing their response. And he couldn't tell Heather—and lose her all over again.

Was he becoming a monster like Mulciber? Would he hurt the others? He bit his lip. Would he hurt Heather?

The thought of that possibility made him sick. He'd do anything to find some peace of mind, some small measure of assurance that the demon heart was truly gone forever.

The others went back to their small groups, some sparring with staves and others practicing the hand-to-hand maneuvers that Knox had taught them.

Zakhart pretended not to have heard Ross' question. Again. Why wasn't he anxious to go find Heather?

Ross had been asking him when for days, but nobody was listening anymore. Like they'd done to him at the great tree.

He watched Diri and Lairz training beside Iznir and Halea, their wings beating the air as they wrestled with the other. Lairz's hair was cropped close and jagged, the color like muted fire, so bright against Diri's rich, dark locks and skin.

Halea struggled through the human maneuvers. Finally, she shuffled back from them in frustration and hurried away from Iznir.

"Halea," said Iznir, disappointment in his tone as he followed behind her. "Don't give up so quickly."

"I can't do it, Iznir! I can't!" Halea shouted, stomping her foot.

Ross had never seen a pale angel so easily rattled. Halea had always seemed a little high-strung (and more human than angel), but unlike the others, she gave up without much of a fight. She seemed troubled and scared since his return. He'd noticed her being increasingly withdrawn from the others, especially the other pale angels.

"Halea, you just need to practice the moves, that's all," said Iznir, following behind her.

"I have practiced them," she snapped.

Iznir was as tall as Knox, statuesque, his long hair drawn back in a thick ponytail of white gold against his brown skin.

"They aren't difficult. See?"

Iznir motioned at sable-haired Diri who seemed comfortable with the moves. She pivoted right and landed a right cross that dropped Lairz to the ground. Iznir folded his wings tightly against his shoulders and walked Halea through the pivot, but Halea pushed him away.

"Halea!" he called. "Wait."

"I just can't do this," she cried and walked away.

Halea rushed past Zakhart who looked distracted, hands behind his back. He didn't say anything to her or try to stop her, but the moment Halea stormed past, Razasha leaned against Zakhart's shoulder and whispered in his ear.

Ross turned, seeing Knox approach him.

"Listen, Shepherd," said Knox in a quiet voice, hand rubbing the nape of his neck.

He glanced at his feet, but finally, he lifted his gaze to Ross' face.

"I'm uh—impressed with how you handle yourself. Ross. Really. Other than Javier, no one else even comes close. Where'd you learn to fight like that? You in the Service?"

"No," said Ross, shaking his head. "You sure you want to hear my answer?"

Frowning, Knox glanced at Lairz as the pale angel hurried past, wings unfurling behind him, but then Knox's gaze returned to Ross' face in a deep, unblinking stare.

"What do you mean by that?"

Ross sighed. "I learned it in the cage. In the demon caves."

"The cage? I—don't understand. You mean there was cage fighting down there? Like MMA or something?"

"MMA?" Ross asked with a shrug. "I don't know what that is. In the demon caves, Mulciber wagered on the souls that he pitted against one another in a big metal cage. They called it SoulSport. No rules. No time limit. It was ugly."

He couldn't stop the cold shudder that rippled through him, the memory so raw and intense.

The curly-haired soldier's light blue eyes widened in a mixture of surprise and compassion, something he hadn't expected from Knox. He reached out and squeezed Ross' shoulder.

"Wow, sorry, bro," Knox replied in a quiet voice. "I had no idea demons did that kind of shit."

"That wasn't even the worst part," Ross replied and shrugged it off.

"What do you mean?" Knox asked, squinting at Ross as he shook his head.

"If Mulciber has Heather now, then he may be planning to put her into that cage. For the SoulSport." Ross gritted his teeth. "I can't let her go through that, Knox. I can't!"

Ross clutched his chest at the sudden memory of the demon heart that had invaded his soul. Three demons had held him down, a fourth carrying that beating monstrosity in its fist. It had a steady rhythm. A deep, hollow rasp that thumped in Ross' ears and resonated through his body, across his skin in a painful, staccato rhythm.

Something shook him. He glanced up.

Knox stared at him, hands on his arms as he shook him again.

"Ross!" he called. "You in there?"

At last, Ross' gaze flitted back to the taller soldier's face. He was vaguely aware that a few moments had passed, but he had no idea how many. From the odd look on the man's face, he must have been far away for a bit.

"Sorry," Ross said, sighing as he glanced down at his feet. "Had a bad flashback from the caves." He looked up, his jaw tightening. "The night they put that horrible demon heart inside me."

He realized he was shaking, Knox looking at him with concern now.

"Damn, dude. That's bad." Knox ran his fingers through his curly, dark hair but didn't look away. "PTSD?"

Ross frowned. "PT-what?"

"Post-traumatic stress disorder," said Knox. "It's basically where you relive the worst moments of something. You get triggered by inane stuff, things you wouldn't expect to set you off. And then you go through those moments again. In real time."

"What kind of triggers?" Ross asked.

Knox shrugged. "Just stupid stuff, really. Like somebody runnin' up to you in a grocery aisle when you're not expecting it. I'm already coverin' my head and gettin' behind a counter because I see a suicide bomber running up to me. Or I'm reaching for my pistol."

"Wow, that's awful, Knox," said Ross in a quiet voice.

"Or somebody pulls something out of their pocket and I see a weapon not a twenty dollar bill. I get the shakes all over, break out in a cold sweat, my heart pounding as I claw my hip for my sidearm or snap my hand to my shoulder for the rifle that isn't there."

Ross nodded, surprised that he understood now.

"Every time I see someone throw a punch or watch two people fight, that demon heart beats in my ears," said Ross in a quiet voice. "My chest shudders and I smell the sulfur clinging to the cage floor. I can't stand the thought of Heather going through that." He grabbed Knox's arm. "Knox. We can't let her go through that. We've got to go out there and find her. Now. Every minute we waste is another moment closer to that cage for her. We can't let that happen."

A look that Ross had been terrified to see washed across Knox's face. His features contorted with worry, his light blue eyes burning with concern. It was obvious that this guy had feelings for her. Strong feelings.

Did he love her? His gut twisted.

Ross felt sick inside now. What had happened between them while he was captured by the demons?

Despite the fiery attraction between them, he and Heather had only shared some kisses, but they'd been inseparable and shared secrets that he had never divulged to another soul. She knew him better than almost anyone.

Even Jessie.

But had she and Knox gotten close like that, too? He winced. Intimate? Had she told Knox that she loved him?

He scrunched his eyes closed, inhaling a sharp breath. No. He couldn't face that thought. Couldn't deal with the possibility that she'd fallen for this guy. Fallen in love with Knox. Even the thought was a sharp, aching stab to his chest.

Knox's stare was piercing, challenging, but Ross met the man's probing gaze. Knox was wondering how close Ross and Heather had been. And measuring his relationship with her against Ross' relationship. Wondering if they'd had sex. Wondering how he could break them apart.

He could see it all burning in Knox's hard blue gaze.

Ross knew that Knox would fight beside him to get Heather back, but after that, Ross was on his own.

Getting Heather back in his arms would be the toughest fight he'd faced. Because he'd have to fight Knox Travers after fighting all these shadow creatures and demons.

Regardless, Ross would fight to the bitter end for her. Because he loved her more than his own life.

six

. . .

"WHY. AM I. HERE?" Heather asked, speaking each word slowly and clearly as she watched Sandriana's reaction.

Would she understand her words? Sandriana's language was bird-like songs and trills. And each note seemed to correspond to the letters and consonants of Heather's language.

The soulstalker crouched in front of her, wings spread wide as she blocked the opening. Her feathers were sleek black and mottled grey with tiny flecks of cream. The leading edge of feathers across her wings was separated, looking like fringe. Heather had read somewhere about how the flight of owls was silent because the edges of their wings had fringe-like feathers designed to break up the airflow. Apparently, Sandriana's wings were similar.

Heather hadn't heard her at all. But she'd heard other soulstalkers approaching. Sandriana was a different type of soulstalker than the others. In many more ways than just the structure of her wings.

Sandriana chirped at Heather, the notes rolling off her tongue in a string of shifting pitches and sharp tones. Heather felt urgency in the soulstalker's response, but she just didn't understand what Sandriana was saying.

Frustrated, Heather sank back against the nest wall. She couldn't follow all the notes, couldn't match them to the crude chart she'd etched into the tree branch. There wasn't even a common word or phrase she could utter, nothing that could tie their languages together.

Learning a new language was tough. Heather remembered struggling through her first high school Italian class. The pronunciations were harder than she'd expected. For the entire semester, Heather had worried that she'd never get them right.

From her limited experiences with these soulstalkers, Heather realized that they communicated through tones and pitches similar to the pale angels, but the soulstalkers' tonal structures seemed more complex and at times, surprisingly subtle, requiring Heather to listen closely to catch the nuances. Angels spoke all languages, but with only one language to communicate, these soulstalkers' tones and notes seemed become elaborate and serpentine. Maybe it was because the angel's tones were designed to communicate as a group with harmonies and discords? Not individually.

She couldn't even make some of the noises these soulstalkers made, much less hit those piercing high notes. And the low notes were impossible for her. How would she ever communicate with them when she couldn't even make the sounds? She wished that Zakhart was here to translate for her.

"Why?" Sandriana forced out in a guttural bark.

She trilled four notes: high note, high note, low note, high again. Her wings quivered as she leaned forward, forcing out another gruff, throaty word.

"Here?"

Heather tried to recreate the notes, repeating the two slightly different high notes, the low note followed by the second high note again.

Screeching, Sandriana rustled her wings, chattering with excitement. The gold flecks in her tortoiseshell eyes intensified, pupils growing large as she clapped her taloned hands together.

Heather smiled. Had she just learned her first word in the soulstalker's tongue? Low-high-low was why. High-high-low-high was here. Then it hit her. The notes were letters!

She sang high note, high note followed by the low one.

"Hey," she said. "It doesn't say an awful lot, but I only know about five letters."

Sandriana reached out with taloned hands and patted Heather's sleeve, tilting her head up and down as she chittered a series of eight notes. The octave changed and she sang more notes. Heather counted. Eight notes. Another octave. Eight more notes.

Heather grabbed a twig off the nest floor and scratched letters into a piece of exposed limb where the bark had worn away, the pale wood soft beneath it. Slowly, she scrawled out another chart of notes and letters. High notes at the end of her alphabet, low ones at the beginning. She'd played the flute in high school, so she could read music. But the highest octaves were beyond her reach. She couldn't create pitches that high.

Sandriana rolled out a series of notes and Heather listened intently, sounding them out one by one as she tried to translate them to her crude little charts. Six notes. She matched the sounds as best she could, singing them back to Sandriana. When she had all six notes, she tried placing them in the four octaves she'd scrawled out.

It was exhausting, but Heather kept at it until finally the word became clear.

"Rescue," she said out loud and repeated most of the notes back, using her index finger to point upward when she couldn't hit the high note.

Sandriana trilled excitedly, wings quivering as she tried to squawk out the word.

"Resku," she said at last. She chimed four notes and rasped out another word. "Save."

Heather clapped, grinning at the soulstalker until the word sank into her brain. Rescue? What did that mean? Was Sandriana trying to tell her that she hadn't meant Heather any harm? Had she been trying to save her from something? Demons had swarmed that area. Along with several soulstalkers nearby, blackening the sky with their dark wings. Soulstalkers controlled by the demons.

"Save. Me?" Heather asked, laying her hand against her chest. "Me? Heh-thur?"

Sandriana tilted her head up and down, squawking out the word, *save* again with low note high note, low note high note.

Heather sang the four notes.

"Save?" she asked and hummed out two more. "Me?" She pulled in a breath. "Heather."

Sandriana tilted her head up and down as she touched Heather's chest with a delicate brush of her taloned hand.

"Why?" Heather asked, singing the three notes in soulstalker song.

Inhaling a quick breath, Sandriana intoned eight notes. She repeated them several times, allowing Heather to process each tone and record it in the chart she'd carved into the soft wood.

"Mulciber," said Heather in a shocked voice. "You saved me from Mulciber?"

Sandriana gave her an awkward nod as she clasped her hands together and settled her body beside Heather in the dry grass.

It was true. These soulstalkers weren't part of the huge flock of soulstalkers that roamed the central part of the Between. And apparently, Sandriana wasn't part of Mulciber's creations either, so Mulciber had no control over her. That also meant that Death didn't control these shadow creatures either. These soulstalkers weren't the ones carrying off human souls and placing them in the poppy fields, to sleep the eternal sleep. She frowned.

But what were they? What sort of function did they serve in the Between? She needed to know.

"An...An.Dray.Alf-us. An-gel," Sandriana struggled with a rasp. "Muls–ibur. Sings to ahn-gel."

Andrealphus? An angel? Mulciber spoke to an angel? Sandriana used the word sing, but Heather knew that meant talk in her language.

"To an angel?"

Sandriana gave her a sharp nod and struggled to explain. "They—send Death. Away. Muls-iber sing—on...fool errand. To...sing to...Sariel."

A chill raced down her back. Demons managed to send Death away from the Between? On what Sandriana described as a fool's errand? She must have heard them talking. Heather winced. Plotting.

Heather struggled through the tones, singing five notes, motioning up or down with her index finger when she couldn't hit the notes.

"Is Death...your maker?" she asked, studying Sandriana's owl-like eyes.

"No," Sandriana snapped. She chirped four notes: high, low, high, high.

Heather glanced at her chart and deciphered the four letters.

"Free," she replied finally.

Sandriana nodded awkwardly, her eyes bright.

"Free," she rasped.

She trilled several more notes and Heather tried to decode them, but Sandriana chittered the the notes so quickly that she couldn't capture them all. Heather shrugged, so Sandriana twittered them again. Slower. Clearer.

"Save Heh'tur," Sandriana said and warbled a small aria, the notes rising and falling.

"Too fast," Heather blurted out, shaking her head as she frantically tried to capture the notes she hadn't heard before in her chart.

Sandriana repeated the notes several times, singing them slower, letting the tones hang in the air before she trilled the next one. Heather sang the notes in a quiet voice, trying to mimic the soulstalker's song until the melody stayed with her. Some of the phrases were just disjointed notes, others sounding repetitive and bland, but others rolled together into a melody that she remembered. These notes hung together in a delicate song that sounded fragile and compelling. She captured it with her makeshift scale and etched the letters beneath the snippet of song.

"To help us," Heather said and she intoned the notes for Sandriana who nodded at her. "You want my help?" she asked.

"Yes," Sandriana spoke, struggling to make the human sounds into words. "To help us. Win."

Help them win what? How could she help them? This place with its massive trees that bordered the boiling lake looked safe and far away from demons and other soulstalkers. What could a lost soul like her possibly do to help them?

Heather sang three notes, asking Sandriana *how*.

The soulstalker pulled in a sharp breath and launched into an aria, beautiful high notes in thick, rich, resonating low tones. Sandriana's pitch and timbre were so clear and bright. A lively, happy tune that floated through the nest, reminding her of a piccolo. Heather had no idea what Sandriana was saying because there were too many notes trilled too fast. She just couldn't process all of them.

"Too many notes," Heather cried, holding up her hands. "I can't hear them all. It's too fast."

Sandriana's song fell silent, her face contorting as she concentrated for several moments. She pulled in a quick breath.

"We fight. With u. Stop demons."

Heather's eyes widened as she processed Sandriana's words in her language. These soulstalkers wanted to fight beside them! They wanted to defeat the demons. Her thoughts rushed back to her flight into the nest. There had been hundreds of soulstalkers. If they wanted to fight alongside the souls and the pale angels, then maybe she could raise an army.

Maybe together they could defeat the demons and stop Mulciber from achieving whatever twisted plan he was trying to set into motion? Right now, this was their best chance to succeed. Maybe Sandriana knew more about Mulciber's plan? It might take Heather a long time to decipher those meanings from the soulstalker, but she'd do her best to find out. Until she could consult with Zakhart.

She smiled at Sandriana and nodded.

"Yes. We're fighting Mulciber. With the pale angels. We need you and your flock." She motioned toward the opening. "We need them. All of them."

Sandriana shook her head, looking frustrated and Heather understood, knowing she couldn't process all those words.

Heather stood up straight, the top of her head brushing against the curved walls of the nest. She put up her fists and threw some punches, miming a fight.

"Mulciber," she said, boxing the air.

She sang two notes that meant *we* and boxed the air. Then she sang five notes, indicating *fight*, and then said, *Mulciber*.

Sandriana stared at her, not quite understanding.

Heather leaned over to the wall and slowly, deliberately chimed the eight notes that were angelsong for Mulciber.

"Mulciber," Heather repeated, throwing a punch in the air. "We. Fight. Mulciber."

One last time, she sang eight angry notes, angelsong for Mulciber.

Sandriana's eyes turned misty, her bottom lip quivering as she approached Heather. Gently, she put her arms around Heather and hugged her, chiming a soft chirring sound. Heather wasn't sure if Sandriana was laughing or crying, but she felt the warmth of the soulstalker's embrace. It was such a strange feeling, hugging a soulstalker, feeling sincerity and concern in that feathery hug, the bloom of emotion within her lean, bony eagle-like body.

Heather put her arms around Sandriana, letting her know that she understood, that she shared the emotion. She wondered how the soulstalker knew to do that. Maybe she'd seen human souls hug each other? She'd probably observed a lifetime of human souls in the Between.

"Fight," Sandriana snarled, the word guttural and raspy. "Muls–ibur. We fight!"

She bared her pointy teeth, the words more of a feral growl, the gold flecks in her eyes sparking as she trilled and chirped, launching into complex strains, simultaneously singing a lilting melody alongside aching harmonies that gave Heather chills. It was beautiful, like a canary's delicate song, but Heather had no idea what Sandriana was saying.

Sandriana lifted Heather into her arms.

"U see."

She growled, one hand unfastening the mat that covered the nest's opening.

The soulstalker slid the mat out of the way and with Heather in her arms, Sandriana leaped into the air. Heather closed her eyes, her stomach plummeting as Sandriana winged her way over the boiling lake, headed northwest. This time, Heather felt a glimmer of trust.

The massive trees and tall, golden grasses fell away as the horizon fanned out into a rich sea of silvery green grasses that flowed in waves across the landscape. The beat of her wings was soft, quiet on the breeze, the steady thump thrumming in her ears. Up ahead, massive, floppy grey blooms poked high into the sky.

Sandriana dipped downward toward the grasslands. Poppies!

Heather's body trembled at the sight of the huge, charcoal-grey blooms that whispered pollen into the air. It fell like snow from the blooms, covering the ground with ash.

The crunch of brush rasped in the silence. Flash of black.

Heather's gaze tracked toward the sound.

Slipping out of the grasses was the lean, black body of a sand runner. It looked like a shadow panther as it prowled through the field of poppies. It dropped back on its haunches, balancing on muscular hind legs as it collected pollen with its thick, shadowy paws and stuffed it into a cloth sack that draped across its lean back.

Heather winced as Sandriana flew in low, hovering above the poppy field.

She had an unobstructed view of the poppies and what lay beneath the huge blooms. She stared at the shrouded figures covered in ashen dust from the poppies, terrified that she'd recognize their faces. But the bodies looked small and squat.

She squinted, taking in all the details as two more sand runners plodded through the poppy field. One lifted its cat-like head upward at Sandriana and let out a quiet mewl at her. The other sand runner crouched on all fours, shadowy ears pressed back against its panther-like head. Their eyes were vivid yellow, startling Heather with their brightness, cat-like pupils giving them such wild and fierce expressions.

Sandriana dipped closer to the ground, finally landing in the ashen soil.

Heather cringed, fearing that the sand runners would leap at her, but the shadowy creatures kept their distance, making no moves toward them. Sandriana set her down, chirping out a lament at the sand runners. They both cocked their heads and sat back on their haunches, watching Heather with alert gazes as Sandriana motioned toward the poppies.

With slow, careful movements, Heather approached the nearest bloom, wanting a closer look at the motionless figure that lay beneath it. The sand runners kept their distance, not moving.

She knelt beside the small figure, studying its face and body size, still puzzled by what it was. It was too small to be an adult human soul, but maybe it was just curled into a ball? Right away, though, she saw its feet and legs stretched out. Its skin had a strange pattern to it, looking leathery. Its head was round, little protrusions on its forehead.

With a gasp, she stumbled backward, a hand over her mouth. They weren't human souls. They were demons!

She turned to stare at Sandriana who bared her teeth into a leering grin. Heather didn't know if Mulciber had originally created this soulstalker or if she'd once done Death's bidding. Regardless of who made her, one thing was clear.

She'd turned on her handlers. Along with her whole flock.

A soft, raspy mewl resounded behind her. Heather turned, her body stiffening, fearing an attack by sand runners.

But the two sand runners hadn't moved. They still sat side-by-side, both on their haunches, shadowy front paws stretched out in front of them. Something small moved between them, shoving forward. A thin growl that ended in a soft mew drew Heather's attention again.

Her mouth fell open when a small, shadowy head pushed out from between the two sand runners. It lifted its smaller panther-like head with its rounded, shadowy ears and bright yellow eyes and propped two thick, heavy paws on one of the sand runner's backs. It had a pale grey smudge on top of its head, the rest of its body was shadow black and mottled charcoal grey.

She gasped, staring. A sand runner cub!

She stared at the cub and then back at Sandriana who was still grinning. Could these shadow creatures reproduce? Was that even possible?

"A cub?" Heather asked, pointing at the little creature.

Sandriana chirped, her wings flattening against her back as she bent down and whistled. The little shadow cub lumbered across the ashen ground toward her. She scratched the little mewling creature behind one ear and patted it on the head.

Mimicking Sandriana's whistle, Heather called to the sand runner cub. It let out a raspy growl and bounded toward Heather. It stopped at her feet, staring up at her with huge yellow eyes.

"Hi there," said Heather, smiling as she sat down in the ashen soil.

The cute little creature pounced on her, jumping into her lap, and standing up on hind legs to press its face to hers. Its little body had some weight to it as she stretched out her hand to stroke the shadowy length of its muscular form. It felt soft, silky. She cuddled it to her chest, feeling a soothing throaty purr against her skin.

"It's adorable," she said out loud, unable to take her eyes off it.

Sandriana rolled through a frantic strain of melody that filled the silence in the poppy field. Both sand runners caterwauled at her in deep, velvet tones, including the little guy in Heather's lap. Heather kept stroking the little sand runner that had settled down against her legs, stretching its thick paws toward her knees.

"We live," Sandriana said finally in a hoarse voice. "We plant. And harvest."

Those words were more than she'd heard Sandriana say, but those few words said so much. Heather understood now. She saw the freedom that Sandriana's flock of soulstalkers had, working together, living their lives as a group. They had planted poppy fields and tended them, harvesting pollen. And they'd planted them to trap their enemies.

Heather saw nothing but demons sleeping the eternal sleep and the sight of so many out of commission made her smile. The sand runners worked and lived alongside these soulstalkers, caring for the poppies, keeping the demons asleep, and living their own lives.

"You hunt...demons," Heather replied, pointing at the nearest demon that was frozen like a statue beneath a huge grey poppy blossom, and chimed the notes back to Sandriana.

Sandriana showed her pointy teeth, the expression on her face light. She gave Heather an awkward nod.

"Demons," she rasped. "No souls," she replied in a hoarse whisper.

Leaning down, Heather hugged the little sand runner, gathering it in her arms. Its tiny purr deepened, gold eyes closing. She touched the little patch of grey.

"I'm gonna call you Smudge," she whispered to the small sand runner.

She watched Sandriana move toward one of the blooms and dig through a pile of ashen soil. She lifted something into her arms and turned toward Heather. From beneath her black wings, Sandriana revealed a grey-speckled egg that was the size of a watermelon. After studying Heather holding the sand runner, Sandriana cradled the egg against her chest.

"Your child?" Heather asked with a smile.

Frowning, Sandriana shook her head and shrugged.

Heather rocked the little sand runner in her arms and pointed at the big egg.

"Child?" she asked again.

At last, Sandriana understood. She nodded, still holding the egg against her chest.

"Child," she said. "My."

These soulstalkers had been created from those demon molds. But now, they were independent. And reproducing. She was amazed.

Was this how Death and the demons forced the other shadow creatures to increase their numbers or was this a new development in the Between? Did the demons even realize what was happening here? Did they know yet that other creatures—besides lost souls—had chosen to fight against them?

seven

· · ·

ROSS STRUGGLED with Zakhart's offer of receiving angel light as a weapon. Part of him wanted to jump at the chance to have wings and powers like some sort of superhero, but a part of him was frightened by it. Didn't Zakhart remember that a demon's heart had once beat in his' chest? That heart had been attached to his soul. Even the memory of it made him feel corrupt inside. Damaged.

He wasn't worthy of wings.

All afternoon, he'd paced the courtyard, watching the others train while he wrestled with his conscience. And a decision. Heather had been gone three nights now and the others were training hard as they prepared to send out a patrol to search for her. Ross knew he couldn't wait much longer. Mulciber had already had enough time to exploit her. Harm her. Infect her with his dark poison.

But if Zakhart's gift would get him out there searching for Heather right now, then he had no choice but to accept it.

The sky was a deep grey, darker than normal—like storm clouds gathered on the horizon. He'd seen these skies for a very long time and knew all its nuances. This sky was different somehow, making him worry what gathered behind those clouds.

A shriek pierced the calm.

"Stay away from me! Stay away!"

He turned.

Cora crouched in the grass, eyes wide with fear, a hand extended up at Knox, blocking his advance.

"Cora, I'm sorry, I—" He reached out to help her up from the ground.

"Stay away from me!"

Her eyes turned misty as she hugged her arms against her body. She was trembling.

Knox looked unnerved, his jaw tightening, muscles in his arms cording as he watched Cora cowering on the ground.

"I was just trying to show you how to throw someone over your shoulder," Knox shouted, his face flushed, eyes filled with anger.

At last, Razasha pushed through the crowd of souls who'd stopped training to watch and knelt beside Cora, enfolding her in her arms. Cora whispered to the pale angel, bottom lip quivering, eyes welling with tears.

Confused, Knox shuffled backward as Razasha helped Cora to her feet and led her toward the soul tree.

The other souls and pale angels gathered around Knox as Cora left the training field.

"What was that all about?" Knox asked Zakhart who watched from the edge of the exercises. "I never even touched her."

Zakhart's gaze didn't stray from Cora.

"She went through hell in her final hours of life, Knox. Not sure how much you know about that, but it was traumatic. None of the angels had been there to comfort her, but believe me, it was awful."

"What do you mean?" Knox asked in a quiet voice, squinting as he glanced around at the other souls. "Everybody, get back to work! Now! Show's over."

The others returned to their sparring, wooden staves cracking together again, souls tumbling across the grass. Ross wandered over to stand beside Knox and Zakhart.

"She died during the battle of Jonesborough," said Zakhart. "Killed herself as Atlanta burned. During the American Civil War."

"So?" Knox snapped. "All wars are terrible! That doesn't give her the right to take it out on me."

Anger was a slow burn as Ross grabbed Knox's shoulder and spun him around.

"So? You do realize that her reaction wasn't about you. That she went through a terribly traumatic experience, Knox. And she's not a soldier."

Knox's expression didn't change, blue eyes still hard. He looked annoyed, staring at Ross' hand on his shoulder.

"Bro, let go."

"Don't you get it?" Ross snapped. "Cora was raped, dumbass! She was burying her little brother when soldiers broke into their cabin. They raped and killed her mother. Then they raped Cora. Afterward, they set the cabin on fire. So yeah, Cora's afraid of soldiers."

"I said let go," Knox snarled through gritted teeth.

Ross held his ground, hand still gripping Knox's shoulder.

"What happens if I don't?"

"You're about to find out."

Knox's voice was low and threatening, but Ross had had enough of Knox Travers. He'd had enough of his arrogance, his swagger, and him calling everyone maggots. Shoving people around like they didn't matter. Acting like he ran the place. What did Heather see in this conceited, self-centered dumbass?

Knox snapped his hand around Ross' wrist, twisting his arm behind his back, his other hand grabbing him around the neck into a headlock.

"You need to learn not to fuck with a truck, Shepherd."

Knox was grinning now, throwing all his weight into the headlock as Ross struggled against his iron grip.

"In case you're not clear, I'm running this show. Not you. You're lucky I haven't run your ass out of this camp for being a demon lover.

Heather's the only reason I haven't, so get used to it, Shepherd. You're washed up here."

Ross stopped struggling. He bared his teeth, waiting a moment or two for the arrogant ass to relax his grip. Just enough to put him in his place. He felt the muscles in Knox's left arm twitch, relaxing into the hold.

With one fluid movement, Ross twisted his body left, slamming all his weight into Knox's left arm. He grabbed that arm, pivoting as he pulled Knox up and over his shoulder, dropping him on the ground.

On his ass.

Ross bent down on his haunches and thumped his hand against Knox's chest.

"Washed up? I'm just getting started, Travers. You can play soldier all day long and try to impress everyone into following you. But you and I both know that you don't give a damn about these souls. All you care about is you. And banging Heather. In time, the others will see it, too. But I'm not going to let you sacrifice them to your ego. So either you start acting like they matter or things are going to get ugly."

With one final glare, Ross let him up.

Fury burned in Knox's eyes as he struggled to his feet, getting in Ross' face. Ross didn't back down.

"You just made an enemy, Shepherd." He glared back at Ross, wiping a hand across his mouth. "A big one."

Ross motioned toward the other souls still practicing.

"I can live with that. As long as they're protected. Because every single one of them matters. Got it?"

Knox shook his head, pointing his finger in Ross' face.

"This isn't over, Shepherd. This is a long way from over."

"Grow up, Travers," Ross said with a snarl. "Stop acting like this is all about you. It was never about you. It's about the team now. Working together. Helping the weaker ones. Thought you soldiers operated on the principle of not leaving anyone behind."

"Only people that have my back," Knox replied, still glaring.

"I'll have you back as soon as you start watching theirs," Ross replied and motioned toward the other souls. "And that includes Cora Abernathy. She's terrified of soldiers, so you shoving boot camp in her face with zero compassion isn't going to get her to train."

At that point, Zakhart stepped between Ross and Knox, hands separating them.

"We don't have enough souls to fight each other, so Ross, Knox, you'd better figure out a way to work together."

The pale angel's face was taut, anger burning in his usually soft, pumpkin-orange eyes.

Knox continued to cast death stares at Ross, but he didn't make another move to attack him. Probably because Zakhart had intervened. With a snort, Knox stormed off toward the souls he'd set up into two-person groups. They traded punches and worked on throws, doing surprisingly well from Ross' viewpoint. Knox had done a good job of instructing the others on how to do these moves, but his smartass superior attitude always managed to ruin any good deed he performed. What was the word that Heather used for people like that...asshat?

"Sorry about that, Zakhart," Ross said, sighing as he ran his fingers through his hair. "I'm tired of his *suck it up* attitude. Cora needs patience and understanding, not someone treating her like she's just being a crybaby. She's not."

"I agree, Ross," the pale angel replied, folding his arms against his chest. "I just wish that the two of you had talked about it maturely instead of dissolving into petty fights like that."

Bowing his head, Ross turned toward the south, his thoughts drifting back to Heather.

"She's been gone three days now," Ross announced, squinting at the horizon. "I'm terrified by what Mulciber's done to her."

The pale angel's hand on his shoulder surprised him. He glanced up as Zakhart stood at his right shoulder and stared toward the south.

"It's already been too long," Zakhart replied. "We need to go out and search for her. I sent Lairz out this morning to scan the southern reaches of the Between. I'm sending Halea north, Razasha west, and Diri east. We need to get some understanding of what's happened to her. Where Mulciber's taken her."

"Send me," Ross whispered. "This waiting is making me crazy, Zakhart."

Zakhart squeezed his shoulder. "Afraid not, Ross. Not yet anyway. Please be patient a little longer."

"It's so hard," he said, glancing at the pale angel. "I'm going out of my mind."

At last, Zakhart smiled, his hand sliding off Ross' shoulder.

"I know. I shepherded Heather through a painful wait. I'll do the same for you, Ross. Trust me."

"I do," said Ross. "But I'm not sure about anyone else here at the moment. Things are so different now. This new tree feels so strange. The souls seem eager to train, but none of them really has any idea of what they're up against. Everyone just seems so detached."

Zakhart turned back to him, a frown on his alabaster face. "By the way, have you seen Javier?"

Ross shook his head.

"Not since yesterday. Why?"

Zakhart thrust his hands into the pockets of his silky robe.

"Barb came to me this morning, worried because Javier wasn't around. He hadn't said anything about leaving the soul tree, but she's worried."

Where had Javier gone? That made no sense. He and Barb were inseparable.

"You think he was taken by demons?" Ross asked. "Like Heather?"

"Perhaps," said Zakhart in a quiet voice. "Except that Lamarr is missing, too."

"What?" Ross was staring at Zakhart now. "He was here last night. Playing hide and seek with Zoe. I watched them goofing off until it got too dark to see. But later, I saw Zoe tagging along behind

Knox again with that pink unicorn of hers. And later, she was annoying Halea. I guess I assumed that Lamarr had followed her inside."

Zakhart looked unnerved now. "He was with Zoe you say?"

"Yeah. Why?"

"Because the last time I saw Javier," said Zakhart, his gaze on the horizon to the south. "He was with Zoe. He and Halea were helping her learn how to use a staff. Javier had been very patient with her, but she was just too little."

Ross turned around, scanning the practice field until he located Zoe. She followed Knox's every step, a wooden staff that Barb had made clutched in her freckled hand. She looked up at Knox with puppy dog eyes and a wistful smile. She either had a bad case of hero worship or a major crush on the curly-haired soldier. Knox seemed to be ignoring her as he barked orders at the other souls. That's when Ross noticed Barb leaning against one of the trees in the circle. She looked distracted and worried, glancing into the woods and back at the training activities again.

"Has anyone seen demons around here? Or anywhere nearby?" Ross asked, watching as Zoe ran around poking people with her staff.

Ian and Gemma were polite even though Zoe had tripped Gemma with it and struck Ian across the shoulders. Thomas glared at her, keeping his distance. Most of the others avoided this girl who had started to behave like a brat. Looked like Knox's personality had rubbed off on her.

"None of my angels reported seeing any demons, Ross," Zakhart replied, sighing. "I can't imagine that any of these souls would wander off though. They know what's out there. I also talked to Avana and she hasn't seen any demons. None of the other smoke people had either. Avana said she and the others would keep careful watch."

Ross smiled. "Javier's a fighter, Zakhart. He wouldn't have gone with those demons without causing a loud ruckus. Believe me."

Zakhart nodded. "I know Javier can take care of himself, but

Lamarr didn't seem the type to put himself in danger like that. Not with so much at stake. And having two of them missing along with Heather? That's too much of a coincidence."

Ross shook his head, watching Zoe pout, arms crossed, staff clutched in one hand as Knox made her stand back while he demonstrated another hand-to-hand combat move.

Zoe was the newest soul Ross had encountered, so he didn't know her at all. New souls appeared all the time. There'd been a time when he'd made it his mission at the great tree to lead newly arrived souls to safety. He doubted anyone had even bothered to look for new souls at this tree.

For the last three days, he'd gone to the entry point, where the forest met the grasslands, to look for newly arrived souls. There had been several and he'd led as many as he could back to the soul tree, but there were too many soulstalkers now. He'd fought them each time, but they managed to carry off a few souls. And he hated losing the newest ones. Who had no idea what had even happened to them.

"Maybe Lamarr and Javier went out to help new souls find the tree?" Ross offered. "I've gone out every evening for three days to lead them here."

Zakhart smiled. "Yes, I noticed there were five or six new souls in the tree. Good work, Ross."

"All these new bands of soulstalkers are making it much harder." He got choked up, turning away. "I couldn't stop them from carrying off some of the new souls. Like when they grabbed Heather. Is there a way to protect the new souls? It's not right. They don't even have a chance."

He felt a comforting hand against his back.

"That's why we're training, Ross. To fight these creatures, to break down their numbers. I can feel how much pain this causes you and I know that every time it happens, you think about Heather. Just know that my angels are doing the best they can."

Ross glanced back at Zakhart.

"If it will make your job easier, I'll take the light's energy. I'll grow wings if it means I can fight those things where they live. And bring back the souls they've captured." He sighed. "And Heather."

He felt the tension drain from the pale angel. Apparently, he'd been waiting for Ross to make that decision. A lot more anxious about it than Ross had realized.

"Words can't express my gratitude, Ross."

"When will you grant me the power?"

"Tomorrow. I'll need time to prepare the transfer."

"And Zakhart," he said, his gaze focusing on the southern horizon. "You know that the first moment I can fly, I will go out and hunt for Heather."

Zakhart grinned, his hand falling away from Ross' shoulder.

"I'm counting on it, Ross."

eight

· · ·

LAMARR DESPAIRED AS THE DARK, rocky underground amphitheater teemed with demons. Rings of seats had been carved into the massive rock walls of the lowest level of the demon caves, the smell of dirt and sulfur sharp in the dank air. They gathered in grey and red droves, squeezing into stone seats. Like a soccer match crowd, they were animated, primed for action, shouting at the cage, feet thumping the hard dirt floor, demanding that the SoulSport match begin.

The cavern was thick with darkness, the only light that burned glowed around the tall metal cage, a rusty gold light illuminating it.

In the distance, the Mechanism thrummed, its bass hum vibrating against the tall metal walls of the cage. Sharp, distant clank of pickaxes punctuated the Mechanism's deep moan.

He and Javier huddled against the metal cage bars, holding each other up, defending each other. Javier stared at him through hooded lids, one arm leaning against the metal cage, chest heaving. Neither Lamarr nor Javier could remember exactly how they had ended up here. There had been demons in the forest by the soul tree, but after that, Lamarr had no memory.

"I don't know how many more of these fights I can take," Lamarr said with a moan, leaning his flushed face against the metal cage.

"Me neither," said Javier, sounding weak and exhausted. "They just keep coming."

Lamarr shook his head. "Can't keep fighting them off," he said, his voice barely above a whisper. "Can't keep this up much longer."

Javier had been trapped here in the caverns when Lamarr arrived. The shorter man picked Lamarr out of the crowd of souls and chose him to be his cage partner. Javier hadn't said much except that he'd been dragged into the woods by demons, just like Lamarr. There hadn't been much time to talk about anything else.

Lamarr had expected to find Heather a prisoner here, too. Mulciber's prisoner. He'd heard the demons talking. Knew that Mulciber was hunting Heather. And that bastard demon was getting ready to flip some switch on some big machine—the Mechanism. The whispers among the lesser demons indicated that when this machine turned some function on, Mulciber would have total control of the Between.

For what, Lamarr had no idea, but having demons in control of anything made him sick inside. He'd heard Heather and Zakhart talking about this Mechanism, but they didn't know what it did. All Lamar knew for certain was that this Mechanism had an addition that was close to being turned on and it would do a lot of harm to human souls when it was activated.

And the Between.

Javier pulled in a labored breath and patted Lamarr on the back, his face bruised and cut, dark hair plastered against his face that dripped with sweat.

"No matter what," said Javier. "Don't give up."

Lamarr nodded, wishing he knew how to escape this cage. Get him and Javier out of here—along with the other trapped souls. He sighed, glancing across the cage as the door rattled.

Demons forced open the door and shoved another soul inside.

This soul clutched a pickaxe in his fists, but a grey-skinned demon stripped it from his hands and closed the gate with a loud clang.

"How many more fights?" Lamarr said with a groan, watching as demons pushed a second soul into the cage. "When is this going to stop?"

"Stay calm, amigo—we've got this," said Javier standing up and stretching his arms, his Spanish accent thick. "I'll bet Barb is worried sick about me."

Lamarr raised an eyebrow and gave him a sharp nod.

"She okay?" he asked, his voice quiet, dark brown eyes sad.

Lamarr had never been sure about Javier's relationship with Barb, but where one was, the other wasn't far away. He'd always thought that they'd been more than friends, although neither Javier nor Barb had ever said a word. They weren't quite like Ross and Heather. Everyone in the great tree felt that fire burning between Ross and Heather, wondering when they would finally admit they were crazy about each other. With Javier and Barb, it felt more like embers than a bonfire. A slow burn.

Now? At the new soul tree, Lamarr wasn't sure. Everything felt jumbled and off kilter.

"She is," said Lamarr. "She's been frantically searching for you."

"Dios Mio," he muttered, crossing himself. "I hope she doesn't end up down here because of me."

Lamarr turned his attention to their next opponents. He'd never seen either of these souls before, but from the way they staggered through the cage and pounded on the door, they were new here. New to the SoulSport. Both souls were men, short and wiry, eyes filled with confusion and fear.

"What the hell is this place?" one of them shouted. "Let me out of here!"

"Where am I? Why am I in here?" the other one raged, pounding his fists against the cage wall. "What is this place? I died. It was a clean shot to the head. I'm not supposed to feel anything! I didn't ask for this!"

Lamarr quickly figured out that the demons used this place in the Demon Veils as a practice ground, testing souls against each other. Trying to find new champions. He was relieved that souls weren't trying to destroy each other in this cage, just fighting, but Lamarr worried that things would soon escalate to a final death struggle like Thraecius had warned them about long ago. And Ross had briefly told him about at the new soul tree.

He knew how scarred Ross was when they brought him back from the Demon Veils, definitely not the same man who left the great tree bound for the Spiral, hopes high, his love for Heather so...

Lamarr struggled for a word, but failed.

Pure? Before, Ross' love for Heather seemed to transcend the Between's emptiness and Lamarr knew it would survive beyond it. But after escaping the demons, Lamarr felt Ross' struggle to find the person he was before. He was trying so hard to hold onto what he'd had before. With Heather at his side.

Lamarr understood Ross better now and he hoped Ross could find his way back again. A journey that he and Javier would have to make, too. A much longer one than finding the Spiral, he realized, but if the two of them could escape, he knew Ross would be there to help them both.

But he also knew that when Barb realized that he and Javier were both missing, she and some of the other lost souls might try to rescue them.

After they found Heather.

"Wagers please!" Mulciber's voice echoed across the amphitheater as the big red and grey demon sauntered around the cage, leering at the crowd. He held his hands high, motioning for the other demons to place their bets. His leathery skin color had changed, looking mottled with both grey and red.

From the carved-out stone seats, demons tossed tokens at Mulciber's feet. Coins clinked and rolled against the metal cage. Some were gold and some were silver. Several smaller grey demons scurried behind Mulciber, gathering up the tokens and collecting them in two black baskets.

When all the coins had been thrown, the two demons sat side-by-side and counted the tokens as a nervous pall descended on the crowd.

Lamarr didn't understand everything that was happening, but he'd been in the cage twice now and both times, they'd counted aloud the number of silver and gold tokens. Mulciber's teams were represented by silver. Apparently, he and Javier were the gold team. He'd wanted to ask Javier more about how the cage worked, but there hadn't been time. The demon crowd voted on which team they thought would win by throwing either a gold or silver token. He hoped the crowd had voted gold.

And he had no idea what happened to teams that lost down here.

With a hiss, a grey demon held up a silver token, displaying it to all sides of the amphitheater. Cheers and rumbles echoed through the massive chamber. Mulciber looked smug.

Lamarr had learned quickly when the crowd favored a team. It set him on edge. His third fight and they were already betting on the newcomers. He feared what happened to souls that fell out of favor. Or lost.

"Guess they think these noobs gonna take this fight," Javier said, wiping his mouth with the back of his hand.

"Bad bet," Lamarr snapped, gritting his teeth as he stared down the panicking souls that watched them from across the cage.

For the last two days, since he awoke in the demon caves and found himself in this cage, he'd fought against other souls that seemed like they'd just arrived in the Between. He'd held his own until the jaded soul alongside him was taken away without explanation. Seeing Javier brought in had filled Lamarr with a mix of anger and relief. Anger that Javier had been taken by the demons, too, but relieved at the familiar face. Together, they'd torn up any and all souls. Partly because of Knox's training and partly because they had nothing else to lose.

Lamarr already knew how this fight would go.

The demons loved these fights, loved watching human souls tear each other up, loved betting on the outcome. Lamarr hated the fights, but for now, there was nothing he could do but participate. He'd come this far trying to restore his soul after his suicide. He wouldn't quit now. He had everything to lose.

Mulciber turned toward the cage and clanged a large metal bell that hung outside it. Signaling for the next SoulSport match to begin.

Lamarr and Javier rushed forward, landing blows on the new souls. Guilt burned in his stomach as they stared at him in shock, confused, and running.

"Hey, get off me, man!" one soul shouted, stumbling back against the cage, clawing at the door, trying to find a way out.

"Why are you doing this?" the other demanded, looking horrified.

"Fight back," Lamarr whispered. "The only way out of the cage is to fight."

Javier chased down the other soul, tackled him, and pummeled him with blows.

"Fight or they'll destroy you! Claro?" Javier told the man.

Lamarr squared off with the other man, throwing punches, shoving him into the cage wall as Javier beat on the other soul. From the rock-lined seats, the demons cheered.

"Fight back!" Javier yelled with a hiss. "You've got to fight back or the demons will destroy you!"

At last, the man that Lamarr fought threw a punch at him. Lamarr didn't move out of the way of the blow, playing up the hit. He fell to his knees, letting the other soul hit him again before he got to his feet and returned fire.

The demons were shouting and beating on the cage walls now, chanting something in their tongue. Lamarr didn't understand their language and the sound of it filled him with rage. He despised them and wanted only to get out of this cage and rip every one of these demons to shreds.

Especially the big blotchy red one. Mulciber.

He despised that demon most of all. Lamarr didn't understand how demons could harm human souls like this—with no one objecting or trying to stop them. His whole life, he'd believed the stories about demons having to be invited in to harm him. He hadn't invited these creatures anywhere. What would they do if he just turned around and walked out of these caves? He sighed. Toss him to the soulstalkers?

But maybe, he realized, that in killing himself, he'd invited in all sorts of things that he hadn't anticipated? A chilling thought.

It seemed like forever until the soul that Javier fought began blocking his blows, but he hadn't thrown a single punch yet. Lamarr feared the demons would throw this one to the soulstalkers if he refused to fight.

He'd seen them do it before.

The rhythmic thump of feet and metallic clang of the cage was almost a hypnotizing anthem, pushing Lamarr into a rage that he couldn't shake. It was like a pulsing heartbeat driving him forward, making him crave more violence.

He lunged at the other soul, landing blow after blow. The other soul kept up with him, dodging and blocking, returning punches. He was making the fight look entertaining.

Lamarr knew that as long as the fight entertained the demons, they would keep them around for the SoulSport. But Lamarr also knew about them carrying champions from the cage and into their lowest realm to fight in a major SoulSport that picked demon leaders and made decisions based on the winners.

Ross told him about the cage fights, of becoming their champion. Lamarr hadn't seen any fights like that yet, but if he and Javier remained here, he knew that they'd see those cage fights, too.

Javier let out a wild howl and beat the other soul back against the cage wall. The other soul had curled into a ball and crumpled against the floor.

Lamarr felt sick inside as he watched the beat down, knowing he couldn't make Javier stop. He feared what would happen to this new soul, wishing he could have led them to the soul tree before the soulstalkers carried them off. To this place.

Before the demons swarmed the Between, soulstalkers carried souls to the poppy fields. But the demons had changed everything. Human souls became their slaves and now, they didn't even have the poppy fields' final sleep to save them.

Lamarr felt sick as cheers roared through the cavern. He and Javier were declared the winners and the other two souls were dragged off, screaming, out of the cage and into the darkness.

nine

. . .

SEEING the egg that Sandriana carried and the little sand runner cub amazed Heather. These soulstalkers and sand runners were either created by Death or the demons, yet they were rebelling against their makers. It gave Heather hope that there might be a way out of the Between again. A path that she and the others could take if they stopped the demons. These demons were an infection in the Between now, one that had to be removed quickly. She needed to let Zakhart meet Sandriana and see these sand runners for himself.

Sandriana moved toward Heather who still held the sand runner cub in her arms. It was feather-light, but it had substance and some weight. She loved snuggling against it, feeling the comfort of its throaty purr and its warm presence. But she had to put it down.

She set down the little cub and it scampered toward the two adult sand runners that sat nearby.

Sandriana studied Heather, a distraught expression on her face as she pointed toward the sky as it darkened with the flutter of wings.

Heather froze. Soulstalkers!

The chirrs and calls of a huge flock of soulstalkers filled the silence as they landed on the poppy field's ashen soil.

Heather held her breath, watching them congregate around the poppies, walking through the fields. Sand runners melted out of the shadows, trotting along beside the soulstalkers as they traversed the huge fields where hundreds of demons slept the final sleep. Heather hadn't seen a single human soul in this field. Only demons.

They were part of Sandriana's flock.

They crowded around Heather, exchanging quiet songs with each other. The others, like Sandriana. looked so different from the grasslands soulstalkers she'd encountered. Owl-like eyes. Eagle-like bodies. They didn't look so frightening, eyes not so wild, faces not so leering and hungry. She felt strange standing before them like this, especially when they all bowed down before her, heads lowered, wings draped like black capes over their shoulders.

As if pledging their support to the soul's fight against the demons.

Sandriana squawked a few notes and moved through the crowd of soulstalkers. She turned and sang a song to them and they lilted a harmony underneath that became a lament, making Heather's eyes well with emotion. When the song drifted away, Sandriana dropped down on her knees in front of Heather, the egg still clutched against her stomach. She lifted her hand toward Heather's face.

"U. Help. Us?" she said, her syllables broken rasps as she motioned at the flock of soulstalkers kneeling before her.

But the look in those intense, gold-flecked eyes sent shivers down Heather's spine. Never had she seen such a look of desperation in her entire life. Not even in her mirror before she took her own life. Sandriana apparently thought that Heather could somehow save them. Protect them from the demons. She needed to get this soulstalker to Zakhart. He would have some answers. And hopefully, he and the pale angels would protect them.

Heather dropped down on her knees and took Sandriana's taloned hands in hers. For a moment, she stared into the soulstalker's intense, owl-like eyes.

"Sandriana," she said. "I will do everything I can to save your flock."

The soulstalker reached up to her long neck and slid a black leather cord free. Dangling on the cord was a dull greenish crystal point that had a rainbow sheen.

"Help. U," said Sandriana, extending the necklace to Heather.

Nodding, she let go of the soulstalker's hands. Sandriana slipped the loose cord over her head. The crystal looked heavy but it nestled gently into the silky grey fabric of her clothes, almost disappearing.

"Thank you," said Heather as she pressed her hand against Sandriana's shoulder then pointed north.

"We must go back. My friends will help. The angels will help."

The soulstalker's mouth fell open, a look of fear contorting her face. She shook her head.

"Yes, Sandriana. Angels. They battle the demons here. They protect souls. They will help you and your flock, too."

Sandriana shook her head, a trill of notes rolling out of her mouth.

"Trust me," said Heather, laying her hand to her chest, where her heart had been.

The soulstalker stared at her, studying her eyes, her expression, and sniffed the air—using everything that she could examine. Finally, she reached out and gripped Heather's arm and let out a breath, nodding.

"We trust," Sandriana said finally, but Heather could tell that the soulstalker was still terrified.

Sandriana and the others were taking a huge risk in trusting her. In leaving their overlooked place beside the boiling lake. Flying into prime demon territory. To fight them. Starting a conflict that might never end.

The soulstalker rose to her feet and the others dispersed, disappearing throughout the poppy field, sand runners shuffling away to the protection of the poppies' huge stalks. Sandriana followed the sand runners, carrying her precious egg off to a hidden nest somewhere safe among the poppies.

When she returned, she moved toward Heather. She wore the

same dull green crystal point that hung from a leather cord around her neck. She patted the crystal that rested against her chest.

"Connects. Us." Sandriana said in a guttural rasp.

Was the crystal a symbol of her flock? Connecting Heather to it?

"Thank you for trusting me, Sandriana," said Heather as she nodded toward the distant forests beyond the sea of grasslands. "I'm ready."

Sandriana lifted Heather into her arms, wings spread wide, black feathers uncurling to their full length. Her wings began thumping against the air as she and Heather rose in the cool greyness. They hovered over the poppy field that stretched far into the distance. It was the biggest one Heather had seen in the Between. The soulstalker chirped two crystal clear notes that echoed in four octaves from the others below as they repeated it back to her. Sandriana turned her body around, Heather wrapped tightly in her arms, and soared across the sky, heading north.

———

IT SEEMED LIKE THEY'D FLOWN FOR HOURS OVER THE GOLDEN, almost sunny, grasslands until finally, the terrain began to change color. The blades of grass grew taller and thinner until wisps of silvery green grass whipped in the wind, cascading in waves across the landscape. The trees still seemed far out of reach, the grasslands endless except for the squares of ashen soil where huge poppies rose into the sky, opening heavy blossoms and shaking pollen like snow across the ground.

Heather hid her face from them, fearing to see people she knew, souls she'd cared about—like Ross—lying fallow beneath the blossoms. Slowly disintegrating like weathered statues.

She hadn't had much time to think about how frantic Ross must be right now. She was terrified that he'd gone charging into the demon caves and gotten himself captured by demons again. There hadn't been any time to talk, to be together. To just hold each other, touch, and be together again. There had never been enough time.

She sighed. And then there was Knox.

How had she managed to have feelings for two men like this? She barely knew Knox, but he'd been there when she'd needed someone. He'd watched her back, comforted her when her thoughts were making her crazy, and helped her get Ross back. How could she just brush him off now? Now that he'd done everything he could to help her save Ross.

Indecision tore at her.

Sandriana rose on an updraft, her form rising high above the fragile grey world below. So strange and delicate. She hated this place, wanting only to find the Spiral again and escape for good, but now, Sandriana and her flock needed her help. Zakhart needed her. She winced. Knox needed her.

But so did Ross.

And her heart had broken at losing him. All she'd wanted was to have him back in her arms. But something felt different between them right now. He seemed so distracted. So distant. And something was tearing him up inside. He'd been through horrible things at Mulciber's hands, things he hadn't spoken about yet, but she hadn't been able to get him to talk about it. She hadn't had time.

Maybe he didn't feel the same way about her anymore? Now, that he'd escaped the hell of those demon caves. Did he even still love her?

Everything in her head felt so jumbled and confused now.

As the forest rose on the horizon, a knot festered in Heather's stomach. Even at this distance, she felt the chaos. All the lost souls struggling to make peace with their own deaths and desperate to reach the Spiral, and now, they had to fight demons to even see it. If they could even see it.

She had the way out wrapped around her wrists, the bracelets' white light illuminating her hands and the way forward. She and Ross had been just steps from it, from leaving this place forever. Again. When Mulciber arrived. Heather was so grateful that Sandriana had saved her from the demons and whatever Mulciber had planned for her.

Then there was Knox. And Ross.

Why did she feel so conflicted? She loved Ross. But she couldn't leave Knox in danger here. A part of her loved Knox, too.

Still, the thought of breaking Ross' heart—of being without him—made her shake all over. But she couldn't bear to look into Knox's hurt blue eyes either. She sighed. She'd never meant for this to happen.

At last, the gentle violet glow of light surrounding the ring of trees near the stream rose out of the forest.

Heather tapped Sandriana's shoulder and pointed toward the ring of trees.

"There," she said.

Sandriana nodded, a shrill call rising on the wind as she edged her flight line a little to the north. The silvery grey grasslands went on in waves and waves until finally, Sandriana flew over the first trees growing at the edge of the thick forest.

Heather held her breath a moment, trying to halt the somersaults in her stomach. She wasn't ready to face the Ross versus Knox question any more than she was ready to face Mulciber's army of demons. Somehow, they had to pull together an opposing force against those demons and try their best to drive them out. Before they did irreparable damage.

But it was too late for that now, she realized. The damage had been done. Somehow, they had to stop Mulciber's plan. Before it destroyed all of these lost souls and spilled into the physical world.

But one question nagged at her. Zakhart was an angel. Why couldn't he bring in a huge force of angels and just stop this whole uprising? He had the power of the light in his hands. Couldn't he invoke it and destroy all the demons here? Get those archangels down here to smite Mulciber and all these demons?

She remembered someone—was it Zakhart—saying that Hell no longer had its king. Was that the Devil himself? What had happened to him? And did that mean that no one was controlling those demons, leaving them free to wreak havoc? Why hadn't the angels anticipated this? And accounted for the swell of demon attacks? Leaving a bunch of confused and lost souls to fight this battle for them?

She and Zakhart needed to talk.

Sandriana soared along on an updraft, wings stretched wide as she floated along the grey sky, dipping closer to the ground as the soul tree's luminous bark appeared in the greyness.

Her hands began to shake. Was she *that* nervous to face Ross and Knox? Would they all look to her for answers again? And action? She had no clue how to fight these demons. Especially since there weren't any creatures of light opposing Mulciber—except a small group of pale angels. As a vulnerable soul, she had everything to lose and little knowledge of how to defeat demons.

Especially Mulciber.

"There," Sandriana squawked, nodding her head toward the jumble of souls crowded onto the grass in the center of the ring of trees.

Heather watched them scurry around, rushing back and forth. Were they training? Or fighting with each other?

Zakhart had kept the peace as best he could, but if she knew Ross and Knox, they were already fighting with each other. Ross wasn't a fighter until his back was against the wall, but she was sure that Knox had been pressing him against that wall since the moment she'd been carried off. But she knew that Ross' captivity by demons had changed him. In ways she was about to learn.

As Sandriana soared closer, Heather saw someone pointing at the sky. The rest of the souls crowded into a group, a handful of pale angels rushing around them. They seemed frozen with surprise—or fear—at the sight of a soulstalker winging toward them.

Could they even see her from this distance?

With a final burst of speed, Sandriana lifted on another updraft, wings spread wide as she floated up and across the shrinking distance between them and the soul tree. The ground was rushing up quickly as Sandriana stretched out her legs and taloned feet, her body stiffening as she used her shiny black wings to brake. Their momentum slowed, the ground so close as Sandriana extended her taloned feet toward the ground like landing gear on a plane, bouncing along the forest floor until the soulstalker dug her talons into the ground, stopping about ten feet away from the soul tree.

A crowd of souls ran toward them as Sandriana set Heather down. Heather kept the soulstalker behind her, arms spread wide, her hands gripping Sandriana's wings.

Would they even listen to her or would they attack Sandriana on sight?

"Heather!" Ross shouted, a grin spilling across his face as he sprinted ahead of the pack, Zakhart and Knox behind him.

She grinned at the warm excitement on his face, the sight of him filling her with relief. He was okay!

As he got within a few feet of her, his expression changed to confusion, but it didn't stop him from throwing his arms around her and holding her against his chest. The heat of his embrace flooded across her skin, making her gasp at how deeply she felt his touch. She slid her right arm around him, her left still stretched out in front of Sandriana.

His mouth found hers in a deep, pulsing kiss that made her lips go numb and her chest flutter. His kisses were frantic, aching, like he hadn't seen her for a thousand years, but Sandriana's chirp shook him out of the embrace.

His beautiful hazel eyes widened and he stared at the soulstalker in shock. He froze in place, watching with wary eyes and slow movements.

"What the hell is that thing doing here?" he asked.

"Relax," said Heather, smiling as she cupped his face. "She saved me."

He frowned as the others reached Heather, Knox and Zakhart

pushing past him. Knox wedged his shoulder between them, edging Ross backward as the curly-haired soldier slid an arm around Heather's neck, a hand against her face.

"I almost lost my mind when that thing carried you off," said Knox in a quiet voice. "You okay?"

She nodded.

Knox grabbed the staff draped across his back and whipped it around, shoving the end into the curve of Sandriana's chin. He gritted his teeth, snarling as he stared at the soulstalker.

"Knox, no!" Heather shouted, pushing him backward, but he wouldn't budge.

"Let me take care of it, Heather," he shouted, teeth gritted as he shoved the staff forward. "Break its ugly neck."

Sandriana dodged the staff, letting out an angry chirr, golden tortoiseshell eyes narrowing. She swiped at the weapon, talons hacking off the end of the staff.

Heather grabbed Knox's sleeve and tried to push him away again.

"No! She's not a threat!" Heather shouted, waving Knox off. "She saved me!"

Knox thrust the staff toward the soulstalker again, the others lifting their staves, moving behind Knox. They shouted and shoved forward.

Spooking Sandriana.

She unfurled her wings wide, talons raised, a screech piercing the air.

"Knox, no!"

Heather screamed as Knox drove forward with the jagged-edged staff, toward Sandriana's chest.

Barely missing the soulstalker's throat.

Heather stood her ground, not moving as Knox tried to shove past her and attack Sandriana.

Ross leaped forward, lunging at Knox, tackling him to the ground. He stripped the staff out of Knox's hands and tossed it behind the soldier.

"Knock it off, Travers! Heather said she wasn't a threat. So, back off."

Ross planted himself beside her, blocking anyone trying to get through. He stretched out his arms wide. And Heather loved him even more for standing beside her, protecting this soulstalker. Because she'd said so.

"All of you, stop!" Ross shouted. "Listen to Heather. She said it's friendly, so I believe her."

Heather stared at Ross a moment, her heart swelling. Based on one statement from her, he'd supported her, believed her. Fought beside her. No questions asked.

She leaned over and kissed him.

"Thank you," she whispered in his ear.

He smiled as Zakhart and Razasha shoved through the group to stand before the soulstalker that stood warily behind Heather and Ross. Knox got to his feet and retrieved the staff, his eyes narrowed, mouth pressed into an angry grimace.

"Heather!" Zakhart cried, stepping forward. "You've escaped the demons!"

"They never had me," Heather replied. "This soulstalker swooped in and rescued me."

"Really?" Zakhart replied.

He looked surprised and exchanged a look with Razasha.

Heather nodded. "She has a name. Sandriana. And she asked me to help her. She and her flock have turned on their demon makers. Along with a large pack of sand runners. They want to fight the demons. Beside us."

Zakhart's pumpkin-orange eyes brightened. "Is this true?"

"Yes. Talk to her. I think you and the other pale angels speak her language. I know a few words, but my voice isn't equipped to hit all those notes."

Nodding, Zakhart stepped forward with slow steps as he sang a few tenor notes in a bright key.

Sandriana's worried expression perked up and she stared at him, cocking her head as he intoned a few more notes. She chirped some notes in response.

Zakhart thought for a moment and then softly responded, throwing out some low and high notes that Heather recognized, but they trilled by so fast she couldn't gather them all. Much less translate them.

This time, Sandriana responded, chirping out a complex aria with melody and harmony. Razasha joined in, laying down another layer of harmony that Zakhart added the melody over in his clear tenor voice until the most achingly beautiful round of music Heather had ever heard filled the forest.

Everyone stopped what they were doing and listened to the mesmerizing composition.

It went on for several minutes, leaving Heather and the others transfixed. It was beautiful. Heather wondered how many stories floated in and around those layers of melodies and harmonies.

Sandriana's face was intense, her pupils nearly blotting out the sharp golden irises that gave her an almost owl-like expression as her taloned hands flashed through the air when she spoke—or sang. Heather wasn't sure which it was, but either way, it was lyrical and moving.

She glanced at Ross whose whole face had lit with intrigue. He seemed moved and entranced by the exchange, a faraway look in his gold-hazel eyes. Even tough-as-nails Knox watched the exchange with watery blue eyes, unable to look away.

Soon, the gorgeous layers of sound faded to silence, only the wind answering through bare tree limbs.

"What a fascinating story," Zakhart said in a quiet voice. "I'm just stunned by it, Heather. All of it."

"Did she tell you that the sand runners are nursing cubs," said Heather. "And that the soulstalkers hide their own eggs among the poppy fields they've planted. They carry off demons and put them into the final sleep. They've been fighting for their freedom, Zakhart, and they have no interest in hunting souls."

"Are you serious?" Ross asked, glancing from Heather to the soulstalker. "Soulstalker eggs and sand runner cubs?"

She nodded. "I held a cub in my arms. The sand runners didn't even try to harm me."

"Friendly soulstalkers?" Ross cried, letting out a hiss of breath as he ran his fingers through his sandy blond hair. "And cuddly sand runner cubs? I'm in awe. And so grateful they were there to save you, Heather."

He took her hand in his and pressed it to his mouth, kissing her fingers. She caressed his face a moment and let go of his hand.

"Sandriana says there are hundreds of soulstalkers in her flock," said Zakhart. "Hundreds! Do you realize what those numbers could do for us?"

Heather grinned at the pale angel.

"Create a real army to fight this demon infestation."

"Exactly," said Zakhart, exchanging a smile with Razasha.

Razasha moved over to the soulstalker and sang gentle soprano tones that were like whispers. Sandriana responded with a series of bright trills, smiling as Razasha led her toward a cluster of pale angels. Halea glared at the soulstalker and walked away, but the others quickly intoned bits and pieces of a melody that Sandriana picked up on quickly, adding her own musical thread to the sounds.

Soon, they were all deep in conversation. Sandriana seemed comfortable with Razasha and the other pale angels, especially when they surrounded her in a protective circle as they spoke to one another.

Heather was amazed and encouraged. They all spoke Sandriana's language just like she'd expected. Maybe it was the same as the pale angels? She couldn't quite tell.

"Heather?"

Heather turned, looking up into Knox's soft blue eyes. He looked sheepish, a mixture of regret and remorse as he rubbed his neck, eyes downcast, shoulders slumped.

"Listen," he said in a quiet voice, his gaze snapping up from his feet. "I'm really sorry about what happened. But I thought you were in danger." He sounded sincere—genuinely sorry for what happened. "I was just trying to protect you from bein' carried off again."

She took his hands in hers, squeezing.

"Knox, it's okay. You had every reason to attack soulstalkers on sight. We all did. There's no way you could have known. It's okay."

She glanced at Ross who looked angry now. Arms crossed against his chest, eyes squinting at Knox as he dug the toe of his shoe into the ground.

"He would have if he'd been listening," Ross muttered, glaring at the soldier.

"Shut up, Shepard," Knox snapped. "You're not involved in this conversation. It's just between us, so stay out of it."

"The only us in this conversation is Heather and me. Travers."

Ross turned toward Knox.

"Tell him, Heather."

Heather winced. She'd never seen Ross territorial like this, but the anger sparking in his eyes made his feelings clear. She glanced at Ross and then Knox, her feelings twisting together and tearing her in both directions. Her soul ached for Ross, but she couldn't deny the pull she felt toward Knox either.

What was she going to do?

Heather sighed, her gaze shifting to Zakhart.

"Heather," said Zakhart, stepping between Knox and Ross and taking hold of her hand. "I need to talk to you. Can we take a walk?"

"Of course," she said, mouthing *thank you* to him as he led her toward a footpath leading out of the ring of trees. "I wanted to talk to you about the soulstalker anyway."

She paused, glancing back at Ross and then Knox.

Ross watched her with an odd expression that she couldn't read.

Was he upset because she hadn't backed up his comments to Knox? That she hadn't had his back like he'd just had hers? There hadn't been time to talk about their relationship, but honestly, could they even have a relationship in a place like this? They were dead.

Fighting to find the way out and back to some sort of a physical life again, but there were no guarantees that would even happen. Or bring them together in the flesh.

Sometimes, she thought that wasn't even possible now. She'd almost given up any hope of living again. But she only had herself to blame. She'd voluntarily given up her new life to save Ross. Because she loved him more than a physical life without him.

Why was that so hard to say to him now? In front of Knox. She'd never felt so confused.

Finally, Ross caught her gaze and held it, his eyes stormy. To her right, Knox stood there with crossed arms and an arrogant sneer on his face. Both of them had expected to be part of this conversation.

She sighed, not wanting to fight with either of them. Right now, she needed Ross' take on all of these new developments. After she spoke to Zakhart. She needed Ross' insights about the demons, too. He was the only person with that knowledge, so Knox would just have to understand. Knox also needed to understand that she'd given up everything to rescue Ross. Even though she couldn't have accomplished it without Knox's assistance. Regardless of who helped her and why, she needed to spend some time with Ross. Alone.

Especially now.

No, she wanted to spend time with him. She loved him.

"Ross," she said, nodding toward the soul tree. "I need your input, too. Soon. About Mulciber and the other demons."

His expression flattened a little and again, she couldn't read his reaction. He almost looked upset and she was afraid she'd hurt him just now.

Knox, looking a little dejected, nodded at her. He turned to leave, but stopped, turning around to face her again.

"Think we could get together later and talk?" Knox asked, hands in his pockets. "After you've had some time to rest?"

Heather glanced at Ross, the anger sizzling in his gold-hazel eyes.

"Sure, Knox. Come find me later, all right?"

He nodded, his expression lightening. "Awesome. Thanks!"

She watched him rush off, wooden staff in hand. He pulled a bunch of the other souls along with him. Back to the practice area to train with some hand-carved staves.

When she turned back toward Ross, his arms were crossed and he looked sullen.

"Sorry," she said, but he just shrugged and walked away from Zakhart.

She'd hurt him. And she felt awful.

"What did you want to discuss, Zakhart?" she asked, turning toward the pale angel whose gaze shifted from Knox to Ross.

"The soulstalkers," he replied. "What did you want to talk to me about?"

"The angel Andrealphus," she said, studying the pale angel's expression.

His mouth twitched, eyes widening. "Fallen angel Andrealphus? He was once among the Maker's most favored angels. Why do you mention Andrealphus?"

"According to Sandriana, Mulciber claims to have his ear. And someone called eosf-something."

The color drained from Zakhart's face, his pupils becoming huge black orbs.

"Archangel Eosphoro?" he said with a stutter, his face looking taut and pinched now.

"That's it," said Heather, studying his fearful expression. "Who is that?"

"The very first of the Maker's archangels," said Zakhart, his voice barely above a whisper. "We don't speak that name very often."

"Why?" Heather asked.

Zakhart glanced around, his face still bone white.

"Eosphoro began the Dusk War rebellion. Some say it was jealousy. Others called it greed. But he wasn't like Lucifer. Eosphoro learned nothing from Lucifer's failed rebellion and his assault on the Maker's throne. And it was no secret that Eosphoro wanted the power of creation above everything."

Apparently, this Archangel Eosphoro had found some way to create creatures in his own image. Shadow creatures and demons. And he'd shared it with Mulciber and some fallen angel. this Andrealphus."

Zakhart's eyebrows pressed into an angry line.

"Eosphoro raged when the Maker refused to share this gift of creation with the angels. So, the archangel entered the fringes of the Heavens—like the Between and the Mortise of Souls—pitting light against dark. Starting the Dusk War. The Maker struck him and his followers down. They fell from the Heavens, wings aflame. Does that answer your question?"

The pale angel seemed on edge.

"It does," said Heather, "Is Death an archangel, too?"

Zakhart nodded. "In a way. She has power equivalent to the archangels, but she inhabited the earliest part of the Creation. Before so many angels existed."

"Does she have a name?"

"I'm sure she does," said Zakhart. "But it was lost to history—unless it's in the Archive. Death was created after the experiment in the Garden failed, becoming part of the elemental spirits that all returned to the Maker when angels took over those duties. Except Death."

Heather felt a chill against her skin. She'd been in Death's presence once and had never felt such dread before. The shadow of her scythe was terrifying, but her past intrigued Heather.

"Does she leave the Between often?" Heather asked.

Zakhart's brow furrowed and he stared at Heather, looking worried.

"Leave the Between? What do you mean? Death must remain in the Between. Always. That's a condition of her penance, forever hunting souls."

Heather shrugged, glancing across the courtyard at Sandriana as she knelt in a circle of angels, chattering away in dulcet tones.

"Sandriana said the demons had somehow sent Death on a fool's errand," said Heather. "Sending word that someone named...Sariel needed to talk to her. They want to keep her gone long enough to get Eosphoro here to take over. Or Andrealphus. Most of this isn't clear and some of it I'm speculating on. I'm sure you can get more information out of Sandriana than I can—speaking her language and all."

Heather had never seen Zakhart's face turn as cloud-white as it did after she'd finished her sentence.

"Andrealphus? Eosphoro? Take over the Between for Death? Death and Eosphoro hate each other. Andrealphus has probably never even seen Death before."

"That's what Sandriana said," Heather replied. "She was made by the demons and probably heard every moment of their planning."

Heather saw the tangle of thoughts rushing through Zakhart's head as he pressed a hand over his mouth and began to pace, eyes focused on the ground as he mumbled to himself.

When she looked up, she saw Ross. Within earshot. Patiently waiting nearby. He'd heard her mention these two archangels. Maybe he'd heard Mulciber mention them?

Ross glanced at Heather who shrugged at him in confusion. She didn't know what was so upsetting about this bit of information, but it deeply unsettled her to see Zakhart react like this.

"What's the matter, Zakhart?" Ross asked finally, moving beside him as the pale angel paced.

"Maybe nothing?" Zakhart muttered, raising his finger into the air, but then he returned to his mumbling and pacing. "Maybe everything?"

"Why everything?" Heather asked.

"If Andrealphus or Eosphoro enter the Between, Sariel will follow," said Zakhart in a hushed voice as his pacing quickened.

"So?" Ross snapped, shrugging. "What does that even mean, Zakhart?"

The pale angel stopped between Heather and Ross, his face flushed.

"It means that our tiny little fight to eject a bunch of freeloading demons has quickly escalated into an official big deal if two archangels join this fight. Sariel and Eosphoro. Alongside demons."

Heather held out her hands. "I still don't understand, Zakhart. Why would two archangels care about the Between?"

Zakhart sighed. "I wish I knew. That's the question we need to answer. Archangels are as high up the chain as field angels go here, so whatever their interest is, it's got to be over something big. Especially traitors like Eosphoro and Andrealphus. But there's more to it than that."

"More to what?" Ross asked. "Is it because one is the light and the other is shadow?" He glanced at Heather. "What? I heard Mulciber talk about Sariel and Eosphoro enough to know that they are bitter enemies. They were on opposite sides of this Dusk War, too."

"That's part of it," said Zakhart, still pacing. "But...they're also brothers. If they escalate this fight, it will stir up the ashes of the Dusk War. That fire died out, but its embers are still hot and easily fanned. Especially here."

Heather felt dread quiver in the pit of her stomach.

"Like a civil war?"

Zakhart nodded. "Brother against brother. Shadow against Light. Waging open warfare. With fallen angels supporting the shadows. And that would threaten everything."

"Everything?" Ross replied.

"Everything," Zakhart repeated. "The Spiral and the physical world all of you so desperately want to rejoin. I'd say that's pretty much everything."

Heather stared into the forest, a million thoughts rushing through her head. If they didn't rid the Between of these demons, before two archangels clashed, everything could be lost. And there just might not be a physical world left to return to. Ever.

ten

. . .

HEATHER STARED AT ZAKHART, her brain whirling with doom and horrific images of archangels battling one another. In the Between of all places. How had all of this escalated so quickly? She needed to understand what all of this meant. And why archangels would lower themselves enough to be interested in Mulciber? Was it the machine he was building?

She'd never understood what Mulciber's machine had been for, much less why archangels would find it important enough to journey to the Between. Had they learned about Mulciber destroying souls and remolding their remains into dark creatures? Was it to stop the SoulSport, where demons pitted souls against each other, and wagered on the outcome? How they acquired power? As horrible as all of these things were, neither of them explained what the Mechanism did.

Wind rose through the bare trees, branches clacking and shifting against the grey sky as it began to darken, night not far off. The air smelled cool and gritty, the pervasive scent of dirty rain clinging to everything. Heather folded her arms against her chest, a sudden chill turning her arms to gooseflesh.

"Why would archangels ever come here?" Heather asked, stepping toward Zakhart.

She motioned toward the forest, feeling frustrated and confused. So much was happening here that made no sense.

"You basically said that no one comes here but lost souls and outcasts. So, how could a bunch of lesser demons—even with angels involved—trick a primordial spirit like Death into going on what Sandriana called a fool's errand."

"Follow me," said Zakhart in a half-whisper, motioning them down the footpath.

"Why?" Heather asked. "Can't we talk here?"

The pale angel gave her one of his *not here* looks and nodded his head toward the darkening forest. Zakhart kept a lot of things to himself. Heather wondered if he kept them from the other pale angels, too.

Zakhart whistled a high-pitched sound and in moments, Lairz landed beside him. His copper eyes were intense, wavy light hair falling against his shoulders, ivory wings curving around him. She'd barely heard his approach. Were his wings stealthy like Sandriana's and the soulstalkers in her flock?

"You need my assistance?" Lairz asked, his baritone voice as silky as his cream-colored robes.

He folded his wings flat against his back and walked beside Zakhart on the path that led toward the small stream and the thick black fog that clung to the trees and floated along the water where the heartlilies grew in glimmers of bright orange.

"Yes," said Zakhart in a quiet voice, his wings curving against his shoulders. "I need your help with something."

Lairz nodded and chimed a series of baritone notes that became a harmony between them. Heather listened to the gentle song with its comforting chords as she walked beside Ross.

Ross reached out and very gingerly—almost timidly—as if she might push him away and took hold of her hand. The heat of his hand softened her uneasiness. It always frightened her whenever the pale angels switched to song. What did Zakhart and Lairz not want them to hear? Or know yet?

Was Zakhart keeping something from them right now?

She glanced at Ross who looked deep in thought, his brow shadowed with creases. He was troubled about something, but the weight of his hand against hers calmed her racing thoughts. His familiar presence was a reassurance she hadn't had in some time. She ached to be close to him again, hungered for some time alone with him. To talk about anything...everything. Especially that heavy two-letter word that meant so much. Us. *Could* they ever be together like that? In the way that they both craved?

And...what about Knox?

She hadn't known Knox long, but he'd been there during one of her darkest hours. Like so many other souls, she knew. Souls like Lamarr and Javier, but as close as she felt to them, she hadn't felt a powerful, raw connection to them. Only Knox—who shared her visceral need. He'd held her, comforted her, fought for her, but he hadn't said the words that every woman dreamed of hearing.

Ross said those words at a time when she'd had everything to live for—and so had he. In those final moments in the Spiral, when Heather knew that something had gone terribly wrong, Ross spoke to her from his heart. He'd said what she desperately wanted—no, needed to hear—what she felt deep in her soul but had been too afraid to say. Words that both of them thought would be his last.

I love you, Heather. You meant more to me than my own life.

Even now, his voice burned in her memory, those words a flame on her lips. There hadn't been any promises—there couldn't have been. No fairytale endings or happily ever afters. Just two sentences from his heart that even now, still shivered through her, made her breath catch, and a lump rise in her throat.

This was far from the daydreams she'd once imagined on those long Saturday nights at home alone, wishing there'd been someone to hold her hand during a scary movie. Someone to snuggle up with on the couch and watch some old 80s movie together.

No, she and Ross were both technically dead, existing somewhere between life and death. Fighting demons and guiding lost souls to a safe zone. Being dead really put a strain on any budding relationship and it certainly didn't translate into anything stable. Us—did that word have any meaning in this place? Did Ross feel that way because there hadn't been anyone else? Was it all just the heat of the moment? Just circumstances putting them together like this?

Regardless, she couldn't deny her feelings for him. She loved him deep into her soul and somehow, that terrified her. She desperately wanted to talk to him about all of this, knowing there were no guarantees of anything.

Even if they got through the Spiral together this time, would they even end up together? Zakhart had found a way to put them together in the very short lives of Hannah Girard-Davies and Rick Ross. Was it against all the odds that it could ever happen again?

Ross leaned down, lifted her chin, and pressed a kiss against her lips.

"I've wanted to do that since that soulstalker brought you back," he said, smiling at last, that familiar twinkle in his eyes again. "Especially in front of Travers."

She smiled, taking in the strong curve of his chin, the slight pout of his warm mouth, and those beautiful gold-hazel eyes that made him look so vulnerable.

"And I've wanted to do this," said Heather, stopping on the path.

She reached up and put her arms around his neck, kissing him hard, nibbling his lips as her arms tightened around him. He grinned against her mouth and tilted his head, lips parting as his arms enfolded her. She lost herself in the warmth of his mouth pressing against hers in a deep kiss, the comfort of his arms so tight around her. She wanted to fall into that embrace and hold onto him forever.

All the horrible nights without him rushed back, the terrifying run through the grasslands with flocks of soulstalkers beating the foliage for new souls. And hers all over again. All the waiting and hoping and hurting, imagining every horrible thing those demons were doing to him.

She laid her head against his shoulder, trembling as the floodgates opened, the memories of rebuilding the soul tree and fighting off soulstalkers that had attacked the tree in waves returned.

All the moments of fighting at Knox's side, trying to gain the tiniest seed of information about where the demons had taken Ross. Searching for him with Knox at her shoulder. Holding her. Protecting her. Keeping her focused and fighting to find Ross. She winced.

Knox. So proud. So much pain.

She held back a sob and let go of Ross, turning away.

"Heather?" he said. "What's the matter?"

He laid his hand on her shoulder. She didn't turn around, instead reaching up, laying her hand on top of his, squeezing.

"Just some awful memories," she said, sniffling, wiping back tears. "Everything that happened when I came back to the Between. Sorry, we haven't had a chance to talk about anything, so you don't know about any of this. It's all so jumbled and painful."

He gripped her shoulder, massaging it.

"I'm so sorry, Heather. I have no idea what you went through to get me out of there. But I want to hear every tiny detail about what you went through. I haven't even had a chance to thank you. To tell you how the memory of your face kept me from going insane in there, kept me hanging on. To even hold you in my arms and feel like, for just a moment, everything's all right. Just for a little while. It's a comfort I haven't felt in a long, long time."

Heather smashed her eyes closed, feeling guilty, remembering when she kissed Knox in the heat of everything, of falling into his embrace after trying to ignore her attraction. She and Knox went through hell to get Ross out and somewhere between the new souls and the demons, she'd developed strong feelings for the tall, curly-haired soldier.

If she still had a heart beating in her chest, it would have been torn in two.

"I'm just so confused right now, Ross," she said, pulling in a deep breath to keep the tears from trickling down her face.

She'd never felt so torn about anything in her entire life. How could she love two guys? How? She felt awful and sick inside.

"I know you are," he said in a quiet voice, his hand still rubbing her shoulder. "I saw how you looked at Knox." His sigh was heavy, aching. "And how you ignored my comment about us. I won't add to your confusion, but I just wanted you to know that I love you. More than my own life. So, no matter what happens, I want you to know, upfront, how I feel."

She couldn't stand it any longer. She turned around, grabbing hold of his forearms, the feel of him so comfortable, so close—a feeling she thought she'd lost forever. A feeling she'd never felt with anyone else before, including Knox.

God, she craved Ross Shepherd!

She couldn't help herself. She threw her arms around him, unable to hold back the tide of emotions drowning her. He just held her face against his chest, stroking her hair and holding her. She closed her eyes against the whirlwind of thoughts bombarding her head, wanting it all to calm down, and leave her alone for just a little while. She needed to clear her head and think logically about the demons and the archangels. The last thing she needed right now was to be in love with two guys. She had to sort this out—or go crazy.

"Heather?" Zakhart called from somewhere up the trail. "Ross? Where are you two?"

The two pale angels rushed back down the path as Heather rubbed her eyes and took Ross' hand in hers again.

"Sorry, we were just talking," Heather replied. "We haven't had any time together since the rescue."

Zakhart smiled. "That's been a problem, hasn't it? Well, hopefully, we can fix that shortly." He motioned them ahead. "Ready? It's not far."

Ross grimaced. "What's not far?"

"The fork in the stream," said Lairz, standing beside Zakhart.

"Fork in the stream?" Heather replied. "Why there?"

"It's a good place to lift off from," Zakhart announced. "Without the others seeing us. We need to take a trip."

Heather glanced at Ross and then Zakhart, frowning, feeling more confused than ever now.

"Where are we going?" Ross asked.

"To the Lake of Despair," said Zakhart. "We need to retrieve some of its essence if we're going to transfer light energies into the two of you."

Heather shook her head, not quite sure she'd heard the pale angel clearly.

"I have no idea what that means."

"You will soon, Heather," said Zakhart, motioning toward the south. "Because for a short time, Lairz and I are going to give the two of you light energies. And perhaps even wings."

"Wings?" Heather could only stare at him with her mouth hanging open.

"Wings," said Zakhart. "With an angel's energies, you'll be strong enough to battle Mulciber. It's obvious to me that he's planning to take over the Between. And block us from the Spiral."

Ross studied Zakhart for a moment. "How do you know that?" he asked. "You just said that we have to figure out what Mulciber's up to. Why he lured Death out of the Between."

Zakhart paced around them a moment, hands behind his back.

"As I was walking, it came to me, Ross. Because I know that there's only one way to lure Death out of the Between. If Death leaves her post, she breaks her oath and there's only one thing that would get her to break her oath."

"What's that?" Heather asked.

"More like who," he said, his tone dark a she paused in his anxious pacing. "More like Sariel."

"What does that mean?" Ross replied, squinting at the pale angel.

"I have what you humans describe as a gut feeling," said Zakhart, a smile lighting his face.

He seemed proud of his human-like hunch.

Lairz stared at Zakhart, a confused expression on his face as he tilted his head to the side. The other pale angel looked concerned and it was obvious that Lairz didn't understand Zakhart's responses.

Ross crossed his arms, fingers rubbing his chin, face a mask of concentration. Like Zakhart's words were a puzzle he was trying to solve.

"Tell us then."

"I'm guessing that with the fallen angel Andrealphus' help, Mulciber faked a missive to Death. Probably got Andrealphus—or perhaps even Eosphoro—to borrow Sariel's celestial seal or something. Used it to send Death word that Sariel wanted a reconciliation."

"What does that mean?" Ross demanded, looking frustrated. "Who's Sariel and the others you mentioned? Okay, I know you said he's an archangel but that's all I know."

"Sariel was Death's husband once," Zakhart replied. "Until Death left him for his brother, Andrealphus. And Eosphoro kept him away until it was too late. Three brothers. Three archangels. One of them fell. One of them oscillates in shadow. And one still holds true to the light."

Heather sucked in a breath, the chill against her skin intensifying.

"Archangels take spouses? And some primordial spirit at that? Are all three archangels fighting over her?"

The last place she wanted to be was in the middle of a love triangle between archangels. She had her own to worry about.

Zakhart nodded. "Spouses are permitted now—as long as the spouse is also an angel. Well, I know of one present-day exception to that rule. But in the days of the Creation, when everything was new and untested, there were only a few rules. And Death wasn't always a primordial spirit."

"Uh, what rules?" Ross asked. "And what do you mean that Death wasn't always a spirit?"

"One angelic rule forbade angels from marrying," said Zakhart.

"Forbade angels from taking spouses outside their own kind. Andrealphus and Sariel—and a few other archangels—defied the rules. They took spouses. Eosphoro, too. But that wasn't the worst part."

What could be worse than an archangel love triangle, Heather wondered. Besides her own.

She studied Lairz's expression. The pale angel had gone quiet, watching Zakhart with a mixture of fear and excitement. It was obvious to Heather that this pale angel had never heard any of these stories before.

"Worse than archangels fighting each other?" Ross replied with a smirk. "Brothers?"

"Yes," said Zakhart, his voice barely above a whisper. "Death was a human in the beginning. A refugee from the Garden, one of the Maker's first experiments. She was beautiful. Terrified. With nowhere to go after the Maker drove these first creations out of the Garden."

"Human!" Heather cried. "An angel married a human despite the rules?"

Lairz looked stunned. His brows pressed into hard lines above his copper eyes, his mouth pursing.

"It happened a lot in the beginning," Zakhart replied. "Quite forbidden now, of course—as I said, despite one exception—but in the early days, it caused a lot of problems. A lot!"

Heather leaned against the trunk of a river birch, its stark white bark looking so surreal against the deep grey sky.

"Like what?" she asked.

Zakhart began to pace again, his footsteps whispering against the dirt path. In the distance, the stream burbled a soothing rhythm against the hush of the wind through the bare trees.

"Offspring for one. Were they human or angelic? Did they belong in the physical realm or one of the spiritual planes? Some had wings. Others inherited an angel's powers. Some got both. Others got nothing. Angels don't age. And they don't die either. The Maker feared losing control of all of these gifts. Any angel caught producing offspring or marrying humans was stripped of their wings and their powers. And cast into the lower realms. Like the Between. Unable to shed her angelic powers, the human that Sariel married was transformed into the spirit of Death and cast into the Between."

So Death had been half human and half angel once?

"What happened to their kids?" Heather asked. "I hope they weren't punished. They had no control over being born."

A heavy sigh slipped through Zakhart's gritted teeth as his pacing quickened. He stared at his feet now, not looking up at Heather. His face was flushed.

"Any child born with wings or displaying angelic abilities was taken away from its human parent and raised in the angelic realms. No exceptions."

"Forever?" Ross asked, his eyes wide as he glanced at Heather, surprise burning in his gaze.

Zakhart nodded. "It broke a lot of hearts and pitted angels against each other. And it turned humans against angels."

"What happened to these—hybrids?" Heather asked. "Were their abilities diluted?"

"Not always the case, but most angels were jealous because humans were favored. So most angels treated these—hybrids badly, relegating them to the lowest levels of the angel flocks. Many angels called them derogatory names. But eventually, they were called...pale angels. And soulstalkers. One, a pale imitation of the light and the other a shadow of the darker fallen ones."

Heather gasped, staring at Zakhart with newfound appreciation. No wonder he'd been so fascinated by humans when he'd first seen them. No wonder he'd been drawn to the Between. He was half-human. Helping the Between's lost souls brought him closer to his human side, something he probably knew little about. Or the hybrid children whose angelic parent had chosen shadows over the light. That had been more like demons to him at first.

"Zakhart," she said, sliding her hand against his arm. "All this time, I wanted to ask what the pale meant in pale angel. I had no idea...so you're half-human?"

He nodded and motioned at Lairz.

"So is Lairz and all the angels I brought here. The other angels don't take us seriously. We're placed in the most menial of spiritual tasks, kept as far from the physical realm as possible." He shrugged "I guess they're afraid we'll defect or spill secrets to our mortal halves. Switch loyalties. That's why they let us come here, thinking we couldn't do any harm. They hoped it would satisfy our curiosity, but all it's done for me is heighten mine."

"Do you have a soul?" Ross asked.

A slight smile touched Zakhart's face.

"The Maker gave humans a soul. It's a human's most prized possession. It's coveted by all dusk and light creatures. Angels live an eternity, but they can also be destroyed. Their light essence eventually returns to its source, but not as a unique being like humans. The human soul is sort of an indestructible blueprint that, when mixed with the right energies, can recreate a human being, exactly as they lived. It's a physical piece of the Maker, not like creatures born of vapor or rays of light. A tangible, physical entity."

A blueprint? Heather had never been exactly sure what the soul was, hadn't really even thought about it before now. But the idea of it being a blueprint—a backup—fascinated her.

"Is that a yes?" Ross asked with a chuckle.

Zakhart smiled. "Honestly, Ross—I don't know. It's one of the questions that has burned inside me since I found out what I was." He shrugged. "I don't know if I'll ever find out the answer to that question. And so many others that I dream of having answered."

Heather took his hand in hers and squeezed it. "What other questions do you have, Zakhart?" she asked.

This was the first time that the pale angel had ever really opened up to her and she didn't want to interrupt him. She wanted him to keep talking so she could keep learning.

"I have so many unanswered questions," said Zakhart in a deathly quiet voice. "Who was my mother? Who was my father? Where was I born—on Earth or in the Heavens? Did I have siblings? A home with a backyard? A cat or a dog? Grandparents?" He laughed, bowing his head now. "So many silly questions, but I wonder about those things every time I help a human being." He sighed. "Every single time I wonder who I might have been if I hadn't sprouted wings between my shoulder blades."

He slid his hand free and patted Heather on the head.

"Guess that's why I have a soft spot for humans," he said as he straightened his robes, wings unfurling into gentle curves at his back. "I understand the things you've lost, the people you hold dear. Most of the pale angels do." He laid his hand against his chest. "We know what it feels like to have a heart beating in our chests."

Heather felt a rush of emotions surge over her. Zakhart had a heart once! He had some memory of it beating and yearning and breaking. She couldn't help herself. She slid her arms around him and hugged him.

"What was that for?" he asked as Heather let him go.

"Just grateful that you're here, Zakhart because you know what it was like to be physically alive once."

He nodded. "It was a very long time ago, but those four years were the most vivid moments in my memory. And I will cherish them for as long as I exist—however long that may be."

Ross sat down by the stream and ran his hand through the cool waters.

"You don't know who your parents are?" he asked.

"I have only vague memories of my mother," said Zakhart. "And I've been told who might be my father, but to be honest, angels make lousy parents."

"So true," said Lairz who walked over to the stream's bank and dropped down beside Ross. "In the earliest days when angels had been allowed to pair, my mother went a little mad. She was fascinated by humans and decided to pair with one. She broke so many hearts. Angels are beautiful. They have compassion, but without a soul, they can't feel human love. They had no concept of human relationships that required faithfulness and loyalty. She desired a child and set out to carry one. I don't think my father was ever aware that he'd sired a child. And she wasn't sure which human he'd been."

"What happened after you were born?" Heather asked, stepping closer to Lairz.

Lairz tossed a stone across the stream, silently watching it skip along the clear, burbling water in three hops and plunk into its depths.

"At first, she was shocked that she'd borne such a helpless creature. After a bit, she grew bored of the helpless child's humanness and how much work it required. Finally, she left me in the hands of other pale angels, instructing them to leave me with a human family if I didn't develop wings or a halo of light by the time I was five."

"How cruel!" Heather cried as she sat down on Ross' right side, leaning against his shoulder. "How could your mother just—give you up like that?"

Lairz's smile didn't fade, but Heather noticed that he exchanged a trill or two with Zakhart, his eyes portraying an emotion that Heather couldn't read.

"Cruel in human terms perhaps," said Lairz, "but angel mothers are different from human mothers. They have to be because a fledgling angel can shift to shadow at any time—depending on their lineage. If a fledgling turns to shadow, they cannot remain in the upper realms."

Zakhart paced behind them.

"Angel parents must relinquish any fledgling," Zakhart began, "with even the slightest hint of shadowing in the hopes that they can be trained out of it. If they can't, they must be removed from the realm. That includes grounded and dull fledglings—those without wings and those without a halo lighting their foreheads."

Lairz nodded. "Fortunately for me, at three, a gold halo appeared around my head, soon followed by wings. I wasn't raised by my parents, but I was raised as an angel. I had a human heart until I sprouted wings. And I felt great heartache at not being with my birth parents. It was actually a relief to shed that human artifact, but its memory remained, including the pain."

Ross skipped a stone across the stream and glanced back at Lairz.

"Do you hold a grudge?" he asked.

"Not now," said Lairz, shaking his head. "I understand now what she had to do. I also understand that she wasn't human and she couldn't feel love like humans. I guess I'm grateful for the experience because it taught me great compassion for humans." He reached out and tugged on Zakhart's robes as the pale angel continued to pace. "Zakhart had it worse though. Having a human mother and all."

Zakhart's wings twitched as he gripped his hands together and cast a dirty look at Lairz. Heather knew that he didn't want to talk about himself. At all.

"I can't deny that it was rough," said Zakhart, halting his pacing that had gotten almost frantic. "It shocked my mother when my father told her what he was, but it broke her heart when they took me away from her at three. I remember her falling to her knees and sobbing, calling my name over and over. Begging for me to stay."

Zakhart's face contorted, wincing at the memory.

"I kept pulling away from my father, running back to my mother, but every time, he'd drag me away from her. When I refused to obey him, he gathered me in his arms and took to the air. I can still see her lying in the dirt, her light blond hair pooled around her as she shrieked my name, her arms stretched out to the sky."

His jaw tightened and he bit his lip, turning his face away from them.

Heather knew that memory had hurt Zakhart much more deeply than he wanted to admit.

"Did you ever see your mother again?" Ross asked, his tone sad.

Zakhart nodded. "Only once. When I was five. Two angels

brought me back to the Earth to see her. She had aged dramatically. I ran to her and threw my arms around her. She held me tighter than I'd ever been held before. And I'd never felt anything so comforting and loving than her embrace. She cried so hard and I remember feeling startled at the beat of her heart against my chest. Until she held me, I'd forgotten that I'd been born with a human heart, but it disappeared when my wings appeared. I remember her laying her hand on my chest and crying. At the absence of that steady rhythm that she shared with me."

"Zakhart," Heather said, getting to her feet.

She moved over to the pale angel and put her arms around him and holding him in a tight embrace.

"That's so sad. Did you get to stay with her?"

He shook his head as she let him go.

"Not long. Only about three days. She read me stories, played games with me, and told me about her life, how she'd met my father. She held me in her arms and told me how much she loved me. I begged her to let me stay with her, but she told me I couldn't, that I had to go with my father because I wouldn't be safe."

"Why's that?" Ross asked, skipping another rock down the stream.

"It was a dark time in Europe," said Zakhart. "Long, long ago."

He began to pace again, shadows darkening his face. For only a moment, those pumpkin-orange eyes were burning flames of pain and regret. Then he turned his back, staring out at the distant grasslands.

"My mother lived in a poor farming village in the region of Aquitaine. She said that if anyone saw my wings or the light around my head, they might harm me. She said that's why my father took me away from her when I was three. When I was five, he brought me back to the village to see her again." He bowed his head, unmoving as he stared at the ground. "For the very last time. I didn't know that at the time. After that, I kept asking for her, but they told me I couldn't see her. Just after I turned seven in human years, they told me, when

I asked for her, that an angel of death had already carried her away to a higher realm. Where I wasn't allowed."

He still had his back to them, but the pain in his voice was unmistakable. Those events had been very traumatic and judging from his words and his tone, he wasn't quite over them yet. Heather had no idea what some of these angels had gone through, but she felt oddly closer to Zakhart and Lairz, now that she knew a bit about their past.

"Was that the last time you could see her?" Heather asked. "Or were they just telling you stories to keep you in line?"

"Funny, Heather," he said, turning around, his gaze settling on Heather, "I thought the same thing. Thought it was just an attempt to control my behavior. Thought when I was older, I could go back there and see her when I got my wings and could control my energies. They let me believe that. Guess no one had the heart to tell me that she was dead because humans die and her soul was in a place where only seraphim could travel." He pasted a smile on his face and motioned for everyone to rise. "Come! Let's talk about more hopeful things. Like wielding the light and defeating demons!"

Lairz grinned and rubbed his hands together. "Are we going hunting, Zakhart?"

"Perhaps," Zakhart said with a chuckle and clapped his hand against Lairz's shoulder.

Zakhart glanced over at Ross who still sat on the stream's bank, dangling his feet above the cool, flowing water, and nudged his knee between Ross' shoulder blades, urging him up from the ground.

"Come, Ross—there's a lot to do."

With a gentle flutter of his wings, the sound echoing across the forest floor, Lairz got to his feet as Ross slid back from the water's edge. He pulled his wiry frame up to his full, six-foot height.

"What does that mean?" Heather asked in a wary voice, glancing at Ross who just shrugged.

Ross paused beside Zakhart, looking stiff and uncertain.

Zakhart motioned her over to him. She walked toward him and stood beside him as the pale angel took hold of her hand.

"Pale angels bridge a gap between humans and the Maker," Zakhart said in a quiet voice. "We are part mentor, part protector. That's one of the reasons why we were assigned to the Between. The archangels thought we could do the most good here—or they at least agreed with me that we could do the most good here."

Heather heard his bitterness. It clung to his words and he made no move to hide it.

"Because some of your—codes if you will—are similar to ours, you can learn some of our safeguards. If given the proper energies." Zakhart cleared his throat. "You can carry—use—some of our abilities. Like the light cores within us—which fuel our light energies."

For a moment, Heather couldn't speak. Was Zakhart saying he would teach her how to use the light as a weapon? But her excitement overpowered her wildly spinning brain with the possibilities and the thought of summoning waves of light.

She held out her hand, palm up.

"Are you saying I could summon the light in my hands—like I watched you do in the demon caves?"

Zakhart grinned as he concentrated his gaze on her hand. In a moment or two, a bright white flame flickered in her hand, its movement tickling her palm. She felt the writhing heat washing over her fingers, seeping into her flesh. The roiling energy built as the flame widened, the wash of blue at its center quickly turning pure white.

"Will I be able to do this?" she asked. "Summon a flame? Use these energies against the demons?"

"Only if you can internalize it," he replied.

Heather frowned. "How do I do that?"

"Internalizing that flame will ignite your soul's core," Lairz answered as he summoned a pure white flame into his hand and placed his flame in Ross' hands.

"To give you a human example," said Zakhart with a wry grin, "it's like lighting the pilot light on a furnace. All the machinery is there. It just needs a spark to set everything in motion. Because you and Ross have touched divine energy within the Spiral, the Between, and the energy of a physical life—almost like pale angels—you are the only two souls in the Between that are capable of summoning this flame."

Heather glanced at Ross and shrugged. She had no idea what to do with this flickering white flame. And judging from Ross' expression, he had no clue what to do either.

She shook her head, holding the flame out toward Zakhart.

"I don't know what to do with it."

Zakhart chirped two notes at Lairz who trilled a note and stepped toward him.

"Lairz and I must return to the soul tree and help Razasha with our new soulstalker recruit," said Zakhart, the hint of a smirk curving up the corners of his mouth. "I'll expect the two of you back...soon."

"Wait!" Heather cried, moving toward Zakhart. "You're just gonna leave us standing here with these flames?"

The pale angels looked at each other and then nodded.

Ross frowned. "I thought we were going to this Lake of Despair you mentioned."

"Eventually, we'll need to fly off to the Lake of Despair, but neither of you is ready for that trip yet. I see that now." Zakhart motioned at the writhing white flames. "Study your flames. Don't let them die out and don't let them explode. But I expect you and Ross to figure out how to use them."

Whistling a tune that Heather didn't recognize, the two pale angels walked along the footpath, headed back toward the soul tree.

"Lairz thinks both of you are ready for this, but I'm not so sure now. Prove me wrong."

"Zakhart, wait!" Heather cried, shuffling away from the stream.

Her flame flickered, the wind catching it and nearly strangling it. She cupped a hand over it, protecting it as she halted on the path.

She turned around and stared at Ross who seemed as lost as she was.

He moved toward her, a hand protecting the flame in his palm. He stared down at her hands and then his and chuckled.

"I think we've been played by a couple of angels," Ross replied.

Heather nodded. "Totally punked. Now what?"

A devious smile rose on Ross' lips. "Let's see what we can do with this—this angel fire."

eleven

. . .

HEATHER FOCUSED her attention on the little white flame dancing across her palm. When it first appeared, she recoiled, expecting the fire to burn her skin, but no heat burned against her skin.

The flame was about the size of a plum, writhing and quivering as if possessed by a spirit. It fluttered softly, guttering like a quilt on a clothesline when the wind touched it.

She cupped her other hand over the little flame and studied the white glow in Ross' hand. He was already cradling the tiny flame from the wind, but he seemed just as mesmerized by it.

"They look exactly the same, don't they?" Ross said as he stared at her hands. "Same height. Same depth of color. But the colors are so fluid, merging and flowing into so many shades of pale yellow and white that I can't even imagine all of them."

Grinning, he reached out and squeezed her arm as his voice filled with wonder.

"And Heather...I can see the life in it. That spark that...I don't know—animates us. That makes us human. We're holding it in our hands."

She watched the flame churn and blossom through endless shades of gold to yellow to pure white. Colors she had no name for but knew they were part of a spectrum of life that somehow breathed spirit and movement into physical creatures. She felt its comforting, familiar essence fill her hand and drift through her soul like the warm, viscous blood that had once surged through arteries and veins, giving her physical body life. Something that, until she'd lost it, she could have never understood or even realized how it felt.

Heather nodded at him, a strange sense of peace settling through her body. She felt connected to something again. Part of something. She felt revived somehow. And she felt hope.

"I've seen Zakhart conjure these little flames a million times," said Heather. "But I had no idea they held this much power. I had no idea how just holding it would make me feel. I have this strange sense of being a part of something again. Was that what Zakhart meant about igniting the core?"

"Something inside ourselves," Ross replied, shrugging, "but I don't know what that means. I feel this weird sense of calm, like everything, no matter what happens, will go on somehow. Even if this flame got extinguished. Its fire isn't alone in the world."

Heather laughed. "Knox would call that cloud storage. I don't know exactly what that means, but Knox always talks a little strange."

Ross' eyes narrowed, his mouth flattening into an angry line.

"Can we please leave Knox Travers out of our conversations?" he said, frustration edging his voice.

"Sorry. Still, I can't quite wrap my brain around this—flame. Wouldn't we have to be in physical form to use it?"

Ross shrugged, his annoyed expression dissipating.

"Maybe that's what makes Zakhart's task possible," said Ross, turning the flame over and over in his hand until it became a tiny ball of white fire. "The fact that we're souls without bodies. Maybe we're more like the angels who can slide from physical form to spirit form with a breath."

"Maybe that core is what makes angels different from humans?" Heather replied. "Souls don't yet have that core?"

"Only part of that core—maybe?"

Heather wandered over to the stream, remembering how Zakhart had once used a small flame like the one in her hand and created an explosive ball of light.

Every time he'd summoned fire, though, the light seemed to manifest like an extension of his body. Had Zakhart been concentrating on a core of light inside, a core that built up a reservoir? A place where he drew his light energies from? Like a well that connected to rivers that ran underground, keeping the well's basin full, allowing endless buckets of water to be drawn out. Did this core somehow create a well of light energies that could be tapped at will?

"Maybe that normally happens when we die? The body turns from earth to air? Or fire?" said Ross, pacing along the stream's bank. "But we came here instead and broke some cycle or something? Interrupted it."

"Maybe our breaking this cycle is what makes this possible now, Ross?" Heather speculated, thinking out loud as she walked along the stream.

"What do you mean?" Ross asked.

"Because we're between," said Heather. "We have the potential to become either physical again or turn into energy." She held out the flame. "Like this."

"That makes sense," Ross muttered. "Keep talking."

She nudged a patch of spiky grass with her foot.

"This fire is our core. Our center. And that's essential, right? When we were alive, what things were essential?"

"Things that would kill us if they stopped?" Ross asked. "Like our brains controlling our bodies' essential functions. Breathing and pumping blood. Cooling or warming the body. Keeping the brain alive. Where all of our thoughts and knowledge existed. Our memories. Our feelings."

"Our physical organs are gone, yet we still have memories and feelings here? Why are hearts and kidneys and lungs so different from our brains?" Heather replied, tilting the little flame until it rolled back and forth in her cupped hand.

"I wish I knew," he said, brushing bangs out of his eyes. "There's so much about this I don't understand."

"Like the heart," said Heather. "It pumped life through our bodies. It kept our blood moving and oxygenated. Blood that made all our systems function."

Ross sighed, shaking his head. "Not needed now that we're in spirit form or halfway between forms. Like you said, those physical organs are gone."

"Maybe they still exist somehow?" she mumbled. "In spirit form?"

"Maybe." He glanced around at the trees and shadows. "If this place exists, then anything is possible," he said, pacing alongside her, still cupping his hands protectively around the little flame. "But how can this little flame ignite something inside us when we're all shadows of our former selves?"

"What makes you and me different from the others in the Between?" Heather asked.

"We both entered the Spiral," Ross offered. "Touched it. Felt its energies flow around us."

"Maybe it changed our bodies somehow? Our souls?"

"Maybe," said Ross, sounding pensive.

They both fell silent, deep in thought as they walked together alongside the stream. Heather watched the water flow over rocks and leaves. The lifeblood of trees and foliage in the same way that her blood had been the energy that fed her physical body.

But she and Ross were spirit now. Or something close to spirit.

What fed spirit? What was its core? Was it this little white flame that Zakhart had given them?

She watched Ross pace, his handsome, chiseled face a mask of concentration, those intense golden hazel eyes so focused on the little flame he carried. He had beautiful hands. Strong and squared, fingers not too thick or too long. They looked like hands that hadn't been afraid of hard work, but gentle enough to play a guitar, delicate enough to put together the tiniest puzzle pieces.

She wanted to feel his hands against her face. Stroking her skin.

The brain was the center of all thought, of all emotions—of everything that made her human. And unique. Like a computer's CPU, processing multiple sets of instructions and conveying them to the eyes, to the hands, and the heart, pumping out blood, memories, sensations, and thoughts to the rest of the body.

Even though she understood the science behind those thoughts and feelings and daydreams—her senses—she couldn't help but associate them with her heart. Its rushing patter. Skipping beats when she'd fallen in love. She sighed. The flush of her face at the memory of Ross' arms around her. The ache in her chest at his absence. All of it came from her brain, she knew—logic and science validating that fact, but her heart was the pump, the life spring—the well—for all of those emotions.

But where did those feelings come from now? Now that she was here—in the Between? Did they come from something like this little white flame? One tiny and coiled deep inside her. Waiting to be ignited?

Was that what Zakhart meant?

He was half-human. He'd had a heart once, felt love and despair, but now that he had wings and a halo of light had manifested around his head, maybe he still felt that empty chasm in his chest where his heart had once been. And he still carried all the memories of his short human life? Especially the ones that had touched his heart. Broken. Pining. Loving. Hoping. Maybe in that empty place where his heart had been, a spark of angel light could bring it all back to life?

Because without love, without compassion, humans were just softer-skinned demons. She sighed. Or wingless angels. Science had broken down those emotions into simple chemical reactions. But maybe there was more to it than that? Something unseen and only felt?

"Whatever the core is," said Ross, "it's gotta be something that humans and angels share, right? Something present in both forms."

"I was thinking the same thing," said Heather.

She'd heard Zakhart say several times that angels lacked compassion because they'd never been human before. They didn't understand humans. The jealous ones even liked to simplify humans by comparing them to children. Or worse.

Maybe this core inside them was some sort of emotional memory, a spirit heart? That sounded totally stupid, didn't it? But it was that core that made her and Ross human. It separated them from the angels—and demons. She smiled. And without it, her physical life would have been as empty and as meaningless as it felt toward the end.

After all those connections had broken.

"Ross, I can't help it, but I keep coming back to the heart."

He stopped beside her, squinting at the tiny flame in her palm and then shifting his gaze to the stream.

"Why's that?" he asked, his gaze fixed on her face—her eyes.

"Compassion," she said, staring into his intense gaze, those hazel eyes so compelling. "Love. Those connections that had been so important to me. The ones that got broken. The ones out of my reach."

She stepped closer until her shoulder was against his.

His mouth looked so warm and kissable in the golden glow of the flame's light that illuminated his eyes and cheeks. His face had a handsome, chiseled look against his sandy blond hair. Looking less and less like the boy next door.

He nodded, leaning closer, his lips pursing.

God, she wanted to kiss him!

"Connection was the one thing we couldn't live without," he said.

That was it! This core was an unseen force that burned inside them, fueled by love and pain and loss and connection!

"That's it," she said, grinning at Ross. "Connections."

He squinted, looking surprised and intrigued.

"What do you mean?" he asked.

"All those emotions and feelings," she whispered, lifting her face toward his. "Compassion. Love. Despair—all of those things come from connecting with each other. And this unseen core still within us."

She brushed her lips against his. And then smashed them against his mouth.

His eyes widened. He kissed back, his warm mouth covering hers in a deep, anxious kiss.

The flame in Heather's hand began to expand, a trail of fire shooting down her arm into Ross' rib cage. Ross' flame crackled and spun wildly in his hand, burning a trail of white fire down his arm.

And into her belly.

They held each other in a tight embrace as trails of white fire encircled them in sizzling waves. The rush of fire undulated across their bodies, burn of emotions intense as the two flames slowly merged into a thick, single coil of dancing white flame.

The energy and light surged up her legs, and his, circling their arms as it burned across his shoulders, then hers, and rushed up to the tops of their heads. With a final hiss, the thrumming wave of fire shot down their bodies, crackling across their arms, and back into their palms.

The air rumbled as a bolt of pure white light shot outward like lightning, arced backward, and struck both of them in the chest. Knocking them to the ground.

A shower of sparks sprayed the darkening sky, cascading around them like fireworks.

The rush of light shot through Ross' chest. And into hers.

It slammed hard against her insides and coiled into a writhing ball of light.

She grinned as warmth filled the empty cavity of her chest—like the memory of her heart that had once beat there—as the ball of light expanded and contracted in a steady rhythm, slowly sinking through layers of skin and disappearing through her rib cage.

With reluctance, Ross let her go. He reached down, brushing away the dimming sparks from the silky, grey fabric of his shirt. He looked at her, a grin on his face.

"I feel something almost beating in my chest, Heather," he said, still grinning. "Sort of like a heart. And it's pumping some kind of energy through me."

He took hold of her hand and gently pressed it against his chest.

"Do you feel it?" he whispered.

She nodded, feeling an almost steady thump—like a heartbeat—reverberate inside his chest. And it made his skin feel so warm, as if blood flowed through his veins again.

She couldn't help it. She laid her other hand against his chest, feeling connected to the warm rush of light. To him. The white light gave his skin a strange radiance that had burned away the grey cast.

He looked up and stared at her, a gasp hissing from his lips.

"God, Heather—the light...you're absolutely stunning."

He laid his fingers against her cheek, caressing her skin.

His touch was like a warm coffee mug against winter-chilled fingers as he drew her face toward his for another kiss.

She slid her arms around his waist and smashed her mouth against his, tasting a raw almost electric power on his lips. Like ozone.

"It's like your body is lit from within," he said in a ragged whisper.

The light energies between them sizzled, bubbling into a haze of white vapor-like steam around them. It settled like fog against their shoulders as Ross pulled Heather into his arms.

His touch was hot, anxious, thrumming with energy as it burned against her skin. Making her ache to feel the press of his body against her skin. The longer they kissed, the more intense the light energies glowed, fluttering inside her in a steady rhythm.

Like a pulse.

At last, Ross pulled back, his breath summer-hot as his chest heaved another breath, those hazel eyes burning for her. He held her out at arm's length, his hands in hers as he gazed into the depths of her eyes.

"I've never seen your green eyes so bright before," he said in a hushed whisper. "They're almost otherworldly."

She smiled at the radiance churning in his golden hazel eyes. Like a flame roiled behind them.

With her thumbs, she traced affectionate little circles against his wrists to the beat of the light energies coursing through her fingers. Like a heartbeat.

He leaned toward her, brushing hot, little kisses along her neck and chin, nibbling his way up toward her mouth.

Heather drank in his touch and the rhythm of his body, the warmth of the churning light energies, and the heat of his affection. His attraction. The intoxication of it all. Something she hadn't felt for a very long time.

But for the first time, she felt the depth of his feelings for her, thrumming in the steady rhythm of light that flowed through him.

Between them.

She laid her index finger against his skin, feeling for the ridges of veins in his wrist. And that pulse.

The first sharp beat against her fingertips made her gasp, his skin physically warm now from the ebb and flow of light within him. Within her own body. And it stirred the memory of being alive again to the surface. What it felt like. How different it felt from the cold, still moment she'd woken up in the Between.

She moved closer to him, lost in the rhythm of life heating his skin. Wanting to feel his heat against her body. Making love to her.

The light energies bore deep as its power rippled through him like swift-moving currents, cycling through his entire body.

Like blood. Like breath. She sighed. And life.

But beyond all the physical sensations, she felt a deep connection to him. And an aching need for him. That need to feel something tying them together.

A thread binding them as one, something she'd never felt so overtly before. It was the closest feeling to physical love she'd ever felt since she'd taken her life on that Bainbridge Island beach.

"Do you feel it?" Ross asked, his voice breathless as he held her tightly against him, his chest pressed against hers.

Heather nodded as she gripped his hand and laid it against her chest where her heart had been. He cupped her breast, stroking it through the silky grey fabric, and she felt the space where the flame of light had replaced her heart.

His touch made her shudder and gasp for breath.

"Light energies are rushing through us," she whispered. "Like a heart pumping warm blood. Between us."

"Zakhart's core," he said, holding her face in his hand, his thumb stroking her chin. "But there's something else."

"What?" Heather asked.

He brushed his fingers through her hair and caressed her neck, sliding his hand to her shoulders in warm, kneading strokes. Helping her to her feet.

"It's like a souped-up human heart. Human emotion times ten, Heather. More than my human heart was ever capable of feeling."

His face flushed and he looked away from her, as if afraid he'd said something wrong.

She leaned up and kissed him in a heated kiss that made her body shudder with need.

"I love you, Ross," she whispered against his ear.

His eyes filled with emotion, burning with need and attraction as he kissed her hard, slow-walking her back against the shadowy white trunk of a river birch growing beside the stream.

He pressed his body against hers, her back against the tree trunk as his hands slid underneath her shirt as he frantically sipped her mouth and neck.

She pushed up his shirt, her hands against his leanly muscled chest as she explored his body.

"I love you more than I can ever put into words, Heather," he whispered, breath huffing.

The heat of his body was intoxicating, his hands so hot against her skin, her breasts, sliding down her stomach into her pants. The silky fabric slid down her thighs, down to her ankles, and she kicked off the pants.

Gasping, she held him tighter, pressing her body against him as his hand slid between her legs, sending waves of heat across her skin, through her belly.

Grabbing hold of his pants, she undid them, pushing them off his slim hips as he picked her up and laid her on the soft carpet of moss growing beside the stream. Into the thick brush edging the water.

After frantically shedding the rest of their clothes, Heather pulled Ross on top of her as the heat radiated between them, his lips cinder-hot against her mouth.

She wrapped her legs around his gorgeous, lean naked body. He was hard and she helped guide him inside her.

The first stroke made her gasp, the sensations so raw, and electric, and intense. Unlike anything she'd felt in such a long time.

She moved against him, wrapping her legs tighter, her breath ragged gasps with his thrusts as she rocked against him. She ran her hands down the curve of his back and held him tighter as his mouth moved to her breasts.

Moaning, she arched her back as his thrusts deepened, his rhythm quickening. She held him tighter, running her fingers down his back and moving her hips with his as the stream rushed alongside them.

Until she felt the first warm wave of orgasm shudder through her, body trembling against Ross' touch, his rhythm frantic, breaths heaving.

He pressed against her body in feverish, deepening thrusts until she felt his first shudder of climax. After a few gasping breaths, he moaned and collapsed against her, arms sliding around her neck. Holding her close.

For a long time, they lay entwined in warmth and the rhythmic quiver of light energies pulsing through them. Around them. Between them. Through them. And for the first time in a long while, she felt content. Loved.

She smiled when Ross entwined his fingers with hers, their white flames sparking as they twisted together and thrummed in a steady, rhythmic flutter.

"I love you, Heather," he whispered against her ear.

"I love you, too," Ross," she answered in a soft voice.

Entwined together in the tall grass and overgrowth, thick carpet of moss soft against their naked bodies, they cuddled and listened to the continuous rush of the stream.

As the sky's greyness began to darken, they rose from the grass and dressed slowly. Pulling on the silky grey layers of shadowy fabric until she felt the distance. And suddenly, she felt cold, wanting Ross against her again.

Heather lifted her hand, concentrating on the white fire of emotion burning through her.

Could she summon Zakhart's fire now? Back into her hand where it had begun?

She focused on the roil of light within her until she felt the shudder and twist of a small flame against her palm. It fluttered against her skin in warm flickers.

"Ross, look!" she cried, nodding toward her hand.

He grinned, reaching out to gently run his finger over the ragged white flame. It sparked and crackled when his skin met the white light, growing wider, taller.

"You did it, Heather!" he said, squeezing her wrist. "You summoned Zakhart's fire!"

She took hold of his right hand and turned his palm up.

"Your turn," she said in a quiet voice, smiling, her gaze focused on his fingers.

He shrugged. "I don't know how you did that," he said.

"You don't have to know how, Ross," she said. "You just have to feel it." She turned her hand upside down and the white flame plummeted toward the ground. It sizzled when it hit, exploding into sparks.

Nodding, he took his left hand and entwined his fingers with

Heather's. Closing his eyes, he concentrated on his outstretched right hand, his jawline sharpening as the muscles tightened, his face taut. He groaned, his grip tightening.

Heather watched his hand, feeling the air shift around them. A trace of ozone tainted the air, pungent and sharp against the dull, dirty smell of rain that carried on the wind. It felt raw and electric. Wild. Ready to ignite.

He exhaled a deep breath and opened his eyes.

The air shimmered and a small white flame appeared in his hand. It flickered, its edges tinged blue as it danced in the wind.

"That's it, Ross—you did it!" She ran her hand through his thick sandy-blond hair. "We did it."

He was grinning now as he rolled the white flame into a shiny sphere in his palm. He turned the ball of fire over in his hand and finally, he plucked it up with thumb and forefinger. Glancing around, he turned toward a tall river birch about thirty feet from the stream. He pulled back his arm and flung the sphere at the river birch, striking its shadowy white trunk dead center.

The sphere sizzled against the darkening sky, leaving a golden trail of light in its wake. It exploded with a thunderclap when it struck the tree, sparks cascading like shooting stars through the growing dusk. The angel light scorched the pasty white bark, leaving behind a deep gouge that steamed in the growing chill.

Ross ran toward the tree, Heather following close behind him. He bent to examine the bark, his fingers measuring the length and depth of the damage. The gash was deep, the damage substantial. He'd almost cut through the tree's trunk. With just that tiny flame!

A cold chill snaked down her spine. She hadn't expected that much damage. It was unbelievable.

She stared at Ross whose face was a mixture of shock and surprise as he traced the length of the damage with his index finger.

"One small flame did that, Heather," he said, shaking his head as he whistled and turned his palm over. "One small flame. Can you imagine how much damage we can do to Mulciber and his horde of demons?" He held up his hand, gritting his teeth as he clenched his fingers into a fist. "The payback will be so sweet."

Payback? Heather pressed her hand against the nape of his neck in a warm caress, hoping to ease his tension—and anger. He'd never been a vengeful person.

"Is that why you're doing this?" she asked. "For the payback?"

"Wouldn't you want to pay them back?" he snapped, anger glinting in his gold-hazel eyes. "They tortured me for months, Heather! Months! Don't you want to hurt them every bit as badly as they hurt you? Me?"

She shuddered at the idea, disturbed that he'd be so focused on that aspect of this fight. It wasn't like Ross to be so self-absorbed—not like him at all. Was that all he cared about now was revenge? Of making those demons hurt worse than he had? Who had he become? She felt scared now. Did she even know him anymore?

"I just think about leaving here, Ross," she replied, taking a step back from him. "And how I can stop them from doing this to anyone else. How I can help the next person who wakes up in the Between. Someone like me that's lost and scared and despondent. Someone that's easy prey for the demons."

The anger slid off his face, replaced by an emotion she couldn't read. But she felt it stir within the connection with him, a sick, confused feeling that she couldn't describe. She knew he'd been ruthlessly tortured and that he still worried about saving newly arrived souls. But the pain he'd gone through for so long at Mulciber's hand had changed him. And she couldn't even fathom the demon heart he'd endured. But it still frightened her.

"Heather, don't you understand?" he asked.

He reached out a hand to her, but she took another step back from him. And the hurt returned to his eyes.

"Can't you feel what they did to me? I've blocked nothing from you. Please—if you see it, you'll understand how I feel. Why do I feel this way?"

Heather winced at the rush of memories and dark emotions

swirling nearby, ready to flood over her if she let them in. But she couldn't do that right now. She couldn't fight against them right now. First , she needed to understand what Zakhart had done to them before she helped Ross confront this darkness. And she wanted this golden warmth to stay with her. Not darken into demonic memories and pain.

She knew Ross had been through something terrible. Something beyond his ability to handle. On top of losing Jessie. And ending his life—like she had. The thought of that demon heart made her tremble. And ache for him.

But right now, she couldn't go back to the cold and numb and empty twilight that had enfolded her all this time. Not with this warm light thrumming through her body. She felt so selfish and she knew that he needed her help, but she needed this core of white fire to take root in her first. And in him. Gain some armor to fight this insidious demonic attack that still caused Ross pain and doubt.

"Let's go find Zakhart," she said, motioning toward the path leading back to the soul tree.

The hurt still burned in his eyes as she stepped onto the path and motioned him alongside her. Back toward the ring of trees.

twelve

. . .

ZAKHART STOOD outside the soul tree, Lairz at his side, listening as Barb raged and paced frantically through the grass. Thankfully, all the others had gone inside except for Knox and Zoe. They stopped twirling a pair of wooden staves in the air and turned to listen, but they didn't approach. Things were already bad enough with hordes of demons and flocks of soulstalkers in constant motion around the area.

He certainly didn't want to cause the other souls more panic. He needed to pull Barb aside and find out what had her so upset.

"I said he's gone!" Barb shouted, a growl in her voice, mahogany brown eyes narrowing, pupils constricting into tiny pinpoints. "Did you hear what I said? Javier's gone!"

Zakhart led Barb away from the soul tree and used his light energy as a buffer, to muffle their conversation. He and the other pale angels had their hands full right now. And right now, Barb needed him. She was upset. And she had good reason to be.

She slapped her arms against her side.

"Why won't anybody listen to me?"

By the Maker, everything was falling apart!

The situation in the Between had grown far beyond his abilities to handle. He'd already bent the rules as far as a pale angel dared. Especially since Archangel Raduriel had sent him to the Between as punishment. For his rebellious behavior. Apparently, the archangel had run out of fledgling angels to break down and had started in on the pale angels. The newest full angels usually got this assignment. But he'd checked the records. None of the others had stayed. Zakhart had been the first angel—pale or otherwise—who had actually stayed long enough in the Between to do something.

And right now, Barb was frantic for his help. Her feelings for Javier were showing through, something he knew that she'd tried to keep quiet since he'd first met her.

He reached out and gripped Barb's shoulders.

"Zakhart, please!" she cried. "He's been gone for three days! Three days!"

Her voice was low for a woman and sounded husky like someone with a nicotine habit.

"I know," Zakhart said in a soothing tone, infusing her with calming energies. "I've had several angels out searching for him. And Lamarr and several other souls that have also disappeared."

It took Zakhart several tries before she calmed down enough that he could talk reasonably with her.

Barb Galki was a strong woman who'd been through a lot. After being a nurse in Vietnam, she came home and tried to put the horrors behind her. When she lost her boyfriend in a flash flood during the summer of 1981, she couldn't go on anymore. She'd tried to save him. She'd done everything and more, but when morning came, she was alone, clinging to the huge tree at their camp.

In the days that followed, she'd gone numb and her indomitable strength began to wane. But in the dark times after, when it was just her in the hundred-year-old Colorado Springs house, she'd broken. When the weeks turned to months and the second anniversary of that night approached, she got tired.

And just gave up.

"What?" she cried, her thick features and strong chin sagging now. "Not Lamarr, too." She pressed her hand to her mouth. "Who else is missing?"

Zakhart listed off the names of souls that included Gemma Bonetti. He'd sent Halea and Razasha out twice now to carry her fiancé, Ian back to the soul tree. Ian was despondent. Ian's brother, Thomas, and Iznir were watching over him, but Ian was in bad shape. And he wouldn't stop trying to go after her.

Zakhart sighed. Like Heather had been when she'd returned to the Between. To save Ross.

"Gemma is the latest to disappear," he said with a sigh. "It happened shortly before the soulstalker brought Heather back to us."

How much does Barb know? Lairz's voice trilled through Zakhart's head.

Nothing yet, Zakhart chirped.

He focused his thoughts on Lairz, pushing away from the cacophony of angel voices, and spoke internally through the light so no one else but Lairz could hear him.

I haven't even told Heather or Ross. I'm afraid Ross will snap if he finds out.

Then it is about the SoulSport, Lairz replied.

Zakhart nodded and spoke in the angel tongue.

I don't know what Mulciber is planning, Lairz, but I sense that he's returning to NetherReach to take power with a new champion or two. And right now, he's testing as many souls as he can to find a soul that can win down there.

To the untrained ear, conversations in the angel language sounded like a choral performance. Humans spoke one at a time and interrupting was considered rude. Angels spoke in layers. In octaves and chords. More voices contributed to deeper, multifaceted melodies. More voices added major and minor harmonies and complex chords to discussions, which was much preferred to solos. Sharing those notes, creating music was every bit as important as the individual parts. And it avoided allowing one voice to speak over the other angels.

Champions? You mean like Ross?

Lairz's baritone voice slid through a series of solemn notes. He folded his arms behind his back and trilled some tenor notes that layered over the lower ones.

What for?

Yes, like Ross, Zakhart said, adding his tenor voice in a soft harmony. *Champions are at the heart of Mulciber's power. And I'm afraid he isn't done with Ross.*

Their conversation lilted across the circle of trees and hung in the breeze in soothing notes that seemed to also soothe Barb's panic—even if she didn't understand what the tones meant.

Her pacing slowed.

"When did you see Javier last, Barb?" Zakhart asked, studying her face as her pupils widened, her furrowed brow relaxing.

She sighed, rubbing her fingers against her forehead.

"We'd just finished doing some drills with the wooden staves we made," she said in a tired voice. "Javier wanted to make more and went into the forest to find suitable tree limbs to carve into weapons. That was three days ago."

Zakhart turned his attention from Lairz to Barb. Barb was solid, stocky, and she stood as tall as Lairz, but she had a much more athletic build. Zakhart had always felt scrawny compared to the other angels, especially being half-angel and half-human. Javier was shorter than Barb, but it never seemed to bother the middle-aged man.

"Besides you, Barb, who does Javier spend the most time with? Who does he train with?"

Frowning again, she propped a hand against her face and stared into Zakhart's eyes, struggling to find some information, anything she could on the Puerto Rican Army Reservist and line cook.

Zakhart learned early on to allow his light energies to deflect attention when speaking to mortals. He had to avoid his human side by allowing his gaze to redirect his wandering attention. Or his eyes became portals of unintended information. Humans called it a poker face.

Through his angel side, Zakhart knew all about how Javier's happy life had fallen apart when his wife left him and took away his two-year-old son, leaving the man with an empty apartment and mountains of debt. When his wife remarried and Javier's son began to call the new husband *Papi*, it was too much.

Losing his son broke Javier.

"Javier was closest to Ross," said Barb. "When you and Heather brought Ross back, Javier was right there beside him again." Her face scrunched and she closed her eyes, concentrating. "He also spent a lot of time with Heather. And Cora. Sometimes Knox. And sometimes that young teen, Zoe practiced with him."

Zakhart listened to Barb's list, gathering names of other souls who might be in danger. None of the missing seemed to show any sort of pattern or connection though.

"Any angels he trained with?" Zakhart asked.

Barb smiled. "You, of course. He really liked Iznir. He was trying to help Halea learn to fight with a staff, too."

"Tell me what he'd been doing that day—before he disappeared?" Zakhart asked.

I thought the SoulSport was just for demonic amusement, Lairz spoke in his head. *Something to pass the time?*

Barb continued with her story, allowing him to focus on Lairz again.

That's what all the angels thought, Lairz, said Zakhart. *They thought these lesser demons—like pale angels—had no major importance. They overlooked the fact that in NetherReach, the demons' ruling structure is based on physical power. And combat. Like the basest humans who fight dogs for money, demons fight souls for importance. Especially with Hell's throne empty.*

Lairz stood stoically beside Barb, watching for any signs of movement in the distant sea of grasses. And from above.

Lots of angels have referenced the SoulSport, but they've all dismissed it as unimportant. But you think otherwise? Why?

Zakhart chewed his bottom lip, listening to Barb tell him about how Javier and Knox had begun training together. Only two days ago. And that he'd argued with Ross about it. Zakhart made a note in his head to follow up with Ross about the disagreement. He needed to keep Knox and Ross as far apart as he could until Heather had settled back into the tree. And he knew how she felt. About Ross. And Knox.

Zakhart was dismayed that she had feelings for both Ross and Knox, especially after bringing her back from a short but wonderful life in the physical world to rescue Ross. That was another conversation for another time.

If they had that long.

I wish I had the answer to that question, Lairz.

Zakhart sang a lament, the notes dark and melancholy.

Let's just call it a gut feeling, Zakhart continued. *The SoulSport here in the Between isn't just for sport. It's practice for NetherReach and it is somehow connected to this Mechanism. I can't prove it yet, but I can feel it. We need to know what this Mechanism does. And quickly.*

So, Mulciber is planning to strike something? Lairz sang. *Use this Mechanism for some purpose? And then what?*

Lairz toned a delicate melody and Zakhart added a minor harmony. Back and forth. In chords and discords.

Whatever it is, you think the souls are somehow connected to it, don't you, Zakhart? Some horrible plan for the Between? By my count, there are five missing souls: Javier, Lamarr, Dominik, Natalia, and Gemma. None of them are strong fighters except Javier and Lamarr. It doesn't make sense why the demons would grab the others.

I agree, Zakhart sang. *Why those five? Were they chosen at random? By opportunity? Or were they selected because of who they were? Or their cage fighting potential?*

Zakhart's lament darkened, sounding like a requiem. He couldn't help the tone and the color. It was how he felt. Some angels couldn't hide their emotions from their voices. Sometimes, it was almost impossible—especially for a half-breed with little control. A Nephilim—he hated that word. Made him sound like some dark, horrible creature. He preferred pale angel.

He had so many questions that needed answers.

"Does Javier usually stay close to the soul tree or does he go off scouting alone?" Lairz asked Barb. "I know you said he went looking for more wood to carve into staves."

"After Ross got taken, he stayed close," said Barb, "but he always ended up scouting the trails and the area for any signs of Ross. A chance to rescue him. Javier was trying to find him on his own. So...I don't really know. Sorry."

Zakhart slid his arm around her shoulders and pulled her into a hug.

"It's okay, Barb," he said. "We'll do our best to find him. Don't give up hope."

Do you think Mulciber's really taking souls just for this Soulsport? Lairz sang in a series of dark tenor notes. *Maybe he's trying to weaken our resolve? Scatter our forces and scare us into a quick defeat.*

I do, Lairz. He's searching for champions—like Ross. It's that simple. Accept it. Zakhart added his voice to Lairz's dark melody, lilting a melancholy harmony that gave the melody an edgy sound.

That doesn't bode well for these souls, Lairz spoke in a baritone harmony.

Mulciber will take them with him to NetherReach, too, Lairz. Use them up to gain power, prestige, and tribute. Unless we stop him somehow. Having trained fighters battle on his behalf is how demons gain favor and influence—now that Hell has no king. Regardless of that, his actions center around that Mechanism. He's been building it a long time now. And we need to figure out what it does before it's too late.

Zakhart didn't know if the Mechanism helped Mulciber win in the SoulSport or whether it had some darker, larger purpose. That's what he'd been trying to learn since he'd discovered the towering monstrosity.

Lairz frowned. *Isn't Mulciber using it to churn out his little demon army?*

Zakhart shook his head and turned his gaze back to Barb.

That was only part of it. He was certain.

"Barb, tell me, where is the last place you remember seeing Javier? Was it when he went after the wood?"

Barb thought for a moment, her brow furrowing again.

"I remember that...he came back with more wood to carve. Then went out for more. Yes, he disappeared after getting that wood."

"Think about what happened next. Which direction did he go? What trail did he take? It's important." Zakhart asked.

"Three days ago," she began, pulling in a sharp breath. "After he'd gathered more wood...we, uh—took a walk in the woods. To practice taking down demons with a wooden staff."

Zakhart listened with his light energies, gathering up her words to refer to later if needed.

Mulciber's army is nothing more than lesser demons and these— these malformed shadow atrocities. Zakhart's voice was a clear tenor melody as he tried to explain more about the demons to Lairz. *They bear little resemblance to Death's sand runners and her soulstalkers.*

Lairz spread his arms, wings twitching at his shoulders. An ivory feather floated gently past Zakhart's face and drifted slowly to the ground.

Mulciber wants us to think that he's armed to the teeth. Lairz's melody floated around Zakhart, dark notes that spoke truth. But not all of it.

Zakhart paused in his chord progression.

Perhaps, Zakhart sang, *but it's worse than that. The Mechanism does something that he doesn't want us to know about. I'm certain of it. And he has no idea about the rebellion of Sandriana's flock.*

He smiled at Lairz, his wings fluttering behind him now.

Lairz, their defection changes everything.

How? Lairz asked, frowning.

The moment the demons release these new shadow creatures, Zakhart explained, *they lose control of them. In a strange irony, the shadow creatures begin developing almost human qualities that they use against the demons trying to control them.*

"So, when I returned to the group, he didn't follow me back. That's why I think he left this as a sign!"

Barb held out something in her left hand, shaking it at Zakhart.

Zakhart frowned, moving closer. Trying to see what Barb carried in her left hand.

"Javier knew he was in trouble and I think he knew what they were going to do to him. So he left this for me to find."

She shook something at Zakhart again.

"He knew I'd find it and do something."

Lairz shifted closer to Zakhart as he studied the shadow in Barb's hand.

Barb laid a shadowy metal ring in Zakhart's palm. It was about eight inches across and hinged in the center. It was made out of a shiny black material that Zakhart recognized from when they rescued Ross.

A shackle cuff! One that fit either wrist or ankle. Cast from that shiny black rock, it felt weightless. He winced. A material created from the destruction of souls.

The sight of it made Zakhart sick.

"Do you know what this is?" Barb asked.

"I do," said a voice behind Zakhart.

He turned around to see Knox and Zoe standing behind them.

Knox stepped forward, reaching out, and taking the small black ring. He turned it over and over in his palm.

"This thing's like the shackles they put on Shepherd back in the demon caves." He dropped it back in Zakhart's palm. "Saw these things all over the place in there."

Barb turned her gaze back to Zakhart.

"Then the demons do have him."

Her voice was low and quiet, the hint of a growl in her voice.

"If he left this thing lyin' around for us to find, that'd be my guess, too," said Knox, turning his gaze to Zakhart. "You need my help with anything?"

Zakhart held back a smile. Knox never shied away from trouble. Always went face-first into everything, something he admired about the young, tall curly-haired soldier. He had such a crush on Heather, too. Zakhart felt it radiating from the young man. It lacked the enduring resonance of Ross' love for the beautiful young woman. She was one of the bravest humans he'd ever met, but every time she stood in the company of Ross or Knox, Zakhart felt her turmoil. Her confused storm of emotions for both men.

"It might come to that," Zakhart replied.

"Javier's missing, Knox," said Barb. "Others are missing, too."

Knox's eyes widened, his pupils nearly blotting out his light blue eyes.

"That true?"

Lairz nodded.

Knox crossed his arms against his chest and studied Barb's expression and then Zakhart's face, looking angry.

"They huntin' souls again? Damned demons."

"This proves it," said Zakhart, holding up the cuff. "They've taken five that we know about. Anyone could be next."

"Knox, I'm scared!"

Zoe threw her arms around his waist. She laid her face against his chest and held on tight, closing her eyes.

"Easy, kid—nothin's gonna drag you off on my watch," said Knox, laying his hand against her back and rubbing her shoulders.

"Mine either," Zakhart replied, leaning toward the freckle-faced young teen.

He felt Heather and Ross approaching the soul tree from the heartlily path and smiled. With the wellspring of light energies growing within them.

They'd figured out his little test after all. He knew they would.

He'd have been disappointed if they hadn't. The two of them would need a lot of training before he could trust them with temporary wings of light, but for now, they had two more souls with light energies.

It was a start.

"So what do we do about this?" Knox asked, glancing from Zakhart to Lairz. "We just gonna stand here and let those bastards pick us off one by one until they have all of us in shackles?"

"No, of course not, Knox," said Zakhart. "We need to act."

"The soulstalker is ready to call her entire flock to the tree, Zakhart," said Lairz, motioning toward the soul tree. "According to Razasha anyway."

"Good," said Zakhart, a smile on his face.

That was very good news.

"Lairz, go to Razasha and ask her to invite Sandriana's entire flock to the soul tree."

"What about the sand runners?" Lairz asked.

"Them too."

This soul tree was quickly becoming some sort of strange zoo. But those creatures would follow Sandriana's lead. And he would welcome any of them as long as they agreed to fight the demons.

"Zakhart," said Knox, his hands waving in the air as he talked. 'I say we pull in all these creatures and immediately march on the demon caves. Take them over. Strike before Mulciber has a chance to execute whatever plan he's working on. A preemptive strike. It's our best move right now. Hell, it's our only move!"

As much as Zakhart didn't want to rush headlong into an impromptu attack like that, deep down, he knew it was the best way to counter Mulciber. Maybe interrupt the demon's final preparations? And save as many souls as they could...including these five missing souls. It was worth a try.

And it was the last thing that Mulciber would expect.

"I agree," said Zakhart. "As soon as Ross and Heather return, I want a small group of us to gather and discuss this attack."

Knox nodded. "Say who attends and I'll spread the word. Meet out here?"

"Yes," Zakhart replied with a sharp nod. "I want Razasha and Lairz to attend. And I want Heather, Ross, Barb, and you, Knox." He winced. "And Ian."

"I'll get the word out," said Knox, stepping away from the group.

He turned toward the tree when Zoe pulled him backward.

"What about me, Knox? I wanna come, too."

Knox grinned, tweaking her cheek with thumb and forefinger.

"Sorry, kid. Not this time. Why don't you go find Halea and Cora?"

Zoe frowned, stamping her feet. She crossed her arms, brow furrowed.

"Cora's upset about Lamarr and hides from you. Halea can't stand all these souls around. She left the tree days ago."

"What?" Zakhart shouted as he moved over to Zoe, gently taking hold of her shoulder. "Zoe, where did Halea go?"

She shrugged. "I'm not exactly sure. She kept complaining about the tree being too crowded. Said she needed air. She ran down that path there."

Zoe pointed at the main footpath that wound into the forest, heading north.

"It was just after Javier carried a staff into the woods."

"Javier?" Barb cried, dropping down on her knees in front of Zoe. "Kid, did you see Javier a few days ago?"

Zoe nodded. "See, he was heading into the woods and Halea was almost right behind him. She had to have seen him. He was about three feet in front of her."

Zakhart felt his body turn cold, a mixture of fear and dread churning inside him. Halea had been acting strange ever since they'd constructed the new soul tree. She had ignored her orders and just... left. Why hadn't she told him about Javier? She had to have seen where he went...and what happened to him. Halea had helped look for Heather, hours before Heather returned. The pale angel had even helped translate Sandriana's words.

What made Halea simply fly away? Leave her post with so many souls in danger?

A queasy feeling quivered in the bottom of his stomach. Something was terribly wrong here. Was Halea somehow involved with the demons?

No. He squeezed his eyes closed. No, he couldn't even think that thought right now.

He turned away from Zoe and moved over to Lairz, speaking through the light now.

Lairz, have you seen Halea?

The other pale angel shook his head.

Sorry, Zakhart. Not for a while.

He'd trained with Lairz in the Heavens, known him since he'd gotten his wings at five. He trusted this man with his light. He'd known Razasha a long time, too. Ever since they'd all trained to use light energies together as fledgling pale angels. But Halea had come to them as a latent. An adult that had been raised as a human. She hadn't displayed any signs of white fire until she was nearly an adult. And much of the time, her human side showed through her light.

Find Halea. Put every angel onto that task.

Why? Lairz asked. *Because some annoying little soul thinks she saw something?*

Sometimes, Lairz had a short fuse with humans. And their souls. Especially young ones like Zoe who tended to get on others' nerves.

It was an innocent observation, Lairz, Zakhart spoke through the light. *One we're fortunate to have uncovered. That's why we need to find Halea. She's abandoned her post, Lairz. Besides...either she knows something that she's not telling us or Mulciber has decided to start kidnapping angels.*

Lairz gave him a slight nod. His wings unfurled like sails at his shoulders and he rose into the greyness, flying off to search for Halea.

Someone tugged on his sleeve.

He turned around.

Zoe, teary-eyed, bowed her head and clutched the folds of her silky grey shirt, that strange fluffy pink thing Heather called a unicorn in her arms.

"Zakhart, don't be mad at Halea," Zoe said, a pout on her freckled face, her voice gaining pitch as she spoke. "She's not in trouble, is she? I wasn't trying to get her into trouble."

He smiled at the teenager, patting her shoulder.

"No, Zoe, she's not in trouble. We're just worried about her, that's all. We have to make sure we locate her and ensure that she's okay."

At last, the teen smiled, wiping her sleeve across her eyes.

"Good."

Zoe looked past him toward the footpath and her eyes narrowed, pupils constricting as a hollow smile rose on her face. When Knox moved toward the path.

"Heather's back," she said in a quiet voice. "Knox, where you going? Knox!"

She ran after him, running past the circle of trees until she was right beside the curly-haired soldier. She slid her hand into his left hand.

Zakhart hadn't realized until now that Zoe was very jealous of Heather. He'd caught that momentary flash of anger in the teen's eyes. He studied Heather and Ross, noticing the incandescence of their eyes.

He smiled. They'd figured out his puzzle.

Heather let go of Ross' hand as they approached the soul tree. Zakhart sighed. And Knox.

He felt guilty now. Had he somehow let Knox come between Heather and Ross? Heather had been so in love with Ross. It hurt his heart to think that she'd gone through so much to rescue Ross and now, she had feelings for Knox, too. Zakhart knew he couldn't interfere, but he just hoped that Ross didn't get hurt in the process. That young man had gone through hell. And he'd given up everything to save Heather.

Ross glared at Knox, remaining right at Heather's shoulder.

"Heather," Knox replied, holding up his hand. "Can we talk?"

Heather glanced at Ross whose face had turned stone-like, eyes narrowed as he looked away.

Zakhart felt the hurt beneath his stone façade, but his poker face slipped a little when Heather responded.

"Sure, Knox," she answered. "Right now?"

Knox nodded and then turned toward Zoe.

"Kid, I need to talk to Heather alone for a bit. I'll catch up with you by the hearth a little later, all right?"

Zoe stamped her foot, smashing the unicorn against her chest.

"Why do I have to leave?" she demanded, glaring at Heather.

Heather seemed unfazed by the teen's tantrum.

"Because it's private," Knox replied. "Like the talks you and I sometimes have. Just you and me, remember?"

Zoe kicked at the dirt, her gaze on the ground now. She shrugged at him and flounced off, tears streaming down her face.

"She's just a kid, Travers," Ross snapped. "Barely a teenager. Why'd you have to send her away like that?"

"Shut up, Shepherd!" His eyes were blue flames. "Mind your own fucking business already!"

Ross slid his arm around Heather's waist.

"I could say the same thing to you, Travers."

Heather held out her hands. "Stop it! Both of you!" She turned to Ross, her voice quiet again. "I'll come find you in a bit, okay?"

Glaring at Knox, he stood his ground for a moment or two. Then finally, he turned his gaze back to Heather. He leaned over and kissed her hard on the lips.

"Sure thing," he said, smiling at her, a hand caressing her cheek.

Zakhart felt relieved when Heather returned Ross' smile and squeezed his hand before he turned and walked away toward the soul tree. He didn't look back as he slid his hands into the pockets of his grey silky pants like all the souls wore.

"Take a walk?" Knox asked Heather, a warm smile on his face.

"Could we just sit out here in the ring of trees?" said Heather, glancing back at the surrounding forest. "It's getting so dark and I'd rather not be out there at night. The Between is much more dangerous now."

He nodded and motioned her to follow him.

Zakhart smiled as they walked past him. And held his breath. If Heather chose Knox, it would break her connection to Ross and she'd lose the angel fire she carried. Ross would lose his angel fire, too. Giving lovers the white fire was an easy task when they'd both touched shadow, life, and light together. But it got complicated fast when they broke up. He hoped that wouldn't happen.

If it did, he'd have to take Heather and Ross separately to the Lake of Despair. His own heart would break at that task. He still had to take them there to give them temporary light wings. He remembered his own rituals: the white fire trial at nine. Flight at fifteen.

As difficult as his Trial of Despair had been, it was nothing compared to the day they'd taken him from his mother. He'd been just three years old, but her frantic cries begging them not to take him would haunt him forever. He ached inside at that separation and the fact that he could never see her or look on her face again. That moment had been centuries ago in human time. She was in a place he could never go.

Wincing, he turned toward the soul tree and tried to focus his mind on something else. He concentrated on the memory of the very first time he'd felt the white fire course through his body and how it had warmed every part of him. Made him feel invincible. And connected. And he remembered his Trial of Despair. He was grateful that he hadn't received his wings here, in the Between, with the Dusk Wars blazing around him. Angels rebelling against angels.

Angels received their wings when they neared adulthood (unless they sprouted early), after enduring the Trial of Despair. There were cases where angels had sprouted wings naturally, but they were rare. Except with pale angels. Fledglings (that weren't half human) could be any age to undergo the first trial, the Trial of Light which connected them to all angels and allowed them to summon the white fire.

The second trial, the Trial of Despair, was a trial by shadow and required angels to let go of weaknesses and break free of earthly baggage weighing them down. Only fledglings approaching adulthood were allowed to even undertake the extremely difficult second trial. Or the third trial, the Trial of Awakening when angels were tested and placed among Heaven's armies.

Ross and Heather had overcome a lot. Together. Zakhart knew they could finish this first trial together. And succeed. They weren't angels, but to touch the same light that angels carried, they had to undergo the first trial.

As much as he wanted to eavesdrop, Zakhart sauntered toward the soul tree to keep a distant eye on Ross and Zoe. He'd try not to worry about Halea until Lairz located her and brought her back to the soul tree. So he could ask her some difficult questions, knowing he didn't want to hear some of the answers. But maybe Zoe was only mistaken? Maybe the teen got her timing wrong? Sometimes, he hated being an angel.

thirteen

· · ·

WHITE FIRE SURGED through Heather's body, gentle warmth tingling against her skin as she walked beside Knox in silence. She felt the steady pump of a heart again, blood flowing, lungs expanding. She almost cried at the whisper of air when she inhaled, a long, slow draw that filled her chest with breath. Life.

Her cheeks flushed, brow beading with sweat as he led her across the ring of trees' courtyard. She folded her arms against her chest and kept a reasonable distance from him, her brain wild with emotions and contradictions. Her heart aching at Ross' absence and now, at her longing to touch Knox. She felt so confused by her conflicted feelings.

"There's a bench over here that Lamarr built for Cora," said Knox, glancing back at Heather. "It's not far and it's on protected ground."

She closed her eyes, holding her breath a moment, delighting in the burn, the urgent need to exhale. At last, she opened her eyes, letting the air slowly whisper out. Again and again. Grinning, she felt overwhelmed by the gentle rise and fall of her chest. She laid her hand against her heart. It was such a comfort against all the Between's shadow and vapor.

"That's good," Heather replied, smiling, doing her best to keep the turmoil out of her face. "I don't mind the walk."

Just moments ago, she'd been connected to Ross in such a deep, enveloping flow of white fire. It made her feel alive—and human—again, something she hadn't felt since she arrived back in the Between. But more than that, she'd felt a familiar, all-consuming rush of emotions, a bond that had connected her solely to Ross. And making love to him had only intensified that bond, despite some of the darkness he still carried from being held hostage by Mulciber. She shuddered. And the demon heart.

But being this close to Knox stirred up her attraction to him along with her confusion. And guilt.

The Trial of White Fire hadn't been a trial at all. It had been an opportunity, an awakening. And it had brought the entire tangle of her emotions to the surface, feelings she'd suppressed when there was only a dim hope of rescuing Ross. Feelings she'd been afraid to feel because, at that time, she had been on a short path to heartache. A loss she couldn't handle—even now. Had she just transferred some of those feelings onto Knox because he was there and Ross was a prisoner with no way out?

Now that she had this strange white fire coursing through her body, she felt a profound deepening of her connection with Ross and his beautiful sandy-haired classic looks. A bond to the man who'd sacrificed his life, his soul to save hers. In those moments when the white fire had first touched her skin like a tropical ocean wave, she'd fallen in love with Ross all over again.

Yet, despite that enduring bond she had with Ross, she feared those shadows of darkness that now lurked in him. And she craved the undercurrents of her attraction to Knox. A strange tie that she couldn't ignore, couldn't dismiss. And it was driving her crazy!

Ahead, illuminated in the protective violet afterglow (when had the color changed from pale gold?) of the soul tree's circle, stood a rustic bench about three feet long and more than a foot deep. Knox stepped toward it and sat down. He patted the bench, smiling as he motioned her to sit down beside him.

"When those demons ambushed us, I thought we'd lost you, Heather," he said as Heather sat down on the bench. "I didn't know how we were gonna get you back again." He sighed, gripping the edge of the bench with both hands, feet flat against the ground. "But I'm so glad you're back safe."

His voice was soft, almost fragile, a glint in those soft blue eyes as he reached out and brushed a lock of coppery brown hair off her forehead. She held her breath but didn't pull away from him.

"I'm not sure what would have happened if Sandriana hadn't saved me, but having her flock on our side will be a huge advantage against Mulciber."

"Actually, that's not what I wanted to talk to you about," Knox replied, staring down at his hands.

"What did you want to talk about?" Heather asked.

He didn't look up at first as he twisted his hands together, licking his lips, beads of sweat on his forehead. Finally, his gaze met hers. He took her hand in his.

Heather gasped. His hands felt so cold now, the grip weaker than she'd expected. Was that what a soul's touch felt like? She hadn't noticed until now.

"Where I stand," he said finally. "I know you told me upfront about Ross and all, but I'll be honest. I didn't expect to rescue him from those demons. And then I got to know you and well,...I thought I could get you to forget him even if we did find him."

"Knox," she began, watching the sadness in his light blue eyes deepen. "You were there for me when I needed someone to watch my back. When I needed a shoulder to cry on." She sighed. "When I thought he was never coming back."

He nodded, his gaze falling.

"Something happened between us, Knox. Something I can't quite identify. Something I can't just dismiss."

A smile curved across his face, his gaze snapping back to her face.

He reached up and cupped her chin with his hand, leaning in for a kiss.

She wanted desperately to kiss him, to know this man who had helped her bring Ross back, but to kiss him was so unfair to Ross. She and Ross hadn't made any promises to each other. Promises weren't possible in the Between because no one knew what tomorrow would bring.

His lips pressed against hers, cool against her mouth, and she couldn't stop herself from kissing back. A soft, gentle kiss against his mouth.

But she couldn't do this. She pulled away.

"Knox, I can't," she said. "I can't promise you anything here. I can't promise you anything beyond this moment on this night—on this bench. I love Ross, you know that. But I care for you very much, Knox. Know that I do."

She exhaled, her chest falling. The sensation startled her. She wasn't used to feeling like her lungs were contracting and expanding like this.

He took her hand in his. "What does that mean?"

"I wish I knew, Knox," she said, not pulling away this time. "Without knowing whether any of us has a future beyond the Between, I can't make any promises. Because even if I fell in love with you and we made it out of this place, it's unlikely that our paths would ever cross again."

He frowned. "Why is it different with Shepherd, Heather? How can you make him any promises when you can't make that promise to me?"

His eyes narrowed, mouth pressed into an angry line. He tried to pull his hand away, but she held onto it.

"Zakhart said that our fates were intertwined when Ross and I entered the Spiral together. If Death hadn't pulled him out of the Spiral, we were to meet again in our next physical lives. The bond I have with Ross would have survived the transition."

This time, Knox yanked his hand away, leaning back on the

bench against the thick bark of an ancient tree. He folded his arms across his chest and stared at her through hooded lids, those thick lashes making his bright blue eyes smolder.

"So, I never really had a chance, did I?" he asked. "Is that what you're saying?"

Heather exhaled an exasperated sigh and covered her face with her hands.

"I don't know what I'm saying anymore, Knox! For all I know, everything has changed again. All I wanted to do was find Ross and head for the Spiral as fast as I could, but now that I've found him...I just can't walk away and leave all of you to fight demons. I can't let Zakhart and Razasha down. And I can't let you down, Knox. I couldn't live with myself if I just turned my back on you and left you here like this."

She rose from the bench, fingers bunched into fists, feeling the white fire throb through her hands.

"I don't know if Ross and I are destined to meet again if we go through the Spiral a second time. In saving me from Death, he might have sacrificed our destiny together."

That sudden realization terrified her. Had Ross truly given up everything—including their happily ever after—to save her? Had he paid a much bigger price than either of them had realized?

She turned around. Knox was leaning forward this time, watching her with those wounded blue eyes.

"I don't know what will happen and I'm terrified that it will all be washed from my memory because I wanna remember this. I want to remember you and Ross and Zakhart and Razasha. I want to carry everything I've learned and experienced with me—well, except for the demons. It's all a part of me now. Something I don't want to just forget and move on from. I want it to last. I want it to color everything that happens from here. Because, without it, I'll never remember how close I came to killing my soul."

Knox was smiling as he slowly stood up and wrapped her in his arms. She slid her arms around his waist and reached up, stroking his hair.

"Damn. I wish I could have met you first—before Shepherd did. Before you came to the Between. Maybe we'd have never even ended up here?"

"Maybe," Heather whispered.

And maybe if Ross had been born in her time, they'd have made it together without these incorporeal sacrifices.

"All right, I won't ask for any promises, Heather. No commitments or labels on anything. All I'll ask for are moments because that's all we really have in this place. Fair enough? A walk to the stream. An hour sitting on this bench. A night by the fireplace. Unless you tell me to stop. Not Shepherd—you."

Heather nodded against his chest, knowing how much this would hurt Ross. But she had to find out. She had to understand this strange connection with Knox first.

"We'll sort the rest out later. Fair enough?"

She looked up at him and nodded.

Knox lightly kissed her on the tip of her nose and let her go.

"Thank you for understanding," she said in a hoarse whisper, stepping back from him.

"It's all I can do right now, kiddo," he said, the smile returning to his face.

She nodded and with arms against her chest, she sat back down beside him on the bench. He put his arm around her and pulled her close. They cuddled and watched the violet gleam of the soul tree's protection shift and flicker across the dark forest like Northern Lights.

fourteen

JAVIER COLLAPSED against the cage wall, Lamarr at his back, fighting off both attackers while Javier tried to get his bearings.

Shadows danced across the cage, the roar of the demon crowd in the caverns deafening, a continuous drone in his ears. Frowning, he shook off the blow. And blinked, trying to clear his head.

A stocky, bearded man slammed his body against Javier. His opponent.

Javier's face smashed against the metal bars and he tried to roll his body sideways to get the man off him. To give Lamarr a step or two of room to maneuver, so, the tall South African could peel this soul and his partner off Javier.

They had to win this fight. They had to.

The long, narrow cage swayed, his vision darkening.

Javier feinted right. Turned, ducking under a punch to the jaw. Whirling around as Lamarr threw an uppercut that leveled the burly soul lunging at him.

Outside the cage, in the dark cavern, demons pounded the ground with their feet, cheering them on as Javier twisted left and delivered a roundhouse kick to the tall, wiry soul. Laying him out on the dusty cage floor.

And it was over.

Demons rushed out of their stone-carved seats and mobbed the cage, a sea of grey and terracotta as they pounded the cage's mesh with their gnarled limbs and cheered through leering mouths and pointy teeth.

Javier dropped to his knees, Lamarr beside him. He slapped the taller man on the back, his mahogany brown skin dusty and mottled black with a strange sort of bruising that hadn't come from blood.

Did souls bruise?

"You okay, jefe?" Javier asked with a smile, slinging his long black bangs out of his face.

Lamarr smirked, thumb raised in the air.

"Bueno, my friend," he said in that smooth South African accent. "We survived another one. But every fight gets harder."

Javier gritted his teeth, sliding into Spanish again as he rattled off a response. "Cabróns! Animales!"

"Whoa, amigo," said Lamarr, holding up his hands. "I'm sure I agree."

Javier twisted his mouth into a grimace, forgetting that his fighting partner didn't speak his language. He was so used to chatting with Barb who was fluent in Spanish, Ross who knew a little, or the pale angels who were fluent in all languages.

"Perdón, jefe—I forget sometimes. I hate these bastardos! They cage us like animales!" He sighed. "They worship us when we win and we beat each other senseless to entertain them. It makes me sick."

"I hear you, friend," said Lamarr. "They do put the winners on a pedestal. They cheer us when we enter the cage like we're gladiators or something. Then we fight until one team drops. And they boo the losers. Forget about them. Win or lose, we're destroying each other for their amusement."

Javier let his anger dissipate before he responded. "None of the new teams are any better, are they?"

Lamarr shook his head. "Have you seen anyone else from our soul tree? I'm terrified I'll look up and see Cora or Knox or someone I know. Where do all of these other souls come from?"

"Wish I knew," Javier muttered, watching the crowd of demons dissipate around the cage. "We must be pretty lucky to have found our soul tree. Look how many souls never found that sort of haven. Hard to believe so many people took their own lives."

"It's unsettling," Lamarr whispered, leaning closer to Javier. "Makes my chest ache a little. So many broken people in pain who just—slipped through. Hurts, man."

"Don't forget, jefe," said Javier as he watched two small grey demons come into the cage and carry off the stocky, bearded soul. "Some of these people did some really bad things before they killed themselves. The guy they just carried off?"

"Yeah?" said Lamarr.

Javier nodded toward the closing cage door.

"That one shot up a school full of little kids but killed himself when the policiá got to him. And that one."

He pointed at the tall, wiry man who lay inert on the dusty cage floor and kicked dust at him.

"That one opened fire in a fast-food restaurant, killing a dozen people then himself."

"Hadn't even thought about that," said Lamarr, his deep brown eyes wide. "That's horrible."

"Not my place to judge," said Javier, struggling to stand. "But I'm glad we kicked their asses. We've beaten everyone. Why don't they just let us go? Barb's probably going out of her mind, wondering where I am."

Barb. Javier slapped a hand against his face. *Dios mío!* She must be fighting mad about now, wondering what had happened to him.

Lamarr patted Javier on the sleeve as he got to his feet and stood up straight, leaning against the outside cage wall. He pulled Lamarr to his feet and they walked over to a bench beside the gate and collapsed on it, leaning their heads back against the mesh.

The air stank with demon sweat and dirt from that pit they called a coalfield. This place always had a slightly acidic smell to it that sometimes burned his nose.

"Barb's not just wondering where you are," Lamarr said with a raucous laugh. "Barb's gotta be completely out of her mind with worry! Probably spitting nails and organizing search parties to comb the forest for you." Lamarr elbowed him in the ribs. "Why, I'll bet she's even got all those angels in the skies searching for you."

Javier grinned.

She was always so good to him, listening to him tell the same sad stories over and over. It didn't matter how many times she'd heard it before, she always listened. Every single time. He'd come to rely on her so much. Not only did she watch his back, but she always watched out for him. He didn't realize how much he missed her until now.

Two more demons entered the cage and carried off the other defeated soul. Javier watched as they tossed the two souls onto a cart and rolled it away toward the rickety lift that led up and out of this pit.

"I wonder where they take them when they lose," Lamarr remarked, watching the demons carry off the last man.

"You don't want to know," Javier snapped, rubbing his eyes.

"I do," said Lamarr, turning toward him. "If you know, tell me, Javier!"

"Okay," said Javier with a sigh.

He stared at Lamarr, noting his usually pleasant expression. By the time he explained, that look would be gone. He took a deep breath and told Lamarr the story.

He'd slipped away once and followed that cart, all the way down a series of passageways that had ended in a huge metal chute.

He shuddered, remembering them dumping souls into the chute.

Flames roared and licked at the opening as the demons slammed the hatch closed. He didn't see everything else they did, but when the cart rolled away, it was filled with a sticky black substance. He had followed the cart into the chamber with that machine, the one that the big red demon always watched over, and into a short hallway. Into a circular room with a bunch of inverted carvings on its stone walls. And on the stones covering the floor. He'd watched the demon dump the black sludge onto the floor. It flowed on its own across the stones, pouring into the carvings, filling them. When all the carvings had filled with black sludge, the demon touched something on the wall.

A horrible grinding sound filled the chamber. Behind him, the Mechanism (what that loco demon called it) belched out black smoke as it shook and made the entire cavern vibrate.

That's when the first moan touched his ears.

When Javier glanced back at the floor, shadows were rising. The whole floor glimmered with a red haze as things took shape in the darkness. Wings. Dark-eyed, four-legged creatures. Red-eyed demons with fleshy skin the color of red clay. He froze, his mouth bone dry, his hands cold as ice as he watched the grey demon approach a wall covered in a white tarp.

Shadows prowled the room now, slowly gaining physical depth and form as the shadowy vapor hardened.

He watched, wide-eyed, mouth hanging open as the demon removed the tarp from the wall, revealing an inverted carving that it approached. The carving had two arms and two legs. A torso and a rounded head. The body was at least as tall as Javier, maybe taller. The demon stepped into it, squeezing its back and legs into the indentations that didn't match its short, gnarled barrel-shaped body. It drew its shriveled legs and arms into the long, graceful limbs of the carving, pressing back into it as best it could. A light in the middle of the floor flashed red as the walls began to move, revolving in a slow circle.

Behind Javier, the Mechanism thundered to life in the main chamber, pistons pumping and groaning as the walls began to spin in a steady, thumping round. He'd closed his eyes, each revolution giving off a loud moan. He felt the shadowy creatures in the room rushing around as the wind from the spinning walls buffeted them across the room, tossing them back and forth.

The wall seemed to turn endlessly, churning as the Mechanism moaned and thumped, the sound filling the cavern.

Slowly, the room's spinning began to slow, allowing him to see a glowing red light outlining the carvings on the wall. Shapes he recognized now. Sand runners, soulstalkers—demons. Only when the wall ground to a stop did the one carving remain lit with red light. The one the demon had pushed its fleshy body into.

A glacial wind tore across him as the demon stepped out. But it was no longer a demon. At least not in form. He couldn't hold back the gasp that had slipped from his mouth.

It looked human. Male. In every way, shape, and form. Even its red eyes had become warm brown, the grey skin a creamy flesh tone.

It had stared past him as it walked out of the chamber, the shadow creatures flowing out behind it.

"It walked out into the chamber with the Mechanism," Javier continued. "Where it went from there, I have no idea. But those dead eyes were terrifying."

Lamarr looked pale now, the smile long gone.

"Why would they be making demons that looked like humans?" Lamarr asked in a shrill whisper as he leaned closer to Javier.

Javier shrugged. "My mind can come up with all kinds of awful things, amigo."

"Mine, too," said Lamarr.

The cage door opened and a grey demon motioned them out. Lamarr was up first and Javier followed in behind him. Just as they walked out of the cage, two demons led a pair of souls past them. Toward the cage. His heart bounced into his throat.

Gemma! Beside her was Natalia, another soul from the tree. Gemma looked thin and frail, her eyes filled with fear and despair. He'd never seen her without Ian at her side.

He reached out to her as they passed.

"Javier," she whispered in her thick Italian accent. "Lamarr. How did you get here?"

"Demons got us in the forest by the tree," said Lamarr.

She nodded. "Sì," she said, bowing her head. "I never saw it until it was too late."

Javier motioned toward the cage. "No matter what happens, just win," he whispered, "Do everything you have to do. Just win."

She gave him a terrified nod and glanced at the fuller-faced Natalia who stood beside her, brown hair long and brown eyes shining with fear. Natalia was tall and a bit stocky. Maybe together, they could get through the cage?

Dios mío! He knew how devastated Ian must be right now. Javier vowed to do what he could to protect Gemma and Natalia. Train them if he could. But seeing her here—alone—made him queasy.

One of the demons poked him in the back, but he resisted. But the demon persisted, forcing him and Lamarr toward the lift.

Had Mulciber attacked the soul tree and brought it down, capturing all the other souls in the process? Including Ross?

"Is the tree still standing?" Javier asked.

Gemma nodded. "As far as I know."

Had they found Heather yet? Javier had looked everywhere in the caverns, but she wasn't there.

"Is Heather with you?" he asked quickly.

Gemma shook her head. "No, she hasn't been found yet."

"Bueno," Javier said with a grin.

Gemma raised an eyebrow, giving him a confused look.

"Don't give up, Gemma," he said. "Heather's our only hope of getting out of here. She won't let us down. She isn't here. That means the demons don't have her either."

Gemma's face brightened as the demons forced her and Natalia toward the cage. The other demons prodded Javier to move along and Javier followed, but he couldn't erase his grin. If Heather was still out there somewhere, she'd do something to help them.

Javier held out some hope now.

He knew that Heather wouldn't let them all down. She'd storm this place with Ross and those pale angels. He smiled. And an army. She'd save them. Like she'd saved Ross.

All of them.

fifteen

. . .

FROM THE NORTH side of the soul tree, where the ring of
dark, gnarled trees bumped against the forest edge, Ross could still
see Heather sitting with Knox. Bathed in the ring's violet aura, Ross
leaned against a stark white river birch, hands shoved in his pockets
as he tried not to watch them, but his heart ached just seeing them
together.

That she'd prefer Travers to him after everything they'd been
through. After loving her like he'd never loved anyone before. After
her telling him how much she loved him. And now, she was with
Travers and he was alone.

God did it hurt.

He looked away, running his hand over the tree's smooth, silvery
white bark. It was the only stand of these spindly, white-trunked trees
he'd seen this deep in the forest. Most of the other trees grew along
the stream, making them look like ghosts against the blackness where
the heartlilies grew. Against this protective glow of violet, the bark
glimmered with ethereal light.

He couldn't think straight right now. Couldn't stop thinking
about her, the warm feel of her skin lit with white fire. Her gentle

touch, fingers against his body, stroking, exploring. He sighed. The huff of her hot breath against his neck. Making love to her, her body pressed against his, the heat of her skin burning right through him. He'd had no idea what it might feel like to have an angel's lifeblood coursing through him like his human blood once did. He felt alive again. Especially after finally making love to Heather.

He'd taken all of it for granted before. Including Heather's love, not realizing how fragile it was. Never dreaming how easily she could shift her feelings away from him. To Travers. And it hurt. Much more than he wanted to admit.

Fighting the urge to glance over at Heather and Knox was impossible. In the end, he gave up and swiveled his body around the tree to get another look at them. Hoping she wasn't kissing him like she'd once kissed him. Or fearing he'd see her entangled in Knox's arms like she'd never leave him.

He groaned. She was in his arms.

It felt like an anvil crushing his chest.

The air rushed out of his lungs and he slumped against the tree, flinching when she kissed him and laid her head on his shoulder.

Everything inside him raged! And ached.

He held in a breath, biting his lip to keep from screaming out his agony, imagining what had happened between Heather and Travers when he'd been trapped in demon hands. Had Travers already made love to her? Was she just trying to let him down easy now that she was with Travers? Now that he was out of the demons' clutches.

He clenched his hands into fists and punched the tree trunk hard. Dammit! He'd given up everything for her!

When they had finally reached the Spiral, he and Heather both stepped into its light together. He'd been free! He could have just let go and the currents would have carried him aloft, taking him out of the Between and on to a new life. With Heather.

He bowed his head. But for her, he'd held on when Death reached into the Spiral. And grabbed Heather. Without Heather, his new life would have been hollow. So, he'd put himself between her and Death, making Death grab him. Instead of Heather.

But in Heather's defense, they hadn't made any promises—as if that was even possible in a place like this. He'd just embraced her and the strength of that roiling connection between them. A burning flame he'd never been able to extinguish, one that had ignited from the first moment he'd met her that night in the tall grasses. Over time, they'd become inseparable. She was always with him, beside him, wanting to be with him.

Had he made an assumption he shouldn't have? It's not like she'd asked him to sacrifice anything for her. Especially his soul.

But it made him feel so sad. First, he'd lost Jessie. Had he lost Heather, too?

"That's got to be hard to take," said a soft southern voice behind him.

He turned around.

Cora stood behind him, looking concerned. She gripped her tan shawl tight around her shoulders as she walked toward him, her gaze on the the bench where Knox and Heather sat.

"Oh, hi, Cora," he said, offering a friendly smile as he walked over to her, turning away from Heather and Knox.

Fighting every emotion he had not to show his pain.

He shrugged. "She doesn't belong to me. And who knows if any of us will ever escape this place."

Cora smiled and took his hand in hers, squeezing.

"Your hand is so warm," she cried.

He hadn't noticed how cool a soul's skin felt (was skin even was it was now) until this moment. And how pallid a soul's skin looked compared to this white-fire-induced complexion. Like the glow of the sun against his skin.

Cora slid her arm around his waist and laid her head against his shoulder. He put his arm around her, holding her close.

"We haven't had a chance to talk much since you came back," she said, walking alongside him. "Can we walk around the circle of trees?"

He smiled. "Wouldn't you prefer the path by the stream?"

She shook her head. "Not since five souls have gone missing. I'd prefer to stay here where it's safe." She glanced over his shoulder, toward the bench and made a face.

"What's the matter?" Ross asked, wincing.

Was Heather in Knox's arms again? Or worse. He pulled in a sharp breath. Held it.

"She—she kissed him!" Cora cried, indignant. "Out here for everyone to see. Like a...common hussy! How scandalous! And mean."

Ross snorted, holding in a laugh. He'd forgotten that Cora had come from a time far removed from his. She died in 1864 and he died in 1961. A kiss in public was nothing to rage over in his day, even if it was his woman being kissed.

"What's so funny?" Cora asked, letting go of him, hands on her hips as she glared at him.

"Cora, I don't think you realize how much the world has changed since you left it."

He led her away from the stand of river birch and around the side toward the footpath, not wanting to hear—or see—any more play-by-plays. It made him sick to his stomach.

"What do you mean?" she said, staring at him.

He put his arm around her shoulders.

"Heather's life ended in 2022, Cora. Do you have any idea how different her world was from yours?" He laid his hand against his chest. "Even from mine."

Her eyes grew wide, the dark blue irises turning purple in the glow of the ring of trees' violet protection light. She was a lovely woman, her fine blonde hair feathering around her face as it swept into a roll against the back of her head. Sweet and pure of heart, she'd always been kind to him.

"Travers died even later," he replied. "So I'd guess that kissing in public is a pretty common thing in their time. And no big deal."

Cora stopped walking. She turned to face him, her hands gripping his.

"Quite frankly, Ross, I don't care if it's acceptable or not. I don't like it because it's hurting you."

He looked down at the ground, not knowing what to say, but she lifted his chin with her hand.

"Ross, I just don't want to see you hurt again." She laid her hand against his face, stroking his cheek with her cool fingers. "When they brought you back, you were so broken. In so much pain. It just broke my heart."

"You're sweet, Cora," he replied, laying his hand against hers.

She sighed. "I know I'm not Heather, but I care about you very much, Ross. I care what happens to you. Besides, that soldier gives me the creeps." She shuddered.

Ross didn't know if it was Travers' amazingly abrasive personality that she didn't like or just the fact that Travers was a soldier. She had every right to fear soldiers after what had happened to her the night that Atlanta burned.

She leaned up, her face close to his.

"Would I be considered a—a hussy in your time if you were to kiss me?"

He laughed and ran his fingers across her freckled cheek and winter-pale skin. He wondered if she'd ever even had a boyfriend. Zakhart said she'd been barely eighteen when she died.

"No, Cora," he said, leaning toward her face. "A kiss was a starting point between two people in my time. It was how we got to know each other after a first date."

"Then I'd like to get to know you better, Ross," she said, lifting her face to kiss him.

He drew her into his arms in a slow, gentle embrace, knowing the terror she'd gone through in her short life. She didn't flinch, but he felt her shaking as he softly pressed his lips to hers.

She closed her eyes as he kissed her. It was a sweet kiss, soft and gentle.

She stood perfectly still, her arms frozen around him as he kissed her full lips, his mouth covering hers.

But the kiss had no spark for him. No flicker of heat, no connection—not even a whisper of deepening. Just two pairs of lips touching each other, hoping for some heat. For something to ignite. He didn't feel much of anything, but he did his best to pretend.

It wasn't a bad kiss. It just wasn't Heather.

Something rustled off to his left as he brushed his mouth over her top lip then her bottom lip. At last, he felt Cora respond, kissing back, her hands sliding up his back to his shoulders.

A flash of shadow danced at the periphery of his vision. He glanced left and then right.

Nothing.

Cora pulled in a breath as his mouth lifted away from hers.

"My first kiss," she said, sounding breathless as she smiled.

He took her face in his hands and pressed another warm kiss against her lips then let her go.

"I hope it was nice," he said, stroking her hair with his hand.

Light danced in her eyes, her smile bright.

"It was wonderful," she said in a husky whisper, reaching out, and clasping his hand in hers.

She was starry-eyed now and he worried that he was feeding some sort of crush. But he'd been very clear with her. His heart belonged to Heather.

Something thumped in the line of trees. He turned.

A black rock hit his foot and rolled across the grass into the tree line.

"What was that?" Cora asked, glancing around.

She gripped his arms tight in her hands.

He shrugged. "Not sure," he replied.

Ahead, in the dark tree line, a figure lurched through the forest, a muffled voice carrying through the trees. He couldn't make out the voice or the face.

With Cora's hand in his, he moved closer to the tree line, trying to identify the bumbling figure in the growing dark. Night had fallen in the Between, turning the forest into an ocean of blackness and spiky bare tree limbs.

White fire rushed through him, pounding at his temples, surging under the skin, into his belly and his chest as he stepped gently through the brush. It beat steadily in his chest, some sort of heart pumping it through his body.

Cora started to speak, but he pressed his index finger to his lips, motioning her to be silent. She nodded, following him.

Ross stepped over a dry, scraggly patch of grass and slid around a thick tree trunk, following a trail of freshly mashed grass—footsteps— until he and Cora caught up to the stumbling figure.

Ian. He stumbled through the brush, calling Gemma's name over and over, his voice carrying through the night. His eyes were rimmed red and he looked barely aware of his surroundings. It broke Ross' heart to watch him struggle so badly. To hurt so much.

"Gemma," Ian called, his voice thin and tear-strained. "Gemma, love, hear me—please!"

"He'll lead anything out hunting right to him," Ross whispered.

Cora nodded and motioned toward Ian.

"Let's get him back inside where he'll be safe."

The hair on Ross' neck bristled as he reached for Ian's arm.

Even as he closed the distance between him and Ian, Ross knew they were no longer alone.

Something hissed past his ear, scraping his shoulder as his hand clamped onto Ian's arm.

"Gemma?" Ian called out. "That you, darling?"

A feral growl rumbled nearby.

Ross turned, holding Ian up.

Cora froze on his right, gripping Ross' arm.

He dropped into a crouch and scanned the horizon for movement, for noise. He winced. For demons.

Bam! Something smacked against his temple and hit the ground, rolling away.

Cora snatched it from the dirt. A shiny black rock.

Ross' stomach twisted, his eyes narrowing. He knew the source of that rock well. The coalfields.

A chill danced along his spine. Demons!

sixteen

. . .

FOOTSTEPS SKITTERED across the forest floor.

Ross pivoted right then left, watching for movement as he held up Ian with his left arm, Cora clinging to his right side.

A limb snapped behind him.

He turned.

Stones pounded the ground.

Ross shifted left, catching a faint red glimmer in the dark woods. Heard the skitter of taloned feet against the hard ground.

"Show yourselves, demons!" he shouted into the darkness.

"Demons?" Ian muttered, glancing up at Ross, glaring, trying to shove him away. "Let go of me, Ross. Gemma? Gemma!"

Ian broke free and then tripped, falling to the ground.

Ross dropped down beside the Englishman, Cora not letting go.

On his knees, palms flat against the ground, Ian scanned the forest.

Ross stayed beside him, watching shadows flit back and forth. Trying to protect the bereaved guy from getting captured by demons.

The first demon was nearly on top of them before Ross saw it.

Cora screamed, dropping to the ground.

Ross let the demon grab his wrist.

He turned, pulling the grey demon up and over his shoulders. And flung it into the brush.

Two more demons flowed out of the forest, growls and snorts filling the silence as Ross flung himself at them. He hammered the first one with blow after blow until it fell to the ground in an inky splatter. The other demon faced off with him, getting Ross around the throat with its arm, choking him as three more demons rushed out of the forest.

Two of them struggled to drag off Ian who didn't put up a struggle while the third one went after Cora.

Cora screamed, scrambling backward from it, kicking and gouging it with her fingernails.

With a twist of his shoulder, Ross broke free of the chokehold.

He slammed his fist into the grey demon's gut and ducked under another blow until he had it on the ground, its face smashed into the grass as he beat it down.

"Ross!" Cora shouted. "Ross, help me!"

He let go of the grey demon, leaping onto the one assaulting Cora. He tore it off her shoulders and she crawled away from it. He had it by the throat, fist cocked, ready to pummel its face when the other demon pulled itself up from the ground.

It stared at him, unblinking, and Ross froze mid-punch, gawking at its eyes. They were bright hazel.

The damaged thing hesitated another moment and then scampered off into the woods.

Ross beat the demon in his grasp senseless and then leaped up to go after the two demons dragging Ian into the woods. Cora rushed after him, grabbing hold of Ian as Ross pulled the demons off, beating them with his fists until they retreated.

And in an instant, the night was quiet again.

Ian lay on the ground, panting, Cora with her arm around his waist as she helped Ross lift him to his feet.

When the Englishman at last opened his eyes and saw Ross, his face contorted in fury.

"No! NO!" He struggled against Ross' hold, turning toward the forest. "Let me go! Let them have me!"

He fought Ross, but Ross was stronger, holding onto him until he collapsed. Ross held him up until the Englishman crumbled. Ross eased him to the ground again.

"Why'd you stop them!" Ian raged. "I'd be with Gemma right now. Why?"

Ross caught the man's face and held it, forcing the Englishman to look at him.

"Ian," he said, shaking the man. "Listen to me. Getting captured won't help you save Gemma. Do you understand?" He shook him again. "It won't save Gemma."

Despair welled in his watery eyes, his face twisting with grief.

"Then help me, Ross," he said in a thin voice, his eyes pleading. "Help me rescue her. Without her, I am nothing."

He wilted in Ross' arms. Ross had to fireman carry him back to the soul tree. Cora was right beside him as he brought Ian across the circle courtyard and into the soul tree. He walked past the rust-colored sofa, where Zoe sat and chattered at Barb, Razasha, and Zakhart. Thomas, Ian's brother, huddled against the wall beside the fireplace, looking a little lost.

Thomas looked up when he saw Ross carrying his brother.

"You found him!" Thomas cried, rising to his feet.

He helped Ross settle Ian onto the floor in front of the hearth.

"Cora and I just fought off four demons," said Ross, pointing at Ian. "He did his best to get them to carry him off, thinking it would reunite him with his fiancé, but I stopped them."

Zakhart was on his feet now, wide eyes staring at Ross.

"Where did this attack occur?" he asked, his voice clipped.

Ross nodded north. "It was just inside the protective circle, Zakhart. It's not repelling the demons anymore."

Zakhart looked disturbed by this news. He motioned at Razasha.

"Find Halea and meet me outside with Lairz. We'll need to create a deeper protective barrier."

"But Zakhart," Razasha cried. "No one has seen Halea!"

Zakhart snapped his wings closed against his shoulders. "Then work with Lairz if you can't find her!"

She nodded, hurrying up into the top of the soul tree.

Ross moved over to Zakhart and spoke barely above a whisper.

"One more thing."

Zakhart nodded for him to continue.

"One of those demons had hazel eyes," he snapped.

The pale angel gasped and covered his mouth.

"What? Hazel? Are you sure, Ross?"

"I've never been more certain in my entire life," Ross said, still whispering. "It looked me right in the eye. Without blinking."

Razasha appeared on the stairs in the warm glow of lantern lights gleaming throughout the soul tree. Her brow was shadowed, eyes filled with worry.

"Zakhart, she still hasn't returned to the tree. I called and called for her."

With a heavy sigh, Zakhart sang a series of notes that Razasha matched then vocalized the harmony until at last, she gave him a quick nod and hurried out of the soul tree.

The notes vibrated through Ross' body, each one carrying an emotion and every crystalline note in the strains reverberated with worry. He hadn't felt emotions from their language before. The sounds—the music—had always been calming. But the music had never carried emotions to him before.

Razasha gave Zakhart a sharp nod and headed out the door.

Ross turned to Cora.

"Cora, help Thomas keep an eye on Ian, will you?"

"Of course," she said and gripped his hand. "You saved me out there just now, Ross. Thank you."

He glanced at her thin, delicate fingers and small, cool hand as he held it a moment.

She squeezed his hand and a sharp pain shot through his fingers. He let go, turning up his palm, seeing a long, red slash that throbbed across his palm.

Had Cora's fingernails done that? Or was it the demons?

He turned his attention back to Cora.

"You're welcome," he answered and gazed at her face.

She still looked terrified and this new chain of events hadn't helped her stay calm either. She'd already been through so much—ending her life to escape a horrific, brutal war and then landing in the middle of a new one had to be weighing heavily on Cora. He saw the weight of her crush in her dark blue eyes, but he just didn't feel the same way. She was like a kid sister to him. A friend at best.

He gripped her shoulders a moment, flashing his best poker-face smile at her.

"Everything's okay right now, Cora. We're safe here with the pale angels, so don't worry, okay?"

"I'll try," she said and moved over to help Thomas get Ian settled.

He glanced at his palm again. The scratch was disturbing. The white fire must allow him to take damage now, something he hadn't realized yet. He needed to have a long talk with Zakhart about this white fire. He needed to know exactly how it had changed him. And Heather.

He sighed. Heather.

The white fire fluttered through his chest, a momentary quiver that took his breath then subsided as the memory of making love to her warmed his soul.

Heather was a whole different matter.

He clutched his chest a moment. When the ache dissipated, he headed toward the door but it opened. And Heather stepped inside with Travers.

She stood just inside the soul tree's threshold, door hanging open as her gaze met his. She held it, not looking through him, looking at him, deep into his eyes as if trying to peel away the layers—the distance—between them. Her green eyes were so intense and piercing.

He held in a breath. Such a beautiful face.

He was melting.

He hadn't put up any barriers between them. He hadn't tried to hide or keep anything from her. But he couldn't deny that there was distance between them now, even though he longed to take her into his arms and kiss the length of her body. Show her how he felt without words or promises. Without Travers or the Between to separate them.

Pain twisted his gut. He hid it, pouring on every ounce of poker face left in him. But all he could manage was a crooked, longing smile. He wouldn't force himself on her. Wouldn't make her feel beholden to him out of guilt or duty. Or demand her time or start a fight over Travers. He'd already fought everything for her, sacrificed everything he had left. He had nothing else left to give but his love.

She knew how he felt. She knew where to find him.

"What's happened?" Heather asked, her alto voice aching through him.

From behind, Zakhart tapped Ross' shoulder.

"Come out and help me with the circle protection, Ross. I could use your assistance."

"Sure thing," said Ross, his gaze still locked with Heather's.

Finally, he looked away, stepping around her and out the door into the darkness.

He hurried around the tree behind Zakhart who'd slipped toward the northern side of the soul tree. He found the pale angel pacing along the edge of the glowing, violet circle, studying the protective lights and the location of the demon attack.

"I see you found the spot," said Ross.

Zakhart nodded. "Yes, you fought off four of them, didn't you?"

"Yep," he replied. "Including Ian who did his best to go with them."

The pale angel made a grunting noise as he traced the demons' steps, his face pinched in concentration. He walked back and forth in silence until finally, his gaze snapped up.

"Hazel eyes you said?"

"Scariest thing I've ever seen," Ross muttered.

"Why's that?" Zakhart said with a frown.

"Because the only eye color I've ever seen those grey demons have is red. Granted, by now I've seen a lot of demons and I haven't seen all of them. But I've seen enough to know that none of them had hazel eyes. Like mine. Something's not right here, Zakhart."

"I agree, Ross," said Zakhart, rubbing his hand against his mouth. "I'm not sure what Mulciber is up to, but human eye colors on demons can only mean something horrible."

"Exactly what I was thinking," said Ross.

How could that thing have human-colored eyes? Like his. Could a demon and human have mated and gave birth to half demon half human child? A chilling thought. But even more chilling was the possibility that Mulciber had found a way to give his demons human traits.

Ross shuddered. Human disguises.

"I'll commune with Archangel Raduriel about it shortly," said Zakhart.

Fragments of memories swirled through Ross' head. Blackness. Spinning walls. Endless parades of grey demons. Floor shifting. Shadows rising. His wrists and ankles ached at the memory of cuffs and chains chafing his skin. Aching against his soul. The memory of shadows flowed over him, into him—around him—smothering him.

He gagged, holding his stomach, and doubled over. Zakhart's arm was around him.

"I've got you," said Zakhart, his hands so hot against Ross' flesh.

He froze. Flesh? Not exactly flesh, but his body almost felt solid again. Just like the pale angels that flitted around the soul tree. Like Zakhart beside him, holding him up. He hadn't noticed how fragile he'd been without this white fire.

"The white fire can be overwhelming at first," said Zakhart, his tenor voice rushing through Ross who could almost feel the words against his skin now. "Most who receive it are children and don't remember the effects."

The pale angel's voice resonated through him and the notes of Zakhart's voice were like the plucks of a guitar string, vibrating in his throat, and into his chest.

"Your voice," Ross gasped. "I—I feel it. Is that right?"

Zakhart got him on his feet. Ross leaned against the soul tree, staring at the pale angel.

"Yes," Zakhart said, smiling. "That musicality will grow with time and you'll be able to pick out bits of our language."

Ross nodded, a hand to his head as he studied the violet glow of the circle protecting the soul tree. The color was deeper, more vibrant than he remembered. He felt the color hum through his body. So strange.

"What's that?" Zakhart asked, pointing at Ross' hand.

Ross held out his right hand, palm up.

"I don't know. I was going to ask you about it."

The pale angel took hold of his palm and ran his finger across it.

"Demon?"

"Maybe," said Ross, shrugging. "Cora's fingernails might have scratched me."

Zakhart let go of his hand.

"Either way, you'd better heal that up quickly. Demons will jump at any chink in our armor, Ross."

Ross squinted. "How do I do that?"

The pale angel smiled. "You've got white fire now, Ross. Use it. Will be a good learning experience for you."

Ross nodded and ran his hand through his hair, brushing bangs out of his eyes.

"So you need my help with this protective circle?" he asked, motioning toward the violet wash of light pulsating in the darkness. "Although I doubt I'll be much help with this."

Zakhart chuckled, shaking his head.

"Not really. I just thought you needed to get out of there and not have to face Heather and Knox just then."

"You are indeed my guardian angel, Zakhart," Ross replied, patting him on the shoulder. "I think I'll stay out here for a while and watch your back for a change. Make sure you aren't attacked by demons. Just to make it look good. Then I'll go in. Thanks."

Just the thought of entering that place and watching Travers touch Heather made him sick to his stomach. Or worse—watch them cuddling. He couldn't look into her eyes right now. He was terrified that he'd see that light she'd always carried for him extinguished. He gritted his teeth. Or burning for Travers. If he had to watch her kiss that guy up close, he was liable to damage Travers.

He stood near Zakhart, pacing around the circle behind the pale angel, and doing his best to clear his head—his anger—before he went inside again.

seventeen

. . .

BUT CLEARING his head was impossible as long Heather was with Knox. Knowing he'd just sit and stew, Ross decided to stay outside a while and talk to Zakhart. Feeling useless, he paced around the circle and avoided going inside for as long as he could. He kept watch for demons, but the night grew quiet except for the constant whisper of soulstalkers winging across the starless sky. And the hushed cries of new souls entering the Between that sparked the whisper of soulstalkers flying low across the distant fields of grass.

The skies were full of them now, the shadows constantly flitting across the ground. Unlike the soulstalker that had rescued Heather. Sandriana had bedded down at the top of the soul tree, watching for demons. And Death. But the other soulstalkers still hunted along the seas of grass and at the edges of the forest. Their screeches and the laments of souls they carried off used to drive him mad. Before the pale angels came here, he and Heather had drawn out a path to the great tree with stones. So the souls could find their way if the others couldn't get to them in time. He had laid out more rocks in the grasses, in an arrow pattern that pointed to the soul tree.

Every morning, there were always new faces at this soul tree. But they never stayed long. He always hoped that they'd found the Spiral and went on again. Whenever anyone asked, he'd answered questions but most of the time, they insisted that they knew more than he did. After a while, he'd just stopped trying.

Like so many others.

By the time he returned to the soul tree, things had quieted down inside, too. The main floor (so much smaller than the great tree he remembered) was sparse. The color of the couch and the walls changed every time he left. And so did the furniture styles. Until he stopped paying attention. Because of Zoe.

None of the smoke people flowed through the room tonight, not even Avana. She'd been so quiet since he'd returned that he'd hardly noticed her or the other wisps of smoke people that had been constant fixtures in the old tree. They seemed to trail off into hidden nooks and corners and fade into the woodwork now. He was beginning to envy that talent.

He glanced around. No sign of Heather. Or Travers. Were they both curled up together in her little nook on the top floor? His heart sank. Where he'd been only a short time ago.

He glanced across the empty sofa at the hearth. Blue. Overstuffed.

Cora was asleep on the floor, Zoe lying beside her, that pink unicorn clutched in her arms. Seeing a teen here that young still made him sick. She looked so pale and fragile. They all did now. Zoe's face seemed almost grey even in the hearth's amber light.

Her eyes rolled open and she stared back at him with sleepy hazel eyes.

Demon eyes flashed in his head. Red and menacing!

He winced at the memory of them crawling over him in the dark, spinning room. Eyes rising out of the night, leering at him. Teeth grinding into his flesh.

Bright hazel eyes glittered from the brush. Leaping at him—talons drilling into his back!

He turned away, gold and brown lights burning through him like flaming tiger's eyes.

Turn on them, it had whispered in the night. *Tear them apart. Devour them, my Champion.*

He gripped his head, eyes smashed closed against the voice in his head. Was it a memory? He shuddered. He couldn't tell.

Consume them all and serve the rebellion, Ross. Lead us into battle. Take all the power that the universe holds.

"No," he hissed, clenching his eyes closed.

You may be out of the caves, Ross, but you'll never be free of us. All the white fire in the universe can't flush us from your soul. You've tasted the demon heart and its essence still beats within you.

He gagged at the memory of the demon heart clinging to his soul like a fat, gorged leech. Tasted the bitter metallic brine that had flowed like bile through him, spreading its nasty black venom through his body. He was trembling now at the memory that clung to his soul, the rhythmic pulsing of the black, tumorous mass in his chest that had throbbed like a boil.

The sound beat in his ears like an infection burning through him and all he wanted to do was to claw through his chest and tear it out all over again.

"Ross, are you all right?"

Zoe was standing in front of him.

He was on the floor now, fingers gouging at his chest. He pulled his hands back.

They were stained red.

He pulled open his shirt, revealing four gashes where he'd torn at his skin.

Laughter rumbled in his head.

You'll never be free of us, Ross. Give in while you're still useful.

"Ross?" she cried, kneeling beside him, unicorn cradled in her left arm. "Do you want me to get somebody? I'll wake up Cora."

"No, no," he said, chest heaving. "I'm fine. Sorry to have woken you up, kid."

Zoe laid her hand on his bare arm and he winced, his skin sizzling. He pulled away, her handprint burning against his left wrist.

She gasped, backing away from him.

"I'm sorry," she said, eyes welling with tears. "I didn't mean to hurt you, Ross. I'm sorry."

"No, you didn't, Zoe," he said, forcing a smile onto his face. "It's okay. I'll be fine. Thanks for your help."

Her hazel eyes were huge, pupils constricting as she averted her gaze to the floor.

"It's okay," he said and stumbled to his feet. "Go on back to sleep, kid. Sorry, I woke you up."

Zoe smiled and went back over to the hearth. She lay down beside Cora as he limped onto the spiral staircase. He glanced down at the main floor when he was halfway up. Travers lay on the couch, stretched out on his stomach, fast asleep.

Grinning, Ross climbed up the stairs to the top. Everything was Christmas Eve quiet, not even a smoke person coiling through the stillness. There were three little nooks up here. His was in the center. The one to the right was dark. On the left was Heather's space.

Soft amber light gleamed from underneath the door.

He paused at the top of the stairs, watching for shadows beneath it, listening for movement. For any reason or excuse he could find to knock on that door.

Everything was so quiet.

He moved to the center space and opened the door. It creaked open and thumped against the wall.

Okay, he'd done that on purpose. Wanting her to know he was there. Giving her an excuse—if she wanted one—to come over to his space.

His room was simple. White walls. Maple wood floors. A ceiling light cast thick, gold light through the room. The wall opposite the door had a comfy, brown leather sofa underneath a big rectangular window overlooking the stream. On the right-hand wall was a small desk and chair that stood beside an archway into a bathroom (that he no longer needed).

His bed was against the other wall. A blue and white quilt draped over it, like the one his grandma had made for him. And four pillows.

Okay, it probably looked like the bedroom he grew up in, a place that had some happy memories. Before Dad died in the Korean War. Mom did her best to fill the void he'd left behind and so did his older brother and older sister, but no one could fill Dad's shoes.

Shiny black shoes. Clacking across the porch. Glistening in the July morning sun like a brand-new Mercury Coup. Warm smell of leather mixed with the waxy, petroleum scent of shoe polish as military men in uniforms walked past him to the screen door. But all he saw was their shiny shoes. And smelled the shoe polish and leather scents that had lingered long after they'd delivered the devastating news and left.

Funny how the memory of those shoes had always stuck with him whenever he remembered that July morning. He'd been nine, sprawled across the porch on his stomach as he'd played with his metal cars.

One of the men had dropped down on his haunches, green uniform glittering with pins and medals and gold piping. A tall, lanky man with angular features and big hands.

"So sorry, little man," he'd said, his grey eyes watery as Ross looked up at him.

"My dad's a soldier," he remembered saying as he pointed at the man's medals. "He's got a medal, too. Momma keeps prayin' he don't get a purple one though."

The lanky officer ruffled Ross' light blond hair with a white-gloved hand, patting him on the head before he stood up, his back board-straight as the other officer rapped on the screen door.

The memory of Momma's shriek still tore through him after all this time. For years after Dad had died in Korea, Ross could still hear her horrid wail, still smell whiffs of leather and shoe polish every time he woke up from a nightmare. Even now, his mouth went dry, muscles seizing, whole body tensing as the faint scents of leather and shoe polish clung to the space. And the shrill, desperate shriek played in his head again.

Like the squeal of tires before a car crash. Scream of a rabbit attacked by a dog.

He winced, shaking off the memory, and walked into the small bathroom. He stared at himself in the oval wall mirror as he took off his shirt.

The scratches he'd inflicted still oozed red liquid. It wasn't thick like blood. More like tinted water that had stained his grey shirt and continued to weep.

He picked up a Navy blue towel from the shelf and carried it and his shirt out of the bathroom. He plopped down on his bed, daubing at the cuts as Zakhart's suggestion came back to him.

Heal it with white fire. It would be a good test.

How would he even use the white fire to heal like that?

Made sense though. Why else would Zakhart have given them the white fire? He needed them to use it, of course. To practice.

Guess it was time he started learning how.

He stared at his wrist where Zoe's hand had burned him, running his fingers across the imprint of her small hand and willowy fingers.

Was he having some sort of odd reaction to the white fire?

Souls seemed so fragile compared to the pale angels, but now, he was beginning to wonder. He'd ask Zakhart about it tomorrow.

Gathering up the pillows he'd conjured (he liked lots of pillows), he propped them against the headboard and laid back against them. Right now, even with the angels' white fire burning through his body, he'd never felt so empty. Blinded.

Had he just ignored the signs? Had he just refused to see her growing feelings for Travers?

Sighing, he dropped his head in his hands, covering his eyes. He couldn't trust his sight anymore. He just couldn't see when or where Heather had stopped loving him.

And it was tearing him apart.

A long, lean shadow stretched across the room from under the door, brushing across the end of his bed.

The white fire in his body spiked, sending sparks of heat along the length of his body.

His connection to her!

He lifted his head, sliding his hands away from his eyes.

Was he seeing things, too, now?

He squinted, elbows propped on his knees as he rested his face in his hands.

"Heather?" he asked in a raspy half-whisper.

The door opened and she stood in the doorway of his room, hand on the doorknob as if she couldn't decide whether to stay or go.

His heart danced in his chest, but he held his breath, fearing it was another trick of the eyes. He sniffed the air for the scent of shoe polish, fearing she was bringing him the worst news of his soul.

"Ross," she said in a quiet voice. "Are you busy?"

He shook his head. "No. Need something?"

He hadn't meant for his voice to sound so drained.

Her steps were timid as she entered the room, closing the door behind her. She stood on the right side of the bed, gazing at him, a mystery in those fathomless green eyes.

She nodded, running her index finger down the curve of his bicep.

"You."

eighteen

HEATHER SAT DOWN BESIDE ROSS, her hands in her lap. He sat up straight, bare back against the headboard, still staring at her in silence. His leanly muscled chest didn't have even a trace of blond hair. But the two groups of bleeding cuts startled her.

"Ross, what happened?" she cried.

She started to reach out and examine the marks, but his distance held her back.

"Cut myself shaving," he said with a chuckle, a smile at last lightening his face.

So, he was still speaking to her.

Tension drained out of her shoulders and she wanted to melt into a puddle right there on the quilt. Her hands were shaking and she kept them in her lap so he wouldn't see. Downstairs was the first time he'd ever looked at her like that before, a mixture of anger and indifference. Knox had gloated all evening after seeing Ross' face. Like it was some game he'd won. But it was a look that had cut right through her.

Hard. Apathetic. Distant.

"Seriously, Ross," she insisted. "What is that? How'd it happen?"

He shrugged, staring at his hands now, avoiding her eyes. Like he didn't want her to know something.

She swallowed hard. Or because she'd lost that place beside him. That thought made her tremble despite the white fire's warmth. She had to make this right with him. She had to.

Finally, he reached over and grabbed a blue towel lying on the bed and pressed it to the seeping cuts.

"I don't exactly know," he said, holding the towel against his chest. "I had this flashback...and I guess I did it to myself."

"Did it to yourself?"

He shrugged, looking at her now. Not through her. There was hope if he was looking into her eyes. She saw the cut on his hand and fear welled inside her.

"Those things are getting inside my head somehow. I don't know how but they are."

The memory of Zakhart ripping that bloated, blackened demon heart from his soul ached through her. It had nearly destroyed him—if the extended time in demon hands hadn't. Those events had nearly torn him apart, but she'd been there beside him, getting him through it. Until she'd ripped out his heart again by kissing Knox right in front of him.

She bowed her head, feeling horrible.

"Are the demons speaking to you?" she asked. "Or sending you pictures in your head?"

With a sigh, he nodded at her. "Both."

He ran his hands through his hair and laid the towel in his lap—like he was trying to find something to keep his hands occupied.

"I think I'm going crazy, Heather. Ever since they attacked Cora and me outside the tree tonight, I've been hearing them in my head."

Me and Cora?

Heather pulled in a breath, feeling a little stunned. Had something happened between him and Cora while she'd been in the soulstalker encampment to the south? Or had Ross just assumed that she'd chosen Knox and no longer wanted him? So, he'd turned to

Cora. Her stomach somersaulted and she felt sick inside. Or maybe he'd just fallen for Cora all along?

Had her confusion just cost her his love?

"Cora?" she asked finally when he didn't explain.

He nodded, changing the subject.

"So how'd your talk with Travers go?" he asked, changing the subject as he sneered the word *Travers*.

"Good," she replied.

Was it good? Or was she just avoiding an answer? Even she didn't know anymore.

He chewed his lower lip, not looking at her now.

"According to some, it looked more than good. I saw you in his arms. I wasn't spying on you, Heather. The circle's a small place."

That stung. But it was true. She'd shared a moment with Knox—just a moment though. Was Ross jealous or angry? Both? She shuddered. Or neither. Maybe he had no feelings left for her now? Were his feelings so easily shaken by a single kiss? In a place where the world was everything but normal? And long-lived?

"He kissed me," she replied. "And I kissed him back."

His face was like stone and she couldn't read those beautiful, gold-hazel eyes that had always melted her with his gaze. She was melting even now. Was he relieved? Happy to be rid of her? Or did he still want her?

"Just like that?" he snapped. "Like you're just reporting the news?"

His voice was bitter now. He grabbed the towel again, gripping it, staring at it like he was avoiding her gaze.

He'd been acting so distant and strange since they'd brought him out of the caves. And they'd had such little time together. She sighed. And then there was Knox. What she desperately needed to know was if those words he'd spoken to her long ago still had meaning.

You meant more to me than my own life. Did he still mean them?

"I wasn't trying to hide anything from you," she said.

Nodding, he glanced up at her, but this time, those beautiful hazel eyes were full of pain.

She winced. That she'd inflicted.

She stared at the raw gashes on his chest, that he'd done to himself, and she wondered if she'd been the cause of those, too.

He slid off the bed, towel in hand, and walked over to the window, his back to her.

"Cora kissed me tonight. Just so you know."

His words were a blow to her gut. She sucked in a breath, not expecting that. She'd deserved it, but she hadn't expected it.

"Okay," she said finally. "Was it to get back at me or because you care for her?"

"Would it matter either way?"

She didn't respond. Did it change anything? Either way, she hated it. And she hated putting him through this. She hadn't planned it. And she hadn't ever wanted to hurt him. Not like this. Especially like this when he'd given up everything for her. But she'd given up everything to come back for him. They were even, but she couldn't help but feel that she was losing something.

Something irreplaceable.

Him.

"An hour before, you're in my arms like everything's okay," he said, the anger seeping out. "Like you'd wanted to be there all along." He sighed. "Like nothing could keep us apart. But the moment we come back to the soul tree, you're in his arms like it's your duty. Or your calling, I'm not sure which. Now, you tell me you can't choose between us? I don't deserve this, Heather."

God, how his voice ached with pain! She'd hurt him badly. Deeply.

"No, of course you don't, Ross," she said, rising from the bed.

She walked toward him, standing behind him, afraid that if she touched him, he'd fling her away in disgust.

"I gave up everything to come back and rescue you. My heart was broken and I did everything to bring you back. Knox was there for every step. He kept me going when I didn't think I could try one more time. I can't just—discard him after everything he did for me. For you."

She couldn't see his face, but she thought she heard him suck in a breath. His hands were shaking as he held the towel to his side.

"Yes, I have feelings for him. I tried not to feel anything, Ross. I tried not to, but I do."

The silence in the room was palpable. Long. Enduring like marble. Finally, he turned around and spoke in a quiet, raspy voice, a defeated voice, a broken voice that made her chest ache.

"Do you love him?"

The ache in his eyes went right through her.

"What?" she replied.

How dare he ask her that question!

Another glacial silence. Demanding that she answer. He had a right to that answer.

"Maybe this whole thing is my fault," he said, a hand gripping his sandy blond hair as if he might tear it out. "Maybe I was blinded the whole time? Thought I saw something that was never there. Thought I felt things that never existed. Maybe I'm deaf, too." His eyes were watery as his anger sparked. "Because I thought I heard you tell me you loved me once. Somewhere in my fevered brain, right next door to a room like this one with all those pale angels around me, you told me that I meant more to you than your own life. But I guess you were just reporting the news then, too—weren't you, Heather? Were you just reading that off a cue card?"

His words tore through her. Sharp, bitter—but every one of them was true.

"What about Jessie, Ross?" she asked.

She hated herself for playing that card, but she had to get him to understand.

He glared at her now. "Jessie?"

She nodded. "There was a time when you were torn between me and Jessie. Remember? You loved both of us then. And you needed time to sort through it while you searched for her. I gave you that time. That's all I'm asking."

He flinched like she'd just struck him in the face, that awful question rolling off his tongue again.

"Do you love him?"

She didn't know the answer. But the emotions were driving her crazy.

"Do I love him?" she repeated, trying to stall her response, but with every repeat, she was gouging his soul deeper.

She saw that now.

He nodded, bowing his head. He bit his lip.

"I don't know." It was an honest answer.

He looked up, jaw set tight.

"Do you love me?" he asked, his whole face tightening.

"Yes, of course I do," she replied. "That was never in doubt, Ross. I love you."

He smashed his eyes closed, wilting a little as he pulled in a breath. Was it relief? Or pain?

Heather took a timid step toward him and he covered the distance between them in two steps, wrapping her in his arms.

She held him as tight as her arms could hold him, trembling as he pressed his face against hers, his arms holding her tighter than he'd ever held her before.

"I love you with everything I've got, Heather," he whispered in her ear. "Everything I am."

Footsteps pounded up the spiral staircase, a fist thumping on Ross' door.

"Ross! It's Zakhart. Open the door."

Heather sighed and let go of him. He took her hand in his as he opened the door.

Zakhart stood there grim-faced.

"Get dressed."

"Why?" Ross asked, glancing at Heather and then the pale angel.

"There's been an attack on the pale angels. By demons. Forgive me, but the Trial of Despair will have to wait. We need to assault the demon stronghold now. Before they get too powerful."

"We're not ready, Zakhart," Ross snapped.

"Can't be helped," said Zakhart. "Raduriel has ordered us to strike now. He's detected a strange buildup of shadow energy in the Between. Enough to threaten the Spiral."

"That's the only way out!" Heather cried.

Zakhart nodded. "That was Raduriel's comment exactly, Heather. The archangel is getting together a force of archangels and full angels, but that will take too long. We need to strike those caves now and destroy the Mechanism before it's too late."

"What about Sandriana's flock?" Heather asked.

"She's flown back south to gather them. As soon as she returns, we'll strike. A force by air and a force on the ground. We'll meet at the mouth of the cave and drive deep into the caverns until we destroy the Mechanism. And rescue all the souls that Mulciber has kidnapped."

"What then?" Ross asked, gripping Heather's hand tighter.

"Then we head to the Spiral to defend it," said Zakhart. "And we hold it until Raduriel's troops arrive. I've called for every pale angel in the realm. More are on the way, but—"

Zakhart stopped in mid-sentence, but Heather felt the finality of his words in the white fire.

"But there won't be enough," she said, finishing the sentence for him.

Zakhart opened his mouth to deny her comment, but he just shook his head.

"No," he said in a tight voice.

Ross squeezed her hand and she glanced down at one of the illuminated bracelets around her wrist.

"Zakhart!" she cried, holding out her hand.

The light of both bracelets had faded as if the batteries had run down.

The pale angel's eyes grew wide, pupils nearly blotting out the pumpkin-orange hue.

"Faded?" He gasped, taking hold of her wrist. "By the Maker —how?"

Ross swallowed hard and Heather felt his turmoil roil through the white fire.

"I'll need to give the two of you a quick lesson in using the white fire as a weapon while we wait for Sandriana's return."

Ross grabbed his shirt off the bed and pulled it over his head. He held the door open, motioning Heather toward the stairs. She stepped out beside him, but she kept a firm grip on his hand, squeezing it which brought a smile to Ross' face.

It was the first one she'd seen on his face tonight.

nineteen

· · ·

THE SOUL TREE was in chaos when Heather and Ross reached the bottom floor. Night had not quite lightened into day on the horizon, but pale angels and souls rushed about, gathering staves and clubs. Barb and Knox herded people into groups, Knox arranging them by practice units, three at a time.

Knox glanced at her from across the room, his wounded blue eyes focused on her holding Ross' hand, and something small changed in his face. A hint of acceptance, a glint of understanding, a spark of anger?

Heather wasn't sure, but he flashed her a smile and kept moving, working beside Barb.

"Let's go!" Barb shouted, anger fiery in her eyes as she concentrated on the assault preparations. "We have to beat these bastards down! Bring back the ones they've taken from us!"

She was thinking about Javier. Heather saw it in her face, in the set of her jaw, the sharpness of her soft brown eyes.

Barb's voice roused Ian from the hearth. Thomas walked beside him, his face intense, his gaze focused on his brother. Ian looked devastated, but there was enough anger burning in his face to get him up and fighting for Gemma.

Heather tugged Ross over beside Ian. She laid her hand on Ian's sleeve and made him look at her, those gentle brown puppy eyes swollen and dull.

"Ian," she said, "if there's a way to save her, we will."

"Thank you, Heather," he said, his gaze wandering to Ross' face and then hers again.

"There is a way," Ross replied. "I'm proof of that, thanks to the three of you."

Ian straightened his body to his full height and smiled, his hollowed face brightening.

The front door sprang open and Diri fell in the door, Lairz behind her. Their robes were torn, angry red marks on Lairz's face and shoulder. The feathers of their wings were torn, smoking, edges singed. The air reeked of burnt hair, sulfury demon stench, and feathers.

Diri lay on her side, a strange, weeping cut on her cheek—like the ones on Ross' chest.

"Lairz! Diri!" Zakhart shouted, rushing toward them.

Razasha was behind him, trying to help them up. Iznir and two other pale angels hurried two steps behind them. Razasha lifted Diri's head, her arm supporting her neck as Diri gasped for breath.

Cora, Zoe, and Knox clustered around the two angels as he slammed the door, his gaze flitting from the angels to the outside. He motioned toward three souls.

"Watch that door," he ordered and then bent over Lairz, helping Zakhart turn the pale angel onto his side.

"No, please—not the angels!" Zoe cried, clasping the pink unicorn to her chest. "Demons can't hurt angels!"

Tears streamed down her face.

Cora knelt beside her, putting her arms around the frightened teen. Zoe turned her face away, pressing it into Cora's tan shawl. Trembling, Cora held her, whispering over and over that everything would be all right. A terrified singsong, her dark blue eyes burning with fear.

Was she reliving the night that Atlanta burned all those years ago? Or something darker that she'd conjured into her memory here in the Between?

Heather knelt beside Razasha, Ross at Diri's shoulder.

"White fire can heal and it can kill," said Razasha, her doe-eyed expression calm as she held out her hand. "Focus the white fire into your hand."

A tiny coppery flame fluttered in her palm.

"Use your voice to attune the flame for healing. Or harm."

Razasha sang a low, steady alto note, adding harmonies until it became a chord.

Heather watched as the coppery flame guttered, its color lightening. The flame seemed to purify itself, shifting from gold to pale yellow and finally into a pure white flame that coiled around Razasha's fingertips.

"As humans," Zakhart said in a quiet voice, "you aren't equipped to create the complex chords and harmonies that we can. You'll have to improvise as best you can." He glanced at Ross and then Heather. "Or create harmonies together. For now, the raw, untempered white fire will have to do."

She and Ross nodded, watching as Razasha laid the swirling flame on Diri's chest. It uncoiled, twisting itself like a fiery vine up Diri's neck to her cheek. It twined its way around her waist, into her wings, and down her legs to her feet.

Kneeling beside Diri, Zakhart chanted a complex chord and unleashed a thicker, ropey coil of white fire onto Lairz's chest. Only when the white fire had been absorbed did their breathing slow.

At last, Diri's eyes opened, brilliant copper orbs—filled with fear and panic—against her ivory complexion, mottled grey now along her cheek and neck. Like bruising.

"Diri!" Zakhart cried, taking hold of her hand. He smoothed her dark sable locks and smiled. "Tell me what happened."

"We were...returning to the circle," Diri replied, her musical alto voice thin. "I remember," she said, lifting her hand to point up at the sky. "A soulstalker flew overhead. Just one. It screeched, diving into a thicket. I remember turning to Halea and bam! They hit us! A dozen or more."

"Demons!" Zakhart cried, eyes wide as he glanced at Razasha.

Heather felt him exchange some fearful thoughts with Razasha through the white fire. She couldn't hear his thoughts or what he'd spoken through the white fire, but she picked up the tone.

And it was dire.

Diri nodded. "Demons, shadow creatures...and dark souls."

Razasha gasped, a hand over her mouth. She intoned a cascade of notes, like an aria that quickly became a duet then a quartet as Diri and Lairz joined them.

It became a dirge. Fragile. Dark. Terrifying.

The notes and chords rushed past so quickly that Heather couldn't even pick up the emotions behind them.

"Wait a moment," Ross replied, interrupting the melody. "What do you mean dark souls? What is that?" He glanced at Heather, frowning, then Zakhart.

Zakhart sank back on his heels and fixed Ross with his gaze.

"It's what you were becoming, Ross. Souls that have been turned to the rebellion, trained to fight as their soldiers. Demons graft demon hearts onto their souls, giving them an almost physical presence again in the Between and other realms."

Barb dropped down beside Diri, gently touching the pale angel's hand.

"Diri, please—did you recognize any of the dark souls?"

Diri stared at Barb, but her gaze drifted to Zakhart who nodded for her to respond.

"No," she said in a weak voice. "None were from this soul tree."

A relieved sigh slipped free as Barb got to her feet. She moved over to the wall where three staves leaned against it and began setting out more.

"Diri, did you say that Halea was with you?" Razasha asked, helping the pale angel sit up.

Diri flattened her wings against her back, curving the ends of her creamy white wings around her waist. She nodded, rubbing a hand against her forehead.

"What? You found Halea?" Zakhart cried as he helped Lairz to his feet.

"In the forest," Diri responded.

"Was she still talking with those other soulstalkers?" Zoe asked.

Everyone turned to stare at the teen as the room fell deadly quiet.

Zakhart moved over to where Zoe crouched beside Cora. His form became luminous, a soft glow emanating as he knelt in front of the teen. Heather felt the calm emanations pulse through the white fire and echo in soothing waves through the room.

Zoe pulled away from him, holding onto Cora now.

"You're scaring me," she cried.

Slowly, the glow faded.

"Sorry, Zoe, was just trying to help."

She smiled, nodding as she sat up, easing her grip on Cora.

"Tell us what you saw, Zoe," said Zakhart in a soothing voice. "When did you see her in the forest? And when did you see her talking to a soulstalker? Was it Sandriana?"

Zoe shook her head adamantly. "It was one of those creepy guys with the jet-black feathers and big pointy teeth. It tumbled out of the sky and landed right in front of her. Like she'd called it or something. Like she knew it."

"Zoe," he said, gripping her shoulders. "Are you sure?"

"Yes, Zakhart! It was just this morning. I was practicing with my staff by the stream when I saw her greet a soulstalker." Zoe slid out of his grasp and huddled against Cora. "That's all I saw!"

"Zakhart, enough," said Cora, "Can't you see she's terrified?"

Finally, Zakhart motioned Cora toward the hearth. "Take her over to the fireplace where it's quieter."

Zoe hid her face in Cora's shawl again, crying softly as Cora led her over to the overstuffed blue sofa.

"Zakhart," said Lairz from behind him.

The pale angel turned toward Lairz.

"Diri and I never actually spoke to Halea," he said with a sigh, gripping his head. "We were walking toward her when demons and dark souls poured onto the trail by the stream. They overwhelmed us. Dragged off Halea. They nearly dragged off Diri, too. I couldn't get to Halea and I barely got to Diri. If I hadn't taken to the air before they could damage my wings, they would have overtaken me, too. There were just too many."

"Zakhart," Diri cried. "They're targeting angels! We have to do something or they'll pick us off one by one. Like Halea."

Zakhart began to pace now. His face looked conflicted, the weight of Zoe's words slumping his shoulders and shadowing his features. Had Halea been consorting with demons?

"Knox," Zakhart called, motioning him over.

Knox moved away from the front door and hurried over to Zakhart. They walked over to the mahogany feasting table where Heather couldn't hear their conversation.

Diri was on her feet now, the slash across her cheek fading to a sooty smudge. She and Lairz followed Razasha over to where Zakhart and Knox stood.

Heather led Ross over to a little nook under the spiral staircase. She knelt on the floor and he sat down beside her. Gently, she opened his shirt and laid her hand against his warm flesh. His shirt was stained red on both sides now from the gashes that continued to weep.

"Let me try and heal these," she said.

He nodded. "We need to learn this."

She held out her palm, concentrating on the warm white fire coursing through her body. Like she'd watched Razasha do for Diri just now.

She had no idea where the pale angels' music came from. She'd never been very musically inclined. She'd suffered through violin and piano lessons as a kid, but never got into playing much.

Focusing on the gashes, Heather concentrated her thoughts on healing him until a sickly red flame flickered in her palm.

"Good job," Ross replied, holding out his hand.

He was silent, his eyes closed, brow furrowed until a coppery-red flame guttered in his hand.

Recalling how Razasha sang until the flame had brightened to white, Heather concentrated on an old folk song that Mom used to sing. In her scratchy alto voice, Heather sang rough notes at the tiny flame.

"The water is wide," she sang.

"I know that song," he replied, humming along with her, his voice soft when he added it to hers.

He picked out notes until he sang a gentle harmony with her. Like Ross, she couldn't remember all the verses and stumbled her way through, singing along with him.

"Look!" Heather gasped.

A tight coil of pure white fire danced in her hand, matching the one in Ross' palm. It made a soft, fluttering sound, like a bird's wings and it felt warm to the touch.

Gently, she held open his shirt and pressed the coil of light to the gashes on the right side of his chest. He applied the small coil in his hand to the gashes on the left side. The coils entwined each other, expanding as they wove their way in and out of the gashes like fiery stitches, knitting the cuts together and sealing them. A small tendril of white fire encircled his wrist and slipped across the cut in his palm, sealing it.

Heather felt someone standing behind her. She turned, seeing Zakhart.

"Great work," he said. "When you're ready, join us outside. I'll teach you how to use the fire as a weapon while we wait for Sandriana."

"Sure," said Heather. "What do you think about Halea?"

She scrambled to her feet as Ross stood. When she glanced at Ross' chest, it was only slightly mottled grey where those heavy gashes had been. The cut on his palm had vanished.

A pained expression tightened Zakhart's features. He shrugged.

"Without her in my presence, I can't know what's truth and what's misunderstanding. I know Zoe means well, but Halea is one of my pale angels. I have to expect the best from her, but at the same time, prepare for the worst. It's all I can do."

Heather and Ross followed him toward the door and out into the circle where the charcoal sky was beginning to lighten.

What would that lightness bring this time?

Zakhart led them past the units of fighters that Knox had created and trained. They moved in step, almost as one now, staves poised and whipping through the air. To her surprise, even Cora held a staff this morning. She struggled to hold it, Barb patiently instructing her, but Heather was surprised to see Knox nearby them, offering Cora tips from a distance. Cora usually left the room whenever Knox was within a few feet of her, but today, Cora must have realized that she needed his help if she was going to get through this thing.

Like always, Zoe was right beside Knox, twirling her staff around and poking the grass with it. She nearly tripped Knox twice who seemed to muster up a lot more courage to train her than Heather would have.

Heather winced as Zoe swung the staff, not realizing how close the other end had come to braining Knox. But they were trying. All of them were trying their best to stop the demons before they destroyed everything in the Between.

"Heather, catch!"

She turned as a white ball of fire careened toward her head. She held up her hands, catching the softball-sized sphere of writhing light. Glancing around, she tried to find the culprit.

Zakhart stood beside Ross, smirking.

Swinging back her arm, Heather heaved the ball of white fire at

Zakhart who caught it. He threw it hard against the ground and it exploded in a shower of sparks.

"You conjure the flame just like you do to heal, Heather," he said and turned to Ross. "But the difference between combat and healing is not tempering the flame."

Ross frowned. "You mean with the music?"

The pale angel nodded. "Exactly. Pale angels can handle the white fire you call up, but the physical world—and the demons— can't. The white fire will explode on contact with these creatures and things." He patted Ross on the shoulder. "Now, you try it."

Heather watched as Ross closed his eyes and held his hand out. He bowed his head, concentrating until a ball about the size of a tennis ball appeared in his hand.

"Not bad," said Zakhart.

Heather closed her eyes and focused on summoning more white fire. She imagined the huge ball of flame fluttering in her hand until she called up a baseball-sized ball of white fire.

Ross cocked his arm and through a fastball at a nearby tree. It sparked through the air and exploded. He grinned at the explosion.

Heather rolled her eyes. Men.

She tossed him the fireball she'd conjured.

He caught it, shifting it from hand to hand a few times until he tossed it back to her. She caught it and fired it back to him. They played catch with it until Heather dropped it and it crackled against the ground, exploding into a shower of sparks.

Again, they created more, passing them back and forth across the courtyard.

A shadow passed overhead, turning the overcast day almost to dusk. Heather looked up.

Sandriana hung in the sky above the soul tree, flanked by at least a hundred soulstalkers.

Everyone on the lawn froze as the soulstalkers landed all around them.

Knox looked horrified, but Ross didn't even flinch as he moved through them toward Sandriana.

She hurried toward Heather, something in her arms. When she got close, Heather smiled. The little sand runner cub! He had a pale grey smudge on top of his head, otherwise, his fur was charcoal grey and black. Except for his hawk-like yellow eyes.

"Smudge!" Heather cried, dropping down on one knee.

She held out her arms and the little cub bounded toward her, throwing itself into her arms. She felt a shadowy rumble against her chest as she lifted the little guy into her arms.

"What is that thing?" Ross asked, brow furrowed as he glanced from it to Heather.

"A sand runner cub," she said, carrying it over to Ross.

Smiling, Ross shook his head as he reached out to pet it.

"It's soft," he said with a gasp. "I wasn't expecting that."

Heather stroked its shadowy panther head and it let out a low, gravelly noise.

"Heh-tour," Sandriana rasped as she moved toward her. "We. Are ready. To fight them." She held out her arm, wings twitching into a gentle arc. "All of us."

Heather hugged Sandriana.

"Thank you," she said. "We couldn't stop the demons without you. Razasha's waiting for you."

The soulstalker nodded and then hurried off to find Razasha.

With the cub in her arms, Heather motioned Ross over to where Zakhart and Knox stood. Her stomach twisted into a knot.

They were making final preparations.

"So we go now?" Knox asked, glancing around him at all the soulstalkers.

Knox pointed at Razasha and Sandriana standing in front of the soul tree.

"Razasha's coordinating the air cover with them right now."

"The sooner we're on the offensive, the better, Knox," said

Zakhart. "We can't let the demons get the upper hand. If we do, we could lose everything."

"So, what's the plan, Zakhart?" Ross asked, folding his arms against his chest as he glanced at Knox. "Travers?"

"We've been training for this moment since I got here," said Knox, nodding toward the huge group of souls on the lawn. "They're as ready as they'll ever be. What about the pale angels, Zak?"

Zakhart seemed to let the nickname go.

"Lairz got another wave of twenty or so pale angels settled and told them what we're up against. They'll be ready to fly with us."

Razasha soared across the lawn and landed beside Zakhart.

"Sandriana's flock is ready. Lairz says his wave of pale angels is ready, too."

Zakhart turned to Ross. "Ross, you, Heather, Knox, and Barb are the advance force, according to Knox. Razasha and I will join you."

"And us."

Ian stepped through the crowd, facing Zakhart with crossed arms, his brother Thomas beside him.

"Ian, no...it's too dangerous now," said Zakhart, a hand on the Englishman's shoulder.

Ian shook his head. "I go where Gemma is. Thomas and I are going in after her. So either you make us part of the advance force or we go alone."

Ian's eyes were filled with desperation and fear, but his resolve burned bright, strengthening him, focusing him. He was deadly serious.

"Welcome aboard, bros," said Knox with a smirk. "It's fine by me. I worked with them before."

Ross nodded. "I owe them my soul," said Ross. "I'm good with them along."

"Same here," said Heather. "Without Ian and Thomas—and Gemma—Knox and I wouldn't have gotten Ross out."

"All right," Zakhart said with a sigh. "Ian and Thomas will join us."

Heather gazed at everyone as a difficult silence descended on them. It was Ross who broke it.

"Let's do this," he said. "We rescue any soul that hasn't been changed and we kill every demon and every dark soul."

Knox gave him a sharp nod.

Zakhart studied the group around him and nodded at Razasha then Knox.

"Give the word," said Knox, "and we move north for the demon caves. Now."

Heather set down the squirming sand runner cub that scampered off toward a pride of sand runners sitting beside a clutch of soulstalkers. Barb handed her and Ross a staff as Knox shouted out orders to the units that filled the courtyard and spilled out into the forest. They were a force of hundreds now with the soulstalkers and sand runners.

Leaning over, Ross pressed a quick kiss to Heather's mouth.

"This time, we stop running," said Heather, gripping the staff.

She kissed Ross back and with her shoulder against his, they followed Zakhart toward the front of the force. She smiled. Their pale army.

The fight had begun.

twenty

. . .

NOT A SOUL STIRRED around the rocky cliffs or outside the entrance to the demon caves to the north. The deathly calm made Heather queasy as she scanned the dusky horizon. The misty swamps were calm, tall grey reedy grasses bending in the slight breeze. No hint of sulfur clung to the cool, gritty wind. Not one metallic squeak from the pushcarts squawked like an injured bird.

Not a single soulstalker patrolled the stark skies. No souls carted out loads of dirt from the demon caves. And no curious grey demons poked their heads out of the dark caves ahead like gophers.

Heather huddled in the brush between Ross and Knox. Ian, Thomas, and Barb crouched behind them, ready to do serious damage. Zakhart and Razasha knelt on either side of the group.

"Do you really think Halea has switched sides?" Heather whispered to Zakhart.

He shrugged. "I wish I knew. But I have to give her a chance to explain. If I find her."

"When will the archangels arrive?" Ross asked.

"Soon," said Razasha.

Knox whistled a bird trill.

Brush crunched behind them. Somewhere off to the right, a twig snapped.

"Let's move," Zakhart whispered and motioned them forward.

They moved through the dark brush with soft steps, sensing the other souls stationed around them, hidden in tall grasses and behind trees, waiting to ambush the demons when their small force of souls retreated from the caves. Knox intended to attack the demons' flank, retreat, and then catch them in a reverse that would trap them between the souls and the pale angels. With pale angels and Sandriana's forces assaulting them from overhead.

Heather hoped the plan worked.

Using white fire, Heather muffled the group's footsteps as they approached the caves. Razasha used it to hide their movements, making them only a shadow against the landscape.

Heather kept a close eye on Ross who seemed to struggle the closer they got to the caves.

"Easy," Heather whispered against his ear and rubbed his shoulder.

He nodded, swallowing hard, but the color he'd gained from the white fire had bled to grey, his gold-hazel eyes full of dread.

The cave was empty, the path to the heavy metal door clear.

Heather scrambled down the path and halted at the door into the caves, waiting for others to catch up.

Ross was the first one at her shoulder. Then Knox. Both men stared at each other in uneasy silence, only broken by Zakhart's approach. Ian and Thomas followed and then Barb and finally, Razasha.

Good. They'd all enter the demon caves together. She hoped they'd all get out together, too.

Heather waited for Zakhart's nod and opened the door.

She stepped into the long, dim-lit rocky corridor, the first one inside.

Ross entered behind her and the rest followed one-by-one until they were all inside.

Not a single cart creaked down the long tunnel that had been carved through the rocks. It was still and silent.

Ross stiffened, his eyes wide as he stared down the empty, forbidding channel.

"Something's wrong," he whispered.

Heather felt it, too.

Ian and Thomas watched every nook and shadow, their faces taut, hands trembling against their staves.

"Ambush," Knox muttered. "Look for trip wires and traps."

Razasha moved beside Knox, white fire in each hand.

"Sweep the perimeter," said Knox in a half-whisper, moving a step into the tunnel.

Heather summoned a coil of flame into her hand and helped them check for traps. Ross called up his own white fire, sweeping the sides of the tunnel and the ceiling as the group moved forward.

They reached the tunnel's end and the next set of doors. Knox motioned everyone down behind him as he crouched against the wall, glancing through a slit where the doors didn't quite close.

Ross covered his ears, rocking back and forth against the wall now.

"Ross, what is it?" Heather asked, worry spilling into her words.

"The Mechanism," he hissed. "I feel it. Beating in my chest."

Zakhart's face turned pale. "Is that what it does?"

"What do you mean?" Heather asked.

"By the Maker," Zakhart said, eyes wide as he stared at Ross. "Does that thing keep all these demons alive? Keep their hearts pumping shadow?"

Heather moved over to Ross, laying her hand against his chest.

"Ross, it's gone," she whispered in his ear. "The demon heart's gone. It's Mulciber. Don't let him trick you."

Zakhart smashed a ball of flame against Ross' chest and he went slack like a worn radiator belt, slumping against Heather.

"That'll shut up that damned demon," Zakhart said with a growl.

Heather grinned and mouthed thank you to him, her arm around Ross' neck.

"You're okay now," she said to him.

A relieved sigh slipped through his gritted teeth as he nodded, chest heaving. Some of the color was returning to his face now.

Where was Mulciber, Heather wondered. Was he watching them right now? Ready to spring some sort of demonic attack?

This time, when they left this place, they were destroying that damned machine. Once and for all. The Mechanism would stop churning.

"Nothing's moving in there," Knox replied. "Wish I had my assault rifle. I'd do this right."

"Let's move out," said Zakhart. "We go through every level, destroying every machine we see and every demon. We send the souls out of the caverns."

Knox smiled. "Let's get this recital started."

He pushed the door open and rolled through the doorway, hand up, telling Heather to hang back while he investigated. He was like a shadow, moving through the main chamber. Heather swallowed a nervous breath. A room that should have been full of souls and demons.

Where had the demons all gone? Were they too late to save anyone?

Knox whistled and the rest of them slipped inside, single file—except Ross. Heather locked her hand in his and pulled him along beside her. She wasn't losing him inside this place again.

She glanced over the railing at the levels below. The Mechanism had grown two more stories at least and the demons had already tunneled through several levels below.

Ross stared at the Mechanism, a mixture of sickness and rage on his face.

It whirred and thumped, wheels squeaking, and rods clacking as something inside the unit turned in a feverish rhythm that clanged throughout the expanse. The rhythm of it was making Ross nervous. Agitating him.

They shifted left, toward the smaller tunnels where all the souls had been forced to work. But they were all empty. Level after level. Empty.

"What happened in here?" Zakhart asked. "The souls. The demons. They're all gone."

"This place was teeming with souls," Ross snapped, eyes narrowing.

Heather held him close.

"Gemma and I were here a long time with Thomas," said Ian, his voice strained. "There were hundreds of souls—maybe thousands. What have they done with them all?"

"Coalfields," said Ross. "And the cage."

Ian frowned, glancing at his brother. "What cage?"

"Where they run their Soulsports," Ross said with a growl.

"Let's move," said Knox.

Ross led them to one of the lifts and they crowded into it. It creaked and rocked as it carried them deeper into the dark earth, the air smelling of fresh-tilled soil and machine oil.

Heather stood beside Ross, listening for the clang of pickaxes. The whisper of voices. But only heavy silence filled the massive caverns.

They moved down through the coalfield, checking its secondary tunnels, but not a single soul or demon walked these spaces.

Knox led them through the darkness, back to the lift, but Ross pointed toward a little alcove to the right. Another lift.

"This one leads down into the amphitheater," he said.

"Where?" Knox asked.

"The cage," said Ross, the bitterness dripping from his voice.

They crowded into the dark lift and Ross pressed the button with a shaking hand.

"I've been in this lift so many times I could find my way here in the dark," he said, staring into the swirling darkness below.

His words were disturbing. Only know was Heather getting a deeper picture of what happened to him in here. And she felt guilty that she hadn't understood the depth of his pain until now.

Heather put her arm around his waist and held him close, wanting to comfort him. Ease as much of that pain as she could.

"When is this nightmare gonna end?" he asked.

At last, his arms enfolded her. He was shaking.

"Soon, I hope," said Heather. "But even if it doesn't, I'm here, Ross."

She felt Knox's gaze on her, but she just held onto Ross as the lift swayed and shook through the long, deep darkness until the thin light below drew her eyes. The air smelled tart and dirty. Gritty.

As the lift settled against the dusty, hard ground, a huge amphitheater took shape out of the rocks. Rows of seats carved into shiny black rock with a huge round metal cage in the center. Thousands of demons sat in the amphitheater, cheering, thumping the ground with their long, leathery feet.

Heather gasped as the lift stopped.

Ross grabbed her arm and pulled her down to the ground. The others were crouched beside him.

With a wave of his hand, Ross motioned them out of the lift and into a small opening to the right.

The musty smell of demons filled the cavern, sulfur thick in the air as they moved down the curving tube of chiseled grey rock.

Four demons guarded the tunnel's entrance and a ten-foot holding cell made of some sort of black metal that stood just past the entrance.

Filled with souls.

Ross threw himself at the demons, white fire in each hand. Heather was at his back, Knox beside her.

They took out the demons with barely a whimper.

"Get the keys!" a familiar voice shouted from behind the bars.

Heather turned toward the cage.

"Gemma!" she cried.

"Heather! I knew you'd come." She glanced past Heather, a grin rising on her face. "Ian?"

She stared past Heather, past Thomas to Ian, her fiancé.

Gemma's face contorted as she gripped the bars.

"Ian? Ian, love, is that you?"

"My love!"

Ian threw himself at the cage, fighting against the bars to try and touch her, to hold her in his arms.

All along the wall of the big room were more cages of souls. A faint gold light on the high ceiling cast a dim glow through the room. It stunk of sulfur, demons, and fear, pungent with something that almost smelled like gasoline.

Heather lifted a sticky chain off one of the grey demons and forced what looked like a key into the lock. The lock clicked and she pulled the door open.

Souls flooded out of the cage, including Natalia, another soul from the soul tree.

And Gemma. Into Ian's arms.

"Head for the lifts and don't stop until you're surrounded by angels," Ross commanded.

Thomas then Barb grabbed more sets of keys that hung on the wall behind the demons that Ross had taken down. As a team, Thomas and Barb worked their way through the chamber, unlocking cells until they'd opened the last of them. Barb looked dejected when they got to the last cage.

"Barb," Heather called. "What's wrong?"

Barb bowed her head. "Javier and Lamarr aren't here."

Outside the tunnel, in the massive amphitheater, a commotion erupted. Demons surged toward the main cage, a fight breaking out.

Zakhart and Razasha gathered fireballs in their hands.

"Let's finish this," said Zakhart.

Knox grinned and swiveled his staff around.

"Anybody who wants to crack some demon skulls, follow me."

Half the souls ran for the lifts, but the other half gathered around Knox and Zakhart.

Heather glanced at Ross. He had a ball of fire in each hand, a fierce expression burning on his face as he stepped toward Knox.

"Thought you'd never ask," said Ross with a grin.

"Count me in, too" said Heather.

She concentrated on the white fire until she felt it writhing in each hand.

Knox glanced at Zakhart and the pale angel aimed a fireball toward the center cage. He flung it hard and rushed out the other side of the tunnel. Ross and Knox ran out behind him, Heather and Razasha following. The crowd of souls followed.

"Lamarr! Duck!" Javier shouted.

The tall, lanky South African dropped to his knees as Javier landed a blow, catching a big red demon in the face. It went down with a crunch.

Javier grinned. "Bueno," he said and grabbed the next grey demon that stormed the cage.

Outside the confines of the cage, the demons crowded the open doorway. Trying to storm inside.

Javier and two other groups of souls had teamed together, destroying demons as they entered the cage. Turning the Soulsport onto the demons. The dusty floor was already sticky with inky blackness as demons fell like dominos.

Javier knew they wouldn't get all the demons, but he'd still see them falling in droves as his own soul expired.

Lamarr was a machine, tearing through them like piñatas. Javier wished they could survive this night just long enough to bask in the glory of destroying so many demons.

At the edge of Javier's vision, something white flashed. And exploded.

He glanced behind him. Demons were on fire, scrambling through the amphitheater in a panic. Running and screeching in all directions.

Explosion after explosion popped as fire rained down on the demonic crowd.

He glanced toward the staging room. A huge group of souls rushed at the demons.

"Mira, amigo!" Javier shouted, tugging Lamarr's sleeve.

A demon grabbed Javier around the throat, dragging him toward the open doorway.

Javier rolled his body into the demon, knocking it over. He slammed his elbows into its fleshy sides and rolled off it. He smashed his hands around its throat, squeezing until its beady red eyes popped out.

Scrambling up from the floor, he faced the doorway again, but no demons poured into the cage now.

Outside the cage, fire kept raining down on the demons. White fireball after white fireball.

Javier grinned, patting Lamarr on the back. He pointed at the open door.

"Vámonos!"

They scrambled over the pile of demons and darted out of the cage as a wave of souls broke through the crowd of flaming demons. Javier couldn't believe his eyes. Zakhart, Knox, Heather, and Ross bludgeoned their way through the squirming mass of demons, Zakhart and Ross flinging fireball after fireball. Heather led the way.

"It's Heather and her army!" Javier shouted, pounding Lamarr on the back. "I told you she wouldn't let us rot in here, amigo!"

Three demons leaped at him.

Lamarr wrestled one to the ground, breaking its neck.

Javier pounded one senseless and knocked another one out cold with an uppercut to its face. He shoved two demons out of the way and sprinted toward Heather, Zakhart, and Ross.

He was staggered a moment when he saw Barb behind them,

pounding demons senseless with her staff. He couldn't hold back his grin. He should have known she was behind this rescue.

"Barb!" he cried, running toward her.

Barb beamed when she saw him.

Javier flung his arms around her.

"Dios mío! You came in for me, Barb!" he cried, reaching out to touch her face.

"What'd you expect, knucklehead?" she said with a snort. "I can't fight demons without my practice partner."

He pulled her face toward him and kissed her. She grinned, her arms sliding around his neck.

Three demons leaped at them. Together, Barb and Javier beat them down.

"Lamarr with you?" Barb asked.

"Sí!"

He glanced around until he pointed toward the tall South African happily bludgeoning demons out of the way.

Heather flung fireballs right and left through the mob of demons that advanced on them, surrounding them in a sea of grey and terracotta. She watched as the souls who'd been trapped in those cages became rabid animals against the demons. They didn't back down, clawing, and punching until they brought two demons down.

She glanced at Ross who fought with the same ferocity, the same commitment. He wouldn't be satisfied until every demon in here was dead at their feet.

Zakhart and Razasha seemed to have endless streams of white fire, but Heather had to move between her staff and the fireballs. It took her a bit to get comfortable with the staff, but it was easy to handle and she repelled a bunch of demons with it, letting the pale angels use their much more powerful white fire to incinerate demons.

When the demons' numbers had dwindled to a hundred or so,

they retreated toward the lifts. Zakhart led the pursuit and the pale army chased after them.

At the lift, Ross shouted in rage and bent toward the ground. He held up a thick, frayed cable.

"They cut the lift cables," he snarled.

"Is there another lift?" Zakhart asked. "Another way out?"

Javier disappeared around the corner but quickly returned.

"It's been cut, too."

Zakhart held his hands in the air as the crowd of souls began to panic. His robes were stained grey and black, sprayed with inky demon fluids. His face was spattered with black spray on one side. The air smelled metallic and warm with sulfur.

"Everyone, calm yourselves!" he shouted until the forces quieted and he turned to Razasha. "Think we can pull this lift back to the surface, Razasha?" he asked.

She flashed a smile at him and nodded.

"Ross?" Zakhart called.

Ross moved toward Zakhart, Heather beside him.

"Help Knox load the lift. Razasha and I will fly them up until everyone's out."

Ross frowned. "That might be a dozen trips or more, Zakhart."

The pale angel shrugged. "It's all we've got."

"You sure," he said, squinting at Zakhart.

"Yes, let's hurry."

Zakhart unfurled his wings as Razasha stretched her wings in a wide arc and grabbed one of the thick cables in her arms. Zakhart lifted the other one from the ground as Ross and Heather began loading souls into the lift.

Over and over, Zakhart and Razasha pulled the lift out of the depths of the cavern. Fourteen trips in all. When they'd towed the last load up, Ross and Heather in the group, Zakhart and Razasha collapsed on the ground, visibly drained.

Heather and Ross called up healing flames. They sang a harmony together until they'd tempered the fire, placing a burgeoning coil of light onto Zakhart and Razasha's chests.

"Let's do one more round of healing after those healing flames sink in," Ross whispered in her ear.

She nodded and glanced around at the other souls. Ian, Gemma, and Thomas crouched beside Razasha, Natalia at her back. Javier, Lamarr, Barb, and Knox stood watch at Zakhart's side.

No one spoke as they listened to the fighting and shouts echoing above from the cavern's main floor. Had the rest of their forces stormed the caves yet? With Lairz and Sandriana leading them?

"We'll head to the Mechanism when you're ready, Zakhart," said Ross.

The pale angel looked weak.

"Did anyone see Halea?" he asked.

Heather knelt beside him, laying a hand on his shoulder.

"Afraid not, Zakhart," she said softly. "But maybe she's outside? With the other pale angels."

His gaze fell to the dirty, sticky floor as he got to his feet, wings shifting. Heather let him lean on her to stand.

Knox and Ross helped Razasha to her feet. She looked exhausted, blond hair tangled around her shoulders.

Zakhart sang a clear string of tenor notes that Razasha matched tone for tone. He paused and resonated some harmonies against her melody until her voice trickled off into a sigh. She nodded at him.

"All right," he said, pointing toward the main tunnel ahead. "Let's do what we came here to do."

Heather smiled and followed Zakhart and Ross down the last tunnel that emptied into the main chamber.

Toward the Mechanism.

The rest of the souls clambered behind them, ready to battle more demons as they surged into the main chamber.

twenty-one

. . .

INSIDE THE CHAMBER, a fierce line of red demons defended the caves as they stood between Heather and her main attack force. It was the only way in or out of the Demon caves.

And the only way to the Mechanism.

Knox shouted commands in a calm, determined voice.

Souls rushed behind carts and equipment while the curly-haired soldier sent groups in waves against the demons.

Heather glanced up at the Mechanism. A grey demon stood at the top, on a dark section of the Mechanism. Was that demon trying to turn something on?

She had to stop it.

She summoned white fire, creating two softball-sized balls of writhing flame. Taking careful aim, she estimated that the creature was about ten to fifteen feet above her. Holding her breath, she flung the fireball as hard as she could propel it, pegging the demon in the head.

It screeched, beating at the fire burning its sparse, coarse hair until it fell over the railing and plummeted several floors into the cavern below.

Ross grinned. "Nice shot, Heather."

"Used to play fast pitch softball in high school," she said with a smile. "I was the starting pitcher."

"And that was right across the plate," he replied. "I'm impressed."

She scanned the Mechanism for any more demons. When she couldn't locate anymore, she aimed the next fireball at a spinning flywheel and let the fireball fly. It exploded, blowing out the flywheel and spewing parts.

The strange green glow caught her attention. She glanced down at the green crystal necklace that Sandriana had given her. It had begun to glow.

A new line of demons surged out of the short hallway where the spinning room stood. Six or seven in all.

Big, fleshy terracotta demons. Scrambling toward her.

"Heather, look out!" Ross shouted, throwing himself between her and the first demon.

He body-slammed it hard against the railing, pummeling it with his fists until it toppled over the side.

And plummeted, hitting with a splat far below.

Heather swung the right end of her staff up and around, catching another red demon in the face. And beat it backward. Left. Right. Left. Toward the railing. Where Ross slammed it over the side.

Razasha slung a series of fireballs at the remaining demons until they exploded into piles of sticky black ooze.

Again, another grey demon climbed the Mechanism.

Heather watched it ascend as she summoned a fireball. Just as it reached a panel with levers, she beaned it with a fireball.

It plunged off the side and disappeared below.

"Find and destroy the pumps!" Ross shouted.

They rushed around the massive machine until Heather noticed a series of piston-like parts that pumped back and forth against some sort of metal housing. The steady thumping reminded her of a beating heart as the deep thrum filled the cavern.

She called up white fire. And took aim as Ross hit the pumps with the first fireball.

It took two more fireballs to destroy the pumping things.

Hoses whipped back and forth from the machine like a dying squid, spraying hot, viscous fluid and steam on the demons surrounding it.

They screeched, burning from the liquid, and ran frantically through the chamber, rolling, and slamming their bodies against the walls to stop the burning. The room smelled like hot machine oil, boiling sulfur, and musty, burning demon skin.

This time, Ross aimed at the Mechanism itself. And fired off three fireballs.

A tall pipe crumbled and fell, panels melting, exposing wires and delicate circuitry.

Heather followed up his throw with two more of her own. The panel exploded, wires catching fire and short-circuiting. Sparks flashed alongside the machine as the whole apparatus caught fire.

As the others took down the last of the red demons.

Iznir appeared at the end of the main tunnel, signaling Zakhart.

"Iznir, what is it?" Zakhart called.

"It's the demons!" he shouted. "They're headed for the Spiral!"

"What about the Mechanism?" Heather asked, flinging another fireball at it.

"We can't let them tamper with the Spiral," said Zakhart. "Or risk them finding a way to enter it."

"Move out, people!" Knox shouted. "We go on defense now!"

Heather grabbed hold of Ross' hand and they charged down the main tunnel, surging out of the caves. Knox caught up to them and ran alongside Heather as Zakhart landed on Ross' right. Together, the four of them led the attack force.

Toward the Spiral.

Before Mulciber and his demons damaged it. Or tried to escape through it.

twenty-two

. . .

THE OUTSIDE WORLD exploded in a blur of demons and screech of soulstalkers—Sandriana's flock. Pale angels soared overhead, tangling with soulstalkers, and knocking them out of the sky. On the ground, demons and souls clashed, staves crackling above shouts and squawks.

Knox threw himself into the fray, staff flashing as he cracked demon skulls and beat the demon's soulstalkers out of the sky. Zakhart and Razasha took flight, surging up to assist Lairz who battled five demonic soulstalkers.

Rolling out of the way, Heather scrambled to her feet, staff in hand, and ran beside Ross as together, they cleared a path through the demons toward the north.

Toward the Spiral.

Demons were everywhere! In writhing masses, clogging the paths, and tangling the vegetation.

"Ross, we'll never get through all of them to reach the Spiral!" Heather shouted. "There's too many!"

"We have to try!" he shouted, knocking demons out of his path, but they grabbed hold of him, climbing onto his back, and shoving him to the ground.

One by one, he pounded them with his fists, but they were overwhelming him. Knox rushed into the fight beside him, but he was quickly inundated by demons.

Heather rushed at them, stave in motion, knocking them off their backs and keeping the demons at bay until Ross and Knox rose from the ground.

She stayed close until Ross summoned white flames and threw them at the ground. The ground caught fire, running along it like it followed a trail of gasoline. It leaped from the ground to the demons, clearing a small opening for them to get through.

She, Knox, and Ross beat demons out of the way as they ran for the opening.

Heather called out for Zakhart.

In moments, the pale angel landed beside her, battling demons alongside them with white flames in both hands.

"Zakhart, we'll never get to the Spiral in time! Not like this! Demons are overwhelming us!"

Zakhart nodded and sang out a piercing high note. A heartbeat later, Razasha and Lairz landed beside him.

"We need to carry a force to the Spiral," Zakhart explained.

Ahead, from the north, a huge flock of demonic soulstalkers descended out of the sky.

Heather gasped, pointing, but Sandriana was already engaging them with her flock of soulstalkers. She and her flock knocked the demonic soulstalkers right out of the sky. Heather grinned, watching Sandriana and her people move through the huge force like it wasn't even there.

A fierce growl rumbled from the northern forest as hundreds of sand runners trotted out from behind the trees, part of Sandriana's shadow flock. They leaped onto the backs of demons, tearing them apart.

Zakhart scooped up Heather and lifted her into the sky. Razasha picked up Ross and Lairz grabbed Knox. They carried them over the top of the demon force, setting them down on a small trail winding upward to the base of the Spiral.

Heather grinned, feeling its soothing vibrations course through her body.

"Let's move!" Ross shouted, grabbing Heather's hand, and running down the path toward the Spiral.

Knox followed close on her left.

Behind them, the tide began to turn, sand runners and soulstalkers tearing through the demon forces, letting the pale army through. They were no more than thirty feet behind Heather, Knox, and Ross now.

The rocky path wound around the steep mountain slope, white with snow, as Heather rushed up it, Ross and Knox on either side of her. Already, her bracelets thrummed with bright white light, pulsing as they got closer to the Spiral.

"What's that sound?" Knox asked, glancing around him. "The voices...I—I hear my unit. What the hell?"

Heather grinned, hearing her mom's voice above the din of the battle. She felt the rush of life, the turn of the Spiral. The way out. A new life. An end to this nightmare of shadows and pain!

"Dad?" Ross grinned at her. "Heather, I hear my dad's voice. He's been gone for so long, I—I'd almost forgotten the sound of it."

He squeezed her hand as the three of them ran full-tilt around the path until the Spiral's turn was a roar in her ears. Like a massive waterfall.

Ahead, it writhed and turned, the whisper of life roiling around them. She gasped. She could almost touch it.

Again.

Grinning, she tugged Ross toward it. And motioned Knox forward.

"Knox, come on!" she shouted.

Smiling, Knox ran harder, legs pumping as he sprinted up the path and caught up to her and Ross again.

To the south, a loud rumbling shook the Between as a deep base thrum, like a jackhammer, quavered through her.

The world shook with a violent earthquake, knocking everyone to the ground. The shaking seemed to last for thirty seconds or more before it finally subsided.

"What was that?" Heather asked.

"Not sure," said Ross, helping Heather to her feet.

"Felt like a blast of some kind," said Knox as he climbed back onto his feet from the rocky ground. "Maybe an earthquake?" He brushed dust off his clothes.

"First one I've ever felt in the Between," Ross muttered, a worried look spreading across his handsome oval face.

"Let's get out of here," said Heather, glancing over at Knox. "Knox, do you see the Spiral ahead?"

He squinted, brow furrowed, those beautiful blue eyes narrowing as he stared straight ahead. Finally, he pointed.

"You mean that big swirling misty thing ahead?"

"You can see it!" she cried, grateful that Knox had a way out of the Between, too, now.

She wondered how many other souls could see the Spiral. Maybe they all could after defeating Mulciber's demons?

Maybe that was their reward?

"Not everyone sees it, Travers," said Ross. "But if you can see it, then you have a ticket out of the Between."

A grin lit the tall, curly-haired soldier's face. "That thing's the way out?"

Heather nodded.

Knox bowed, motioning her forward with the sweep of his arm.

"Lead the way, Heather."

Heather turned toward the Spiral, still gripping Ross' hand, and hurried along the path that wound toward it.

Halfway up the path, they slammed headfirst into something blocking it.

Heather bounced backward, rolling to a stop against some snow-dusted brush. Dazed, she lay there a moment, Ross and Knox on the ground beside her.

"What the hell was that?" Knox shouted.

Ross scrambled to his feet and lunged forward.

Heather climbed up from the rocky ground and rushed forward behind him, smashing into an unseen barrier. It knocked her to her knees a second time. Ross was on the ground again, too.

She shook her head, staring at the unseen force keeping them away from the Spiral.

"No," she cried, clawing at the air. "No! NO!"

Turning, Heather grabbed Ross by the hand and motioned Knox alongside her. The three of them ran west then swerved north toward the Spiral, slamming face-first into another barrier.

They traversed an entire circle around the Spiral, but the barrier encased its circumference, blocking anyone from approaching it.

"They've cut us off from the Spiral!" Ross shouted, fury burning in those golden hazel eyes.

Again, the three of them tried every direction and every height they could reach, but they could only get within ten feet of the Spiral.

Defeated, Heather sank to the ground, kicking, and pounding the invisible barrier, but she couldn't get past it.

Behind her, the rest of the pale army surged up the path, footfalls pounding against the hard ground as they ran toward the Spiral.

Stopped by the crunch of the energy barrier.

They turned south, rushing down the hill back toward the Demon caves, but another barrier had materialized behind them. Shoving them backward.

Into an unseen cage.

They were surrounded. It had been a trap all along!

Heather beat the ground with her fists. The demons had herded them right into this invisible box. Why hadn't they caught it? Why?

Zakhart and Razasha soared out of the sky and landed in the middle of the invisible cage.

She winced. And she couldn't warn them. Now, the pale angels were trapped, too!

Souls pounded and clawed at the unseen cage around them, trying to find a way out, but it was impossible. They were trapped.

Heather crawled over to Zakhart and Ross.

"Zakhart, what happened?" she cried. "We're trapped in here."

Ross gritted his teeth, fury blazing in his gold-hazel eyes.

"No," he snapped, shaking his head. "We were herded."

He knew it, too.

Zakhart sighed. "So were Razasha and I. I've warned the others to stay back. Lairz and Sandriana's forces are trying to locate the boundaries of this cage. They're also trying to break through it. Nothing's worked so far."

Knox dropped down beside Zakhart.

"Shepherd's right, Zak. We were herded up here. Quite effectively, I might add."

Zakhart's pumpkin-orange eyes were shadowed with anger, a dark realization burning on his face.

"Because someone betrayed us," he spat. "Told Mulciber everything we were planning. Right down to the paths we'd be taking."

"Are you sure?" Heather asked.

The pale angel nodded.

Razasha slid beside Zakhart and called up healing light. But no flame lit her hand. Frowning, she tried again, her brow furrowing, teeth gritted as she struggled.

Nothing.

"This cage won't let me use my abilities," said Razasha.

"What?" Zakhart cried.

Frantically, he tried to summon the white fire within him. But he came up empty-handed. Looking defeated, he covered his face in his hands.

"Razasha and I are powerless in here," he said with a moan.

Razasha flew out of the barrier and landed outside it. She summoned white fire, throwing it at the barrier. The white fire sizzled and dissipated.

The barrier was to trap souls. The pale angels could escape!

"We're at their mercy now," said Heather.

"At the mercy of demons?" Knox snapped, making a sour face. "We're screwed."

Ross pounded on the barrier. "Not without a fight," he replied. "They'll have to destroy me first."

What if that's what the demons intended all along? Destroy souls like Ross who refused to cooperate. She was afraid for him now.

"Licking your wounds?" Mulciber called from the other side of the barrier.

The demon snickered, hands on his hips as he paced along the edge of the invisible barrier, a leering grin on his face. And clicked his forked tongue, his red eyes glowing. His demon skin had changed. It was now a mix of grey that faded to terracotta and finally ruby red around his faces and hands and feet. He had grown larger since she'd last encountered him, taller than the red demons, his body appearing almost human with male features. But that smooth, scaly skin persisted.

"Tsk, tsk, tsk. If only Raduriel had sent archangels instead of half-breeds and misfit souls to do his job for him. How unfortunate."

Mulciber's corpulent laughter resonated around them, burning Heather's ears. The demon folded his arms behind his back and approached the Spiral. Studying it a moment and then he walked to the edge of their cage again. He held his gnarled hands up, like he was pressing them against a solid surface.

Opening some sort of portal.

Heather gasped as grey demons poured out of the portal, plodding single file toward the Spiral. One by one, they leaped into the stream and vanished.

"No!" Zakhart cried, scrambling to his feet. "NO!"

Zakhart soared over the barrier. He lunged at Mulciber, but the red and grey demon was behind some sort of invisible protective energy barrier now. Furious, Zakhart ran along the length of the crackling mass of dark energy encircling the demon until he was face-to-face with Mulciber.

"Stop this!" he shouted. "Stop this now, Mulciber!"

Mulciber slapped his leg, a thick belly laugh rumbling through his fleshy red and grey body, horn buds quivering above his large red eyes as he stood as tall as Zakhart now. Tall as a human. A pale angel.

And looked Zakhart in the eye.

"Or what? Half-breed." Mulciber's expression turned deadly as he flicked an invisible switch on the portal. "Why stop when we're having so much fun?"

The red and grey demons' forms shifted. Into human form. There were no demon scales, no mottled demon skin. He looked just like the other souls. And he could blend into any group of humans.

Heather shuddered as the stream of demons changed, too. They all looked as human as she did!

"What have you done?" Zakhart raged, throwing himself at the shield protecting Mulciber.

Mulciber laughed and pointed at Heather and then Ross.

"Thanks to Heather for carrying the poppy bloom into the physical world and back again, I have a path through the Spiral now. To plant poppies and harvest souls." He motioned at Ross. "And thanks to Ross, I was able to perfectly copy his likeness and I used him as the model to make my human mold. I regret that I couldn't use him further. As my champion. He was a master at the Soulsport. NetherReach would have loved him. But they'll love this accomplishment, too."

Something flashed behind them.

Heather glanced back as the edges of their cage appeared, glowing with an eerie red light. A shiny black crystal the size of a basketball gleamed in one corner of the cage, pulsing red as the cage walls began moving forward. Slowly.

"What's happening?" Heather shouted, pushing against the barrier as it slowly shifted forward.

"The barrier?" Mulciber asked with a chuckle. "Just a little housecleaning. Need to get rid of all these useless human souls. You get to watch, half-breed."

About two dozen souls clustered together in the center of the cage, Heather between Ross and Knox as the edges began to close in on them.

Barb and Javier pressed closer to Ian, Gemma, and Thomas. And the others. The rest of her pale army had escaped this horrible cage. They were still below, battling demons.

The barrier buzzed, both walls only four feet away from them now.

And inching closer. All within feet of the Spiral. Where they would have been free of the Between—and Mulciber—forever. It made her rage inside.

"Zakhart!" Heather called as she pressed closer to Knox and Ross. "We could use some help here."

"I'm trying, Heather!" he shouted.

"Enjoy being crushed and erased," Mulciber said with a chuckle and slipped through the portal as the last of his human/demon creatures disappeared into the Spiral.

Still, the barrier crept closer, energy building as the distance between the walls grew shorter and shorter.

Heather turned her gaze toward the black crystal in the cage's corner as it pulsated red.

"Zakhart, the crystal!" Heather shouted. "Destroy it!"

Zakhart and Razasha lurched into the barrier and stood over the crystal. Razasha tried to knock it free and shatter it while Zakhart flung white fire at it. But they couldn't even move the crystal.

Or damage it.

"Can't," he shouted.

Zakhart and Razasha moved outside the barriers again, both showering it with white fire, but it had no effect. Both barriers continued to move each other until a red glow washed over the cage.

Zakhart flew over top of the barrier as the group of souls shifted closer together and tried to land beside Heather. But something blocked him. Heather winced.

The red glow.

"I can't pass through the barrier anymore!"

Heather rushed toward Zakhart as he stood outside with Razasha and tried to knock the black crystal over. It slumped to one side, lying across the pedestal but still connected to the cage.

She grabbed hold of one end of the crystal, fingers closing around the bottom point. When her hand interrupted its connection to the pedestal, the dull green crystal around her neck brightened.

The necklace that Sandriana had given her was reacting to this black crystal!

For a moment, the barriers stopped moving.

"Try to enter the cage again, Zakhart," said Heather, blocking the beam shooting through the crystal with her hand. "In the space right in front of me."

Zakhart slid his body halfway through the barrier. "Yes, that works!"

Heather glanced over at Gemma.

"Gemma, when I say go, run through the barrier. Right where Zakhart stands. Hurry!"

Heather grabbed hold of the crystal, blocking the beam with her body.

"Now!"

Gemma ran toward Zakhart and leaped out of the barrier.

"Heather, it worked!" Gemma shouted.

"Interrupting the beam from the crystal works," said Heather.

Ross and Knox were beside her now as she stepped out of the red light and let go of the crystal.

The walls began moving again. Closing fast.

"I'll do it," said Ross. "I'll block the beam. Both of you—go through. Hurry!"

Knox shoved past him. "I'll do it. Both of you go through. Now."

"Why?" Heather asked Knox.

Knox grinned. "Because I love you."

"Why, Ross?" she asked, turning to Ross.

He winced, gazing from Knox to her and she felt his pain.

"Because you mean more to me than my soul."

She gritted her teeth. That bastard Mulciber was forcing her to choose. Ross or Knox.

She leaned up and kissed Knox.

"Heather, you go on through," said Ross, his voice breaking, the pain sharp in his hazel-gold gaze. "With Knox...you've made your choice."

The watery pain in his eyes cut through her like a razor. He didn't think she wanted him anymore. That she didn't love him anymore. She bit her lip. That she'd chosen Knox over him.

She threw her arms around Ross and smashed her mouth against his in the hottest kiss she could summon.

When she let him go, he looked confused.

The barriers crackled, lightning flashing around them. In a few more moments, it would destroy their souls.

"If I have to choose between Knox and Ross," she shouted, stepping between the crystal and its eerie red light. Blocking the beam and halting the barriers. "I choose...me!"

Grabbing Ross and Knox by the arms, she pushed them both through the wall of the barrier. And dropped to the ground, the safe ground between the barriers disappearing rapidly.

"The rest of you go, now!" she ordered and put her body between the beam again.

The remaining souls surged out of the barrier in front of her, through the only escape route from the cage.

"Heather!" Ross shouted, clawing at the barrier, pounding it with his fist. "Heather, no! NO!"

"Heather, what did you do?" Knox snarled, his hand against the barrier as he stood beside Zakhart who looked stricken.

"Don't do this, Heather," Zakhart pleaded.

He didn't understand. Someone had to interrupt the beam so that the others could escape. By design. Anger swelled in her. By Mulciber's design.

Ross slammed his body against the barrier between them, his face contorted. He pounded the obstruction with his fists as both walls slid closer to each other. It a few moments, it would crush her soul between the two walls and destroy it.

In agony, he sank against the barrier, his hands pressed against it. Still trying to get to her.

"Heather! Why? Why!"

She pressed her hands against his, the barrier still between them.

"Because you mean more to me than my own life. And soul. I love you, Ross."

Like a madman, Zakhart slammed fireballs against the barrier, howling in desperation.

Heather wrapped her arms around the crystal and huddled in the corner as the barriers began to pres against her body. The green crystal necklace was moon-bright against her throat as lightning flashed and arced, making her hair stand on end.

"Heather, I love you!" Ross screamed. "Heather!"

She closed her eyes, clutching the crystal tighter against her chest as the barriers were on top of her now. Almost touching.

Click.

Click.

Connect.

And the world exploded red and green around her.

The End of Avenge, Book 3: The Spiral Series

The story continues in...
Ruin, Book 4: The Spiral Series

Subscribe to the Reader's Club

An exclusive reader club dedicated to the fiction of Lisa Silverthorne, including her series: **A Game of Lost Souls, The Resurrectionist Papers, The Spiral,** and **Experiencing True Purple**.

When you subscribe to the reader's club:

- *Receive exclusive updates from Lisa on Ream*
- *Influence future works through Reader Polls*
- *Get early access to new books*
- *Read stories only available on Ream!*
- *Acquire Book swag!*
- *And more!*

JOIN THE CLUB AND SUPPORT A WRITER!

For Book Swag & Ebooks Direct,
visit Lisa's online store!

NOVELS BY LISA SILVERTHORNE

Standalones:

ISABEL'S TEARS

LANDFALL

PACIFIC BLUE TATTOO

A Game of Lost Souls series:

THE CINDERELLA HOUR

THE PRINCE CHARMING HOUR

THE EVER AFTER HOUR

THE FALLEN HEARTS SEASON

THE RISING SPIRITS SEASON

THE ETERNAL SOULS SEASON

THE ROYAL WEDDING HOUR

THE HEAVENLY HONEYMOON HOUR

THE DIVINE NEWLYWEDS SHOW

THE CELESTIAL COUPLES SHOW

THE ENOCHIAN APOCALYPSE SHOW

The Spiral series:

BETWEEN

REPRISE

AVENGE

The Resurrectionist Papers

GRAVE RECKONING

SHORT STORY COLLECTIONS

THE SOUND OF ANGELS

THE MAGIC OF ORDINARY THINGS

SCIENCE FICTION WRITING AS L.S. SILVERTHORNE

Standalones:

REDISCOVERY

Experiencing True Purple series:

RECOMBINANT, Book 1

HELIX, Book 2

SPLICE, Book 3

FORTHCOMING

A Game of Lost Souls series:

The Angelic Anniversary Hour, Book Twelve

The Perdition Picture Show, Book Thirteen

The Spiral series:

Ruin, Book 4

Descent, Book 5

The Resurrectionist Papers:

A ROMANTIC FANTASY MYSTERY SERIES

Corpses Delicti

Stiffed Again

Cease and Deceased

SCIENCE FICTION WRITING AS L.S. SILVERTHORNE

Experiencing True Purple series:

Cipher, Book 4

Renascence, Book 5

SHORT STORY COLLECTIONS

Timeless: 8 Time Travel Romances (Dec 2023)

about the author

LISA SILVERTHORNE has published over 20 novels and 150 short stories and novelettes in many genres. She is the author of *A Game of Lost Souls* series, *Experiencing True Purple* series, *The Spiral*, and the upcoming series, *The Resurrectionist Papers*. She lives in Las Vegas, Nevada.

Before you go, you are invited to please leave a **review of this book**!

Reviews are a wonderful way to help an author. They are also an exciting opportunity to share your honest thoughts with other readers, so **please post yours,** in as many places as possible!